DANGER IN
THE KEYS

By Ernest Francis Schanilec

Also by Ernest Francis Schanilec

Blue Darkness

The Towers

DANGER IN THE KEYS

Author - Ernest Francis Schanilec
Publisher - McCleery & Sons Publishing

International Standard Book Number: 1-931916-28-4

Printed in the United States of America

ACKNOWLEDGEMENTS

MY GRATITUDE GOES OUT TO my reader-critics, editors and proof-readers: Lois Ring, Vern Schanilec, Faye Schanilec, Nancy Dashner, Rob Schanilec, Joe Dashner and Clayton Schanilec.

DEDICATIONS

THIS NOVEL IS DEDICATED TO all the people who are suffering with cancer and to those who are serving and supporting them. This author wishes them all well.

1

Tom Hastings was driving south in his Pontiac on Interstate 75 in the southern part of Tennessee. His speedometer read eighty-two, a sure bet for a speeding ticket. Looking in the rear view mirror, hoping not to see flashing lights, he noticed a small red car approaching at a tremendous speed. Looks like a Chevy, he thought.

Tom's car was in the middle lane. Glancing into the mirror again, the red Chevy was almost in his trunk before it switched to the passing lane. As the car passed him, he noticed a woman was driving. She was hunched forward, barely seeing over the dash. Tom watched in horror as the Chevy struck a guardrail, soared over the top and disappeared into the wooded slope below.

After slowing down, Hastings brought his car to a stop onto the far right shoulder, as did a pickup truck. It pulled up right behind Tom's Pontiac. Tom got out and walked back to the truck. The driver, a man wearing a baseball cap, opened the window.

"Did you see that?" the pickup driver asked.

"I sure as heck did. The woman driver must have been doing at least a hundred-per—the car just sailed through the air. I'm afraid to even think about what may have happened to her," added Tom. He had a cell phone in his hand. "I'll call for help."

After punching in the number and waiting for a response, he looked west and saw a deep valley of fields appearing to be the size of postage stamps. A partial fog hung over the valley preventing a view of the far slope. After Tom put his cell phone in his pocket, the pickup driver said, "I don't see any smoke coming from below. I'll go down and have a look."

"Wait a second and I'll go with you," answered Tom. "I'll put my flashers on first."

"Yeah, I better do the same," responded the pickup driver.

After setting their lights to blink, the two men cautiously worked their way down the steep slope, led by the younger of the two, the pickup truck driver. Slipping and falling into a crevice, he cursed and grabbed onto a small shrub. Hastings established secure footing and reached down with his hand.

"Here, grab on. Are you all right?"

"Thanks. I'm fine."

"Ah, my name is Tom Hastings and I'm headed for Florida. You might call me a snowbird."

"Ben Pierce. Atlanta is my destination."

"Look at those broken branches. Do you see the red smear on that tree trunk?" asked Ben. "Good God, no way could there be any survivors."

"I think there was only one person in the car, a young woman," responded Tom.

"Let's follow that trail." Ben sounded anxious.

The two men worked their way down about another hundred feet when Ben exclaimed, "There it is! Up against that tree!"

Hurrying along as rapidly as possible, they reached the red Chevy, still upright and crunched against the trunk of a huge tree, its front axle embedded into the bark.

"Look, air bag," said Ben.

He jerked on the driver's side door. It was stuck. Tom went around to the other side and pulled on the passenger door handle and it opened.

He leaned down and said excitedly, "She's alive! I can hear her breathing."

Tom noticed the blonde hair. In spite of the fact that the woman looked short when she passed, her legs were quite long. She was dressed in gray slacks and a white blouse, which was sprinkled with red drops of blood. Her eyes were closed, exposing a thin long dark set of eyebrows.

Tom slid onto the front seat of the car and pulled out the ignition keys. After dropping them on the seat, he placed a finger on the woman's wrist, feeling for a pulse. Ben was standing behind the car, not paying much attention to Tom or the victim.

After failing to feel a pulse in the wrist, Tom touched her neck and responded, "Ah, great—a strong heart beat...she's got a good chance to make it."

He was pondering an attempt to remove her from the car when he felt it move—a bouncing motion. Looking back, he could see through the rear window that Ben was leaning over the trunk. Why would he be lifting? Tom asked himself.

"Hey, Ben," Tom yelled, "She needs help and fast!"

2

BRAGEN'S PUB, IN THE BACK STREETS OF BOSTON, had a back room where frequent poker games took place. Serin and Terrance Duggin were among the players that evening in the smoke-filled room. The middle of the table was heaped with money. All chatter stopped when Vince laid down his five cards, face up—aces and queens-full house. Quincy, one of the other players, lost his temper and swept his arm across an array of empty beer bottles. The sound of breaking glass didn't seem to phase the moods of the remaining players.

"I've had it with you guys!" shouted Quincy as he rose from his chair and left the room.

"Good riddance, bad loser," said Vince, as the door slammed shut.

Vince was not a big guy, standing about five-nine in stocking feet. His hair was kinky and still black except for a splash of gray in the sideburns. The slight hump in his back required personal tailoring of his sport coats. His complexion and eyes were dark. When Vince looked at someone, he would lock on their eyes.

The remaining players, except for Serin, Terrance and Vince, also left the room. Vince stood with both palms on the table. "Men, I brought you two here for a much bigger reason than poker." He put an arm on a shoulder of each of the two men. "I've got a deal for each of you guys...it's going to take some finesse and doesn't come without some risk. Could mean a million each...are you interested?" asked Vince, sweeping the bills from the middle of the table.

"Let's hear it," said Serin anxiously. "I'm busted."

"This coming Tuesday, an Arabian Prince, Omar Vallif, is coming to New York City. Word has it, he will be wearing his birthday present, the Guni. It's a gem worth at least twenty-five million, probably closer to fifty.

"The Prince is going to attend an Arabic Club meeting in lower Manhattan on Thursday. Arab princes wear their finest jewelry to political and social functions, but not to events such as ethnic meetings.

"My Sicilian cousin has been in touch with me. He has a good connection in Saudi Arabia with one of the Prince's enemies. They need someone in America to oversee separating the Guni from the Prince. I feel honored that my cousin respects me enough to offer me the opportunity.

"I have it all set, a foolproof plan on how to get into the Prince's hotel suite. The gem will be stashed in there somewhere. I made sure the hotel safe would not be available that evening. We'll have about two hours to find it. What do you men think?"

———

OMAR VALLIF WAS DESPONDENT, sitting in his hotel suite in New York. He stood up and walked to the windows that overlooked the skyline. Dominating the view were the Twin Towers. His personal gem had disappeared. It had been taken from his jewelry case that was in the top drawer of the ornate dresser in his bedroom. Who would do such a thing...*meen*...who?

Along with his entourage last night, he had gone to an Arabic Club meeting in lower Manhattan. Not wanting to chance a loss, he left the gem behind in his suite. Must be worth thirty million in US, he thought, probably a lot more. My father and mother will kill me, being it was a birthday gift last year. Well, perhaps they may not need to know.

The peridots, known by ancient Egyptians as "the gems of the sun" were mined in Zeberget near the Red Sea long before the time of Christ. The gem had a reputation for its alleged powers, including successes in marriages and relationships. Cleopatra reportedly had a collection of Peridot gems. The Ottomon sultans gathered the largest collection of Peridot gems during their six hundred-year reign from 1300-1918.

Sauli Vallif, Omar's father, had purchased the Guni gem from a dealer in Pakistan in 1996. It was discovered in a mine in the Nanga Parbat region of the Pakistan part of Kashmir, about 15,000 feet above sea level. The Guni topped 400 carats in size, at least 100 carats larger than the previously largest known Peridot gem stored at the Smithsonian Institute in Washington, DC.

The Prince pushed a button and an aide entered. "Get our embassy security on the phone. Tell them I wish to speak to whoever is in charge."

A minute later the aide brought the Prince a phone. "Ah, Malinas...good to hear your voice. I wish for you to contact Rhoul Massif in Saudi Arabia. It's of utmost importance. Have him call me back immediately."

"Yes, master."

Twenty minutes later, the Prince's phone rang. "This is Rhoul Massif. What can I do for you?"

"I am in need of a master investigator here in America. Select an assistant and get on the next flight. You are to keep our communication confidential. When you get to New York, report to me at the embassy, immediately."

"I'm on my way," responded Rhoul. "Bern Tallin is available. He will accompany me."

3

TWO AIRLINERS LANDED AT INDIANAPOLIS INTER-
NATIONAL AIRPORT, half-an-hour apart. Serin was on the first
one and he intentionally mingled at the gate, hoping not to see officials
waiting.

The seats in the gate area were rapidly filling with people awaiting
the next flight. Serin paused at the exit to the concourse. The coast is
clear, he thought. Walking rapidly, he remained near the wall,
occasionally slipping into a shop. At last he came to the escalator
that led to the baggage pickup areas. He plucked the piece of paper
from his breast pocket that established Terrance Duggin's flight
number.

The successful heist in New York was the biggest thing that had
happened in their lifetimes. Serin smiled feeling the bulge of the gem
in the money belt strapped to his waist. He thought about Vince
awaiting delivery in Atlanta, a cool million each for him and
Terrance—not exactly chicken feed.

His long, blond ponytail was secured with a red, plastic hair-tie.
His whisker-laden face narrowed to a rather pointed triangular chin.
Large, crowded middle front teeth protruded when he began to speak.

Passengers were gathering and mingling at the baggage pickup
station as the conveyer belt began to move. Serin nervously looked
up and down the concourse, watching and waiting for the appearance
of Terrance. He didn't have any baggage beyond his carry-on, but he
knew that Terrance did. Round and round the conveyer went—
passengers plucking their luggage and packages from the moving
belt. Looking at his watch, a whole hour had passed since the conveyer

began moving and still no sight of Terrance. There were only a handful of parcels left on the carousel. Serin was getting worried.

His instinct told him something was wrong. Serin walked away from the baggage retrieval area and sat on a bench next to a young mother and a boy of preschool age. The mother didn't appear pleased when he patted the youngster on the head.

"Hi, mister," said the youngster, looking up at Serin and smiling.

"How's it with you, buddy?" asked Serin, his voice trailing to a whisper, watching two uniformed police officers coming up the concourse. The concourse was crowded, but it became apparent to Serin that the two men walking behind the officers were with them.

The little boy's toy dropped to the floor. Serin reached down and picked it up. He handed it to the boy and said, "Here you are, sonny."

Getting up off the bench he moved into a telephone stall. Serin had the receiver snuggled against his ear, anxiously watching the police officers. He saw another man, a fifth person. One of the non-uniformed men who walked behind the officers had his arm tucked between the fifth man's elbow and side. Serin saw a glint of silver, a reflection from an overhead light—handcuffs, he thought. Serin watched anxiously, straining to get a look at the fifth man's face— it's Terrance. "They caught 'em," Serin whispered.

After they passed, Serin mingled among a group of people for a couple of minutes and then headed for the taxicab station. A short distance from the station, he noticed two police officers scanning the arrivals. One of the officers was holding up a photograph. Serin suspected the photograph was of him.

Ducking into a bar, he took a stool and ordered a whiskey. His feelings of apprehension were mounting by the moment. If I get caught in the airport with the stone, my life is over, he thought. A woman came into the bar and sat down two barstools away from him.

"Hi, miss, how's the day goin'?" Serin asked.

"Great, I had a very good flight."

"My name is Ben Pierce, I'm headed for Florida, how about you?"

"I'm headed for Florida too, the upper Keys. I'm Pamela Zachary."

"Excuse me, miss, I'll be right back," Serin said as he saw two officers pause by the door of the bar.

He wasted no time getting to the men's room. Inside, he removed the money belt, unzipped the compartment and grasped the gem. He dumped the money belt in the trash container and put the gem in his pocket. Peeking around the partly opened men's room door, he became alarmed. The two police officers had entered the barroom. They were obviously looking for someone, he thought. *They are looking for me*!

Serin reentered the men's room and waited for another five minutes, after which he peeked around the door again. Much to his relief, the officers had gone. He headed back to his stool and tried to look calm.

"I thought you had forgotten your drink and left," Pamela said.

"Ah, no, just ran into someone I know."

"Excuse me, my turn. Would you keep an eye on this?" Pamela asked as she gestured toward her carry-on bag that she had laid on the barstool. "Just makeup in there," she added and smiled.

The police officers were loitering in the concourse, near the door. It's going to be difficult to get out of here, Serin thought. Noticing the woman's carry-on bag tag, he reached across the bar and picked up a pen. After writing down Pamela Zachary's name, phone number and address, he pulled open an outside zipper and dropped the gem into the compartment.

When Pamela returned, Serin said, "Miss, blast it, my transportation hasn't shown up. You wouldn't have a vehicle available, by any chance?"

He watched her light a cigarette and contemplate his request. She is obviously attempting to decide if I'm on the level, Serin thought. He watched her facial expression show approval—my lucky day.

"Yeah, I'll give you a ride. Where do you need to go?"

"Only the Budget Car Rental place—about half-a-mile. Here, let me help you with that," said Serin as he grabbed Pamela's carry-on. "Lead the way."

Slinging the strap of his own carry-on over his shoulder, he grabbed her carry-on with one hand and tucked his other hand between Pamela's elbow and waist. Serin escorted her through the door and into the concourse. One of the officers glanced at them for a moment, his eyes darted away, looking to-and-fro across the concourse. Perfect, thought Serin, they're not looking for a couple.

Serin looked straight ahead, his heart beating rapidly, as they walked by police officers and security people and passed through a terminal exit. They walked out the door onto the sidewalk. The sounds and smells of vehicles revitalized his confidence. They crossed the busy street on a pedestrian right-of-way and entered the massive parking area.

"It's a long walk and I do appreciate you carrying my heavy bag. You would think it's full of gold," laughed Pamela.

"Oh, it's no problem, I appreciate your offer of a ride."

"It's that red Chevy over there," said Pamela as she clicked her trunk button.

She pulled up the trunk lid and said, "Drop it in here and take the load off your shoulder."

"Always glad to help a lady," said Serin as he carefully set the carry-on down in the trunk.

Pamela opened the back door of her car and threw her purse down on the seat. She looked back and saw Serin fiddling with her carry-on bag.

"What are you doing, mister?"

"Oh, I thought it was mine."

"Yours, hell, that's hanging on your shoulder. You get out of here. I've changed my mind, I'm not giving you a ride."

Serin looked up and scoffed. He grabbed the zipper tag between two fingers and pulled.

"Leave that alone. Get away from here or I'll yell," she shouted.

Lucky for Pamela, two extremely tall men happened by. "Hey, you leave the lady alone. Get lost or you're in big trouble," one of them said firmly.

Serin looked up into the threatening face of a big man. After glancing at the tall man's partner, who was even bigger, he turned and walked a short distance away and paused, but not before memorizing the letters and numbers on Pamela's license plate.

"Thank you, gentlemen. Next time I'll know better than to trust someone in a bar," said Pamela.

Serin reluctantly created distance between himself and Pamela

Zachary's car. He could see the red Chevy back out of the parking space and head down the corridor. The two tall men began walking in his direction. Skulking away, Serin began looking for a vehicle. Damn the luck, he thought. Sure as hell, those two guys were basketball players, probably on the Indiana Pacers pro basketball team.

Serin had been a basketball player in high school. On occasion, he would watch pro games.

Angry and frustrated, Serin strolled over to a pickup truck that had just parked. After the driver lifted a suitcase out of the box, Serin pushed him to the ground and drove off with the truck, not paying any attention to the yells. *Okay, so she got away, but I've got her name and address, plus the car license.*

4

AFTER THE AIRPORT INCIDENT, Serin successfully followed the red Chevy onto Interstate 75. After crossing the Tennessee border, heavy traffic caused him to lose sight of Pamela's car.

She's got to stop at a rest stop, he thought anxiously. It's been non-stop since the airport. There's one up ahead. He pulled off the highway and slowly cruised by a number of vehicles.

Near the far end of the row, he spotted it. That's it! The red Chevy. There she is...anyhow that sure looks like her, he thought. That's her standing by that white receptacle...the one with blue and red markings.

After finding her, Serin was exhilarated. He drove by and parked at the next available place, several vehicles down. He got out of the pickup truck and hastened toward the Chevy, approaching on the parking lot side. Serin was only a few steps away when he heard an engine start. The Chevy was backing out. He paused and watched as the car jerked before moving forward.

As it came broadside, their eyes locked for a moment. Wheels squealed as the car sped toward the ramp that led back to the highway. She recognized me, he said to himself. Serin quickly returned to the truck and followed.

Serin thought how critical it was keep that Chevy in sight. It could mean life or death for me. After the rest stop, he stayed close behind until it crashed through a guardrail and went down a slope, north of Chattanooga.

———

STANDING NEXT TO THE RED CHEVY ON THE SLOPE, Serin's thoughts were interrupted by stomping sounds above. Two Tennessee highway patrol officers were working their way down. When they arrived, he stepped away from the car. .

"Any people in there?" one of the officers asked Serin.

"Yeah, seems to be only one, a woman."

One officer went over to assist Tom Hastings in helping the victim. The other one looked up when he heard the whirling blades of a helicopter. "Here it comes!" he exclaimed.

Because of the steep slope, the helicopter had no place to land. One of the officers communicated with the crew with a phone and anxiously watched as one of the crew was lowered to the ground via a cable. The troopers assisted him in removing the woman from the wrecked Chevy and securing her in a basket dangling from the cable.

Serin asked one of the officers, "What happens to the car?"

The officer gave Serin an inquisitive look, shook his head and answered, "Likely it will end up in one of the salvage lots in Chattanooga."

Serin remained on the scene with the two officers until a second helicopter arrived. As they were hooking the cable to the car, Serin was hoping that somehow the trunk lid would pop open and he could sneak out the carry-on bag—it didn't happen.

Hastings had left the group and was making his way up the slope. Serin watched with anxiety as the small red car, twisting and turning, disappeared over the tree line.

"Are they going to haul that car all the way to Chattanooga like that?" asked Serin.

"Oh no, they'll drop it off on the road, somewhere up there. A wrecker will come by and pick it up."

The fact that she wasn't killed was a miracle. He hoped that the Hastings guy didn't notice him trying to open the trunk. He may have been too occupied looking after the woman, Serin thought. My fingers just fit into that space—under the trunk lid. It had distorted from the impact. All my yanks on that stupid trunk lid had failed— damn-it.

Serin thought of Vince in Atlanta awaiting the stone. If I don't show up with it soon, there was a sure chance of getting roughed up, even killed. He began the climb, realizing that it was going to take a long time to get up to the road. The stone is in that lousy little car, already up there on the road somewhere. Getting into that trunk was not going to work right now, especially with the patrolmen around.

Vince Gulloti was capable of pulling off big deals, more than anyone else that Serin knew of. He was good to work for as long as you didn't cross him. Serin thought about a couple of guys he knew in the past that double-crossed Vince. They were both pushing up daisies.

Serin arrived in Chattanooga. Immediately, he called Vince to tell him about Terrance getting caught in Indianapolis. The news didn't seem to upset Vince much.

Staying cool, Vince said, "No problem as long as you have it."

Serin's stomach felt the tension—*as long as you have it*. He didn't dare tell Vince that he didn't have the stone. It was either still in the bag in the trunk, or maybe the blonde had it with her in the hospital in Chattanooga.

"Vince, my pickup truck got bashed at an intersection, here in Chattanooga. It's going to take some fixin', that's going to delay my arrival in Atlanta."

"What! You get your butt down here...right now!"

"Can't help it, Vince, the cops found an empty beer bottle in my pickup," he lied.

"Jesus, man, you still have the stone, don't you?"

"Of course...how would I not have it?"

"Where are you staying?"

"Dunno yet."

Serin's gamble was that the he would get away with the lie. It totally depended on getting the Guni back. He felt it was worth the risk.

———

DIRECTLY AHEAD WAS THE FLORIDA STATE LINE. Tom Hastings was playing a Judy Collins CD and thinking about the dramatic rescue that he witnessed back in Tennessee. It took a helicopter and a crew of six to lift the unconscious woman off the slope.

Pamela Zachary is her name...forty-two years old, I heard someone say. How in the heck she survived sure beats me, Tom thought. Surely the spirits are on her side.

One of the Tennessee highway patrolmen, back up on the highway, had told Tom, "The young woman has your name and phone number in Florida. Don't be surprised if you get a call."

Tom thought about Ben Pierce, his cohort in finding the car on the slope. Twice...twice the man tried to get into the trunk. *Why?* Tom thought as the highway signs changed from Georgia to Florida.

"Perhaps we can all get together. The Florida Keys aren't that far away," Ben Pierce had said.

The man was interested in something more than the victim's well being, thought Tom. He had lifted the car, probably by the trunk lid. *What was in that trunk?*

———

TOM HASTINGS' CURRENT HOME was in the Towers apartment complex in Minneapolis. He had moved there two years ago from a lake home in central Minnesota. The reason for moving was the traumatic memory of the tragic murder of three of his neighbors and friends.

His girlfriend, Julie Huffman, lived in St. Paul. One of the benefits of moving to Minneapolis was a reduction in travel miles. Julie had a good job working for a high-tech company in Minneapolis. Tom was retired, but maintained a part-time computer consulting business.

The violence he escaped up north in the lake country followed him to Minneapolis. He lived at the Towers for only six months when a psychopath murdered a woman resident. Four other's lost their lives in or near the Towers building. Tom Hastings was directly involved in the capture of the serial killer. Instead of running away a second time, he remained a resident of the Towers and was currently looking forward to spending a month in Florida. Not only would he escape the wintry weather of March in Minnesota, but take in some baseball spring training games.

Tom Hastings was a senior, over sixty years old. His career in computer science ended a few years ago. Working with computers, especially accounting was one of his favorite pastimes. Because of sports and outdoor activities, he remained in good physical condition—no medications or ailments of any kind.

By 4:00 that afternoon, Tom was approaching his destination on Key Marie, south of Tampa Bay, Florida. The drive from Minneapolis took only two days, in spite of some road construction and the accident incident in Tennessee. He was anxious to move into the condo at Park Place and get on a tennis court. Park Place had two of them.

Watching the street signs, he was pleased to find Beach Street easily—it was right where his Internet-generated map showed it would be. Taking a right, he drove slowly, glancing at the building numbers. At last, he saw number 7660. He parked his car in a space directly in front of the office at Park Place.

The woman at the desk said, "Greetings, Mr. Hastings, right on time. Your place was ready to move into an hour ago."

5

KEY MARIE WAS ONE OF THE NORTHERN ISLANDS off the gulf coast of Florida, just south of Tampa. It connected to the mainland by two drawbridges and to another island by a single drawbridge.

The landmass of Key Marie was long and narrow. Keys Highway, running up the middle, allowed vehicle access from one end to the other. Half way between the mainland drawbridges was a wharf consisting of a restaurant and a long pier. It had been primarily used to slip boats, to fish and to sightsee.

There were numerous strip malls that lined the terrain along Keys Highway. The closest one to Park Place was at the junction of the northernmost bridge and Keys Highway.

Park Place condo complex was on Beach Street, which forked off Keys Highway about two miles north of the strip mall.

Because Keys Highway and adjoining streets and avenues were single lane, the traffic moved very slowly. Adding to the traffic jam-ups were the take-your-time drivers from the northern states, spending the winter in Florida.

———

UNIT 230 WAS LOCATED ON THE SECOND FLOOR of Park Place. It overlooked the beach and was Tom's new temporary home. Stacking his luggage next to the small elevator, he managed to squeeze it all in after the door opened. He pressed the 2nd floor button and patiently waited for the humming hydraulics across the hall to move the cables. The elevator slowly made its way to the second floor.

A noisy clunk and sudden jerk announced that he had reached his destination. The elevator door began to slide open, but stuck before opening completely. It needed a push to continue its slide. Tom placed one of his largest bags in the path of the door to prevent it from closing. He removed his luggage and other belongings from the elevator and placed them on the foyer floor.

The door to Unit 230 was visible. After unlocking the door, he walked inside. The room straight ahead was the kitchen—looks inviting, he thought. The first door to his left opened into a small bedroom. The two other doors in the room accessed a walk-in closet and a bathroom. The living room, just past the kitchen, was equipped with a television and stereo, which were setting on the top shelf of a large open-shelf cabinet. The other furnishings featured an attractive large blue sectional, two easy chairs and a central coffee table.

The master bedroom, off the living room, was much larger than the other bedroom. It had a bathroom with a huge shower. Walking to the window, he pulled the cord attached to the drapes and exposed large sliding glass doors that accessed a long narrow balcony. Walking out on it, he saw a dense patch of high plants below and the beach beyond. Tom noticed that the balcony had another set of sliding doors. Probably open from the living room, he thought.

After bringing in his belongings, he walked out onto the balcony and watched the fascinating surf that was splashing up on the sand. There was a never-ending parade of beach walkers. Looking to his left, he could see into the balcony of the building next door—it was empty. On his right, across the courtyard, the balcony was identical to his. A woman sitting there looked over and waved. Tom returned the wave.

The never-ending sound of the surf was a perpetual reminder that he had arrived. Tom inhaled and experienced the smell of the ocean. He felt exhilarated after thinking about the half-mile of his former roadway in central Minnesota being blanketed with a couple feet of snow. Tom stood at the railing and watched the breakers spread out over the sand. A flock of large dark pelicans set their wings and settled into the water. Their expertise at finding fish was so good that invariably gulls would follow them.

Tom took the stairway down to pick up miscellaneous items from his car, noticing it had a dull, dusty look compared to the other shiny vehicles parked there. I'll need to get a car wash, he thought. The license plates represented many of the upper Midwest states including Illinois, Iowa, Ohio and Indiana.

Looking across the street, he saw the two tennis courts and was reminded of Julie. She needed to work the coming week and would be flying to Tampa next Saturday. Their plan was for her to join him for two weeks and share Unit 230. Tom was looking forward to her visit and the extra tennis.

He spent the rest of the evening unpacking and getting accustomed to the features of Unit 230. The kitchen was well equipped with a large refrigerator, dishwasher and garbage disposal. He flicked on the television and laid the remote control on the coffee table. After stretching out on the sectional, he channel-flipped for a few minutes. He had the choice of a DVD or VCR player and a large selection of movie tapes and disks. Tom fell asleep watching a DVD movie.

6

THE YELLOW PAGES IN THE PHONE BOOK showed six impound lots. On Saturday morning, Serin began by calling the AAA Impound Lot—no luck with that one or the next three.

The fourth on the list, Kerrigan's had the car. "Oh yeah, that must be that red Chevy over there. Came in yesterday."

"Thanks," said a smiling Serin, hanging up the phone. Ask and you shall receive, he thought.

Arriving at Kerrigan's in his pickup truck, Serin used his charm in the office to access the red Chevy. The trunk had not been opened. Excited, he returned to his pickup truck and got a crowbar. Three pries and the trunk popped open. Overwhelmed with excitement, he reached down to touch the carry-on bag. With shaking fingers, he managed to pull open the zipper. Reaching into the compartment, he groped inside and felt panicky—the stone wasn't there.

Lifting the carry-on bag out and sitting it on the back ledge of the trunk, he opened the main compartment. Flipping it over, he dumped the contents onto the floor of the trunk. Probing, he failed to find the stone. Damn, he thought. I bet the broad has it. *She may have found it at the airport after those tall hunks showed up.*

An envelope was nestled amongst all the other junk. It was addressed to Pamela Zachary. There was a return address—Melissa Buntrock, Park Place, 7660 Beach Street, Unit No. 150. Inside was a short note—signed by her aunt, Melissa. The note said, "Pam, please stay at my place until your job starts."

Stuffing the envelope and letter into his pocket, Serin knew his only chance to get the stone back was to head for Florida, check out that address. I need to find that broad at all costs, he thought. That means I will pass through Atlanta without stopping to see Vince. Showing up there without the stone would be fatal.

———

VINCE GULLOTI WAS SITTING AT HIS DESK in an office in Atlanta. Now, where the hell is that guy? He should have been here by now. Oh yeah, the pickup was crunched at an intersection. That could take some time. Wonder if I should head down there and pick up the stone, he thought. Damn, I don't know where he's staying.

Vince had sent out a feeler via e-mail, about the Guni to Vordi, an underground gem dealer in West Atlanta. Amazing, but Vordi already knew the Guni was stolen and could become available. He was ready to pay twenty million dollars.

To Vince, that meant two million for Terrance and Serin, plus the up-front one-and-a-half he paid the other guys to get into the Prince's room. That left a cool, potential sixteen-plus million in his pocket. Elation transformed to frustration—next a sinking feeling that he was never going to see that stone. Gotta cool it, he thought.

I'll give that gook another day or two. If he doesn't show up by then, I'll go looking for him.

Vince had selected Serin and Terrance for the heist because they were both calm and smart men. He knew from their past history that either one was capable of cheating. Yet he trusted that Serin would do everything possible to deliver the Guni. Neither Serin nor Terrance were capable of brokering it—they both knew that. They needed me to make money.

Vince didn't pay any attention to a story in the newspaper about the dramatic rescue of a woman by helicopter from a treed slope in the Smoky Mountains in Tennessee. He saw the headline but wasn't interested.

He had been born to wealthy parents in the northern part of Chicago. Life was good. The private Catholic school that he had attended was managed by the Scholastica order of nuns. He would never forget that day in the fifth grade when Sister Constant called him into her office. His dad had been killed—assassinated in the parking lot next to the Sears Tower.

From that day on, Vince vowed he would revenge his father's murder. Just a fifth grader, but Vince had already learned that money was power. Someday, he would get lots of it, even if he had to steal.

His mother always said that he had inherited his dad's black hair. The dark blackish eyes and heavy black eyebrows were also his. His mother didn't care for his narrow black mustache. His dad never had one.

Vince was a senior in high school, surrounded by relatives and friends, when he tossed a clump of dirt on his mother's coffin. She had died of cancer, much too young.

After graduating from high school, he took a job with his Uncle Bert, who owned a used car business in a Chicago suburb. Selling vehicles was a natural for young Vince. His uncle taught him the ins-and-outs of buying and selling. Eventually Vince started his own business in Atlanta. His lot, always full of vehicles, took up most of a block. He employed seven salesmen, two were cousins from Chicago.

Being middle-aged and not getting much exercise, his waist-line was expanding, much to his displeasure. On his desk lay a brochure from the West Side Athletic Club. He intentionally kept it in view, hoping that it would inspire him to join.

Vince was fussy about how he dressed. Always wearing a white shirt and black bow tie to work, he alternated between six different colored suspenders. Dark trousers, never light—never jeans.

7

TOM HASTINGS TOOK THE STAIRS DOWN and picked up a newspaper from the vending machine next to the postal boxes, near the parking garage. It was Saturday morning, his first full day in

Florida. He had found enough fresh coffee in the cabinet to brew up a full pot. While sipping, he searched for a spring training schedule in the newspaper. The Yankees had a game in Tampa on Tuesday— it's a must-go, he thought.

He headed down a second time, just before the lunch hour, on his way to the grocery and liquor stores. Approaching his car, he encountered an Illinois couple removing packages from their trunk.

"Hi there, do you belong to that Minnesota car?"

"Yeah, sure do, just came in last night."

"I'm Grady Prichard and this is my wife, Helen. We're from Rockville, Illinois."

"I'm Tom Hastings, from Minneapolis."

"How long you staying?" asked Helen Prichard.

She was a tall woman with a tan, good-looking face, wearing glasses that hung down slightly on her nose. Her hair was short, mostly gray and fell partly over her ears, from which dangled a pair of long earrings.

"A month. All of March," responded Tom.

Grady's narrow shoulders were bent slightly forward. His thinning gray hair was combed straight back. When he straightened up to shake hands, he towered over his wife. Must be six-five or more, thought Tom.

"You're in that front unit above, aren't you, Tom?" asked Grady.

"Yup, Unit 230. As I mentioned before—all of March. I am expecting a guest next Saturday."

"Uh-oh, isn't that nice," responded Helen. "A woman guest, perhaps?"

Tom laughed and said, "Yeah, Helen, you guessed right. Her name is Julie, she lives in St. Paul and is going to spend a couple of weeks here."

"I'll look forward to meeting her," Helen responded and smiled.

"Well, people, I've got shopping to do. The fridge and pantry are empty."

"Good meeting you, Tom, I'm sure we'll see you around. By the way, we're in the unit directly underneath you. We bought it over twenty years ago, so we know our way around," said Grady.

Tom noticed Grady's left arm was shaking. Hopefully not Parkinson's, he thought.

Tom parked in the six-row parking lot that served the grocery store plus the occupants of the strip mall, which was about six blocks long. It was busy—vehicles in constant motion and grocery carts abandoned in many places. A wide sidewalk fronted the entire length of the mall. In the very first unit Tom was pleased to see a hardware store. He chuckled when spotting colorful wheelbarrows on display. He knew Julie would laugh when he offered to give her one for Christmas.

Tom's first look at the checkout lines staggered him. All six lines were at least ten people deep, practically all of them seniors. He thought about the small corner grocery store in New Dresden, his former home. It had only two checkout stations and both of them moved customers a great deal faster.

Tom checked the outdoor thermometer after returning from shopping. He had been readying for a stint on the beach—the temperature eighty degrees. After gathering needed items, he donned his swim trunks, put on a beach shirt and headed down the steps. The first wrought-iron gate allowed access to the courtyard area where the swimming pool and hot tub spa were located. A second gate separated the courtyard from the beach. After unlocking it, he held it open for two attractive women coming from the beach.

"You must be new," the brunette said to Tom.

"Yeah, I arrived last night. I'm Tom Hastings."

"I'm Corrith Schweitzer and this is my friend, Lucy Barrows. We're taking a break, too much sun. We'll be back out for cocktail hour, just before sundown, though. Why don't you join us?"

"Hi, Corrith, nice meeting you," said Tom as he shook her hand. "I'll be happy to join you."

"I'm Lucy. Happy to meet you, Tom."

Tom shook Lucy's hand and said, "Well, I'm off to get my new burn. See you two later."

Lucy Barrows had long blond hair and blue eyes. Her long, lanky legs had obviously spent a lot of time in the sun. They were tanned, perfectly. Tom winced and glanced at the bruise he suffered on his palm from the handshake and her long fingernails.

Corrith Schweitzer wasn't as tall. Her dark brown hair partially covered the left side of her face. Brown eyes complimented her brunette features. Neither woman wore glasses.

Hastings settled into a tan metallic lounge and stored his accessories on a small table nearby. He took off his shirt, applied sunscreen and lay on his back. Hatless, wearing a pair of overlay sunglasses and propped up slightly, he could see the beach walkers as they passed by. Noticeable was a senior gentleman, dressed in shorts and a wide brim straw hat. He used a cane and struggled while working his way along the beach. His generous, grayish beard covered most of his face. A pair of sunglasses almost covered the rest.

At close to 4:00 p.m., Tom adjusted the lounge and sat up straight. Reaching into a freezer bag, he brought out a bottle of beer. The ice had melted, but the bottle felt cool. Flocks of small sea birds were working the surf, feeding on some type of sea worm deposited by each receding wave. The small worms elevated themselves from the wet sand in amazing numbers. It was fascinating to Tom how those little birds flew in tight mimicking patterns. He wondered how those little brains knew exactly what turn that the leader bird was going to make—they moved in unison, every single time.

"Hello there, you're new here, aren't you?" asked a masculine voice off to Tom's left.

Tom turned and saw a man, dressed only in shorts, a dark baseball cap and no shirt.

"Oh, yeah, just arrived last night." He extended his right hand and said, "I'm Tom Hastings."

"Glad to have you aboard. I'm Richard Schweitzer. You've probably already met my wife, Corrith. She's the one that isn't blonde."

"Name sounds familiar. Does she hang around with a woman by the name of Lucy?"

"Yup, that's the one. They spend a lot of time together on the beach and other places. We're from Peoria, Illinois. I see your car has Minnesota plates. What part of the state are you from?"

"Minneapolis."

Richard Schweitzer had an air about him, a man in charge—the boss. Considering his age, upper fifties or lower sixties, he was in good physical condition. His dark skin showed the fruits of spending a lot of time in Florida. The ring finger of his left hand sported a large diamond, set in a complex gold ring.

"We're Packer fans. I imagine you support the Vikings." Richard said.

"Yup, you're right. Vikings fan I am, and a disgruntled one at that."

"That last season was a tough one for you guys. Ours wasn't so hot, either."

Tom took a long swig from his beer and Richard said, "Hey that looks good. It's time for me to go home and prepare for cocktail hour. Perhaps you'll join us down by the pool just before sunset."

"Yeah, that sounds good. Maybe I'll just do that."

———

COCKTAIL HOUR KICKED OFF with a loud laugh coming from the direction of the pool. Tom was sitting on his balcony watching the calming surf. A formation of pelicans was approaching from the south. Tom watched as the birds swooped, and landed in the water about fifty yards to his left. I wonder why they land in pairs, he thought. There's that similar laugh, deep and aggressive again. It's coming from around the corner in the courtyard.

Walking to the north end of the balcony and peering around the corner, Tom could see seven people had gathered. Retrieving a bottle of Chardonnay from the refrigerator, he filled a wineglass and headed down the stairs. The wrought iron gate was slightly open—no need for a key. The first person to greet Tom in the commons area was Corrith Schweitzer.

"My husband tells me you are from Minneapolis," she told Tom while reaching out her hand to grasp his.

"Yup, he's right. I met you earlier today. Your name is Corrith, is that right?"

"Hey, what a memory. Are you getting settled in?"

"Yes, I sure am. It doesn't take much to supply one person. Things are going to change. I'm expecting a friend next weekend."

"Ah, a friend. A lady, may I presume?"

"Yes, her name is Julie. She's flying into Tampa on Saturday."

"Well, if it isn't sweet, sexy Corrith," a voice interrupted. Tom had heard that type of voice before—a carnival barker. The man approaching was holding a mixed drink in one hand, a cheesy-looking nacho in the other. Beady, dark eyes were complimented by wavy, pepper-colored thick hair. The grin on his face seemed to be fixed.

He put the arm holding the drink around Corrith's shoulder, trumpeted a loud laugh and looked up at Tom.

"Your new here; don't remember seeing you before," the man said to Tom.

"Dale, this is Tom Hastings from Minneapolis. He just arrived yesterday," Corrith said attempting to wriggle free of Dale's arm.

After escaping Dale's grasp, she added, "Tom, this is Dale Strong."

Tom knew the type, playing the crowd, checking out all the women.

"I am pleased to meet you, Dale. I guess I'll go over and get something to eat," Tom responded.

Tom approached the appetizer table and saw Richard Schweitzer loading up his plate. Richard turned and said, "I see you've met the Dale. Help yourself, there's plenty to eat here."

"Hi, Richard, yes, I have met Dale. Where's he from?"

"New York, always comes alone, rents a place for three months. He's been doing that for the last ten years."

"Seems like quite the character," responded Tom.

"Yeah, he's pretty darn loose with his hands. Did you notice my wife breaking free? Come over here. I want you to meet some more people."

Tom followed Richard to the other side of the pool where a couple was sitting at a table, munching from a plate of appetizers.

"Hey guys, I want you to meet Tom Hastings from Minneapolis. He came in last night. This is Marv Plum, and his better half, Ann. They live in the mirror unit of yours, across the courtyard. That's their balcony, right over there," Richard pointed, smiling.

Marv had a large chest with short, thick, hairy arms. His dark, wide eyebrows stood out on his dark skin. His wife appeared younger by about twenty years. She had dark hair and wore glasses. Marv didn't get up but nodded. He put his hand on Ann's shoulder, an obvious signal not to rise.

Sure a mean looking guy, Tom thought. I wouldn't want to meet him alone in a dark alley.

Ann smiled and said, "Hi, how are you?"

Tom was amused by the sound of her high-pitched voice. "Glad to meet you two," he said while wondering if she was an opera singer.

Tom met another half-dozen people before the cocktail party began to dissipate.

Getting back to his room, just before nightfall, he called Julie.

"It's so nice to hear from you. How was the trip?" she asked.

"Fine, except for a nasty accident. A woman, doing about a hundred and twenty, went off the road. By some miracle, she survived. It happened in southern Tennessee, near Chattanooga."

"My heavens, did you stop?"

"Yeah, I did. I've never seen something like that before. It stopped my breath. That little red car went sailing out into space and disappeared. Another guy and I went down the slope and found the car. I was the first to find the woman. She was alive. The highway patrol showed up and they called a helicopter to take her to a hospital. It was rather weird to see a car dangling on a cable and floating through the air after a second helicopter arrived."

"It must have been quite the experience. How's the condo? Meet any new people?"

"The condo unit is fine, real nice place. Yes, I met some of the residents by the pool this evening during cocktail hour. Apparently that's a tradition around here, cocktail hour at sunset."

They talked for another half-hour. After Tom hung up, he went to bed and fell asleep watching a movie.

8

PAMELA ZACHARY KNEW SHE WAS LUCKY TO BE A-LIVE, surviving the steep slide and the abrupt stop of her car. She remembered looking through her rear-view mirror while passing a car. She was aware that someone was following her the last fifty miles—a pickup truck. The curve came too fast and she felt the temporary resistance of the guardrail. The speed at impact was such that the car went over the rail and down the slope.

Oh, what a feeling it was to sail into space. Her whole life flashed through her mind, knowing it was going to end when her car landed. The miserable part of my life would be gone and never come back, she thought. Dying will be easy. All the people that I hate and fear will disappear in a flash. For just a moment, Pamela wished the end would come.

Strange noises had awakened her. It took close to a half-hour before realizing she was in a helicopter, lying on a stretcher. Pamela's dark brown eyes opened and she saw the face of a woman squatting next to the stretcher. My body feels so cold compared to her warm hand, Pamela thought. What's that stinging feeling in my shoulder? She asked herself. Oh, it hurts....

When the helicopter landed on a hospital rooftop in Chattanooga and the noisy blades stopped rotating, Pamela had passed out.

Hunger was the first feeling that she experienced after waking in a hospital bed. She looked into the smiling face of a nurse who was standing next to the bed. "Glad to see that you are awake, Miss Zachory. How do you feel?"

Pamela didn't return the smile. This is a hospital room. Why am I here? She thought.

"I'm hungry," she tried to say, her words muffled by the roughness of her vocal chords.

"Now, you just rest. The doctor will be here soon," the nurse responded.

Pamela closed her eyes and imagined looking in the dresser mirror that reflected her image, just before going downstairs to meet her date for the senior high school prom. I was so beautiful and only a sophomore, she thought. Why did my father growl and say those terrible things after I got down into the foyer? "You're not going out in that! Are you? Damn-it, you're half naked."

Brett didn't say a word after we got into the car. I was so ashamed of my father. The evening was ruined even though four of my friends told me how pretty I looked. Brett was an awful dancer, but he stepped back and said I was the best looking girl at the prom. Brett never asked me out again. It was all down hill for my life after that. I hated my father after the prom. My mother didn't help me much either. Her drunkenness was disgusting. She would drink the evenings away and fall asleep in a chair. Sometimes her glass would fall onto the carpet and the gin would create a stain.

Pamela's eyes moistened when she thought about the long bus ride after she ran away from home. Working in a greasy restaurant was the only way I could make money enough to eat and sleep. My life really wasn't worth living.

She heard a man's voice. A doctor in a long white gown was looking down at here. "Miss, I'm going to check those bruises on your shoulder. Relax."

The doctor's hands were gentle and his voice was kind, she thought. The nurse replaced the gown after the doctor was finished with the shoulder. Pamela looked up and saw him smile. "Miss Zachory, you are a physical wonder, considering what you went through as a result of the accident. You were saved by technology— the air bags totally absorbed the impact."

"Thank you doctor." responded Pamela, smiling.

Instead of calling her parents, she called her Aunt Melissa, who lived in one of the Keys islands in that part of Florida where Pamela had planned to live and work. After spending two days in the hospital, Pamela was released to her aunt, Melissa Buntrock.

Melissa had responded to Pamela's call and agreed to drive to Chattanooga. Before running away from home, Pamela overheard her father say that Melissa didn't like us very much. "She thinks she's so high and mighty. Just because she went to college...called us a bunch of losers."

I don't like my aunt, but she's my best bet for getting out of here, Pamela thought. Besides when her husband divorced her, she got a lot of money.

Pamela told Melissa that some of her baggage was still in the wrecked car. Information from the police sent them to Kerrigan's Impound Lot in the suburbs of western Chattanooga.

Looking at the trunk lid, she realized that she didn't need a key. It was slightly opened. After lifting the lid, she was startled to see her carry-on bag lying upside down on the trunk floor with the contents spread all over.

She had felt relieved that all her money and valuables were in her purse, which was returned to her by the police when she was in the hospital. The carry-on bag contained only reading material, makeup and other personal things.

Pamela was confused when discovering a FedEx claim check in the bottom of her purse. Scratching the side of her head, she tried to remember what that was all about.

"Now, how could that have happened in the accident?" she said angrily.

"What, Pam, what?"

"Well, look at this! Accidents don't unzip travel bags."

Melissa surveyed the trunk and said, "My heavens, your things are all over the trunk. Can you tell if anything is missing?"

"Not really, but I'm sure someone went through my stuff." *Someone did that*? Pamela asked herself fearfully. She had been chased in her dreams many times before. Is this more than a dream? A man...yes, a man...the airport! Is he after me? They were so tall...two men. The trunk...there was another man.

Her aunt interrupted her thoughts. "Why don't you check at the office?"

"Yeah, I'll do that."

Melissa helped her gather the items and place them back into the bag.

"Ah, lady, lots of people check in here every day to look for spare parts. We don't keep track of them unless they buy something."

"Well, someone was in my trunk and went through my carry-on bag," responded Pamela angrily.

"Oh, wait a minute—there was this guy. He described a vehicle—a red Chevy, saying it was his."

Melissa put her arm around Pamela's shoulder and calmly said, "Pam, let's get out of here. This place gives me the creeps. What's done is done."

Pamela felt her skin cringe as the puffy arm lay against her neck. She began to move her head from side to side, trying to shake the arm off. That woman has always treated me like a child she thought. Things haven't changed—she body's me to death. Even though I never liked being around her aunt, I have not choice but to play along. I need a place to stay right now.

"Auntie, I'm scared and don't know why. Someone had been following me. I have no idea who or why. Whoever it was may have emptied my carry-on bag."

"Your memory will come back, sweetie. Then you can go to the police if necessary."

Pamela heard her aunt express anger at the owner-operator of Kerrigan's. "You're a stupid idiot."

After the man spit on the ground and returned to his office, the two women drove onto I-75 toward Florida in Melissa's green Toyota.

"Can I stay at your place until I find one of my own?" Pamela asked her aunt, thinking that she owed me. Pamela's dad supported Melissa and put her up at his house when she was going through a divorce. Melissa should be grateful and she had an extra bedroom that was likely not doing much more than collecting dust.

"Of course you can stay at my place. The spare bedroom is available. You can relax on the beach and do whatever you want. You need time to heal." Melissa said, her voice tailing off.

They spent an entire day driving across Georgia and the northern part of Florida, arriving at Key Marie during the evening hours.

Pamela's memory of what happened in Indianapolis and on the highway after the crash was absent. She vaguely remembered meeting a man in a bar at the airport. There were actually three men, two of them very tall. Flying through space after passing a maroon Pontiac was her last recollection until waking up in the helicopter.

The next day, Monday, with the assistance of her auto insurance company, Pamela obtained a temporary car to use until the insurance claim was settled. Remembering the FedEx ticket in her purse, Pamela drove her rental blue Honda to the station identified in the claim check.

"Sign right here please," said the woman behind the counter.

Resisting the temptation to open the package right there, Pamela returned to Melissa's condo with it unopened.

Sliding a kitchen knife under the paper flap, she anxiously peeled it away. "What could this be?" She thought. Perhaps it's money. She stood there, stunned, after opening it in Melissa's kitchen. The huge green gem was something beyond her imagination. The circumference was close to that of a baseball. Taking it out on the deck, she was astonished at how it absorbed the sunlight. Where did it come from? Searching her memory over and over again, she drew a blank.

It wasn't exactly money, but it could be very valuable, she thought excitedly. Oh, what to do—tell my aunt? Show it to the police? She carried it into the living room and paced the room for a few moments. She felt her heart pounding. I'm not sure what to do.

Meanwhile, she needed a hiding place. Entering her bedroom, she looked around and walked into the bathroom. She retrieved a large box of cotton balls from the medicine cabinet. The gem fit in the box and was nicely secured by the cotton. Returning the box onto a shelf in the medicine cabinet, she left the room.

9

SERIN WAS BORN IN PORTLAND, OREGON, to an unwed mother. She was an alcoholic and he was forced to fend for himself after the age of eleven. Turning to crime for a living was the only viable choice he had. In later years he met Vince Gulloti at a poker game in Chicago. As time went by, Serin did odd jobs for Vince. One of the jobs resulted in a two year prison term.

He was christened with the name Benjamin Marshall Parks. The name Serin was given to him while in prison by one of the guards—he never did learn why. The name Ben Pierce was used by Serin whenever needed. The million dollars he was promised for the Guni job would set him up for five years or more. He was determined to turn over the stone to Vince at all costs.

He began his search for Pamela Zachary, at the Park Place condo units, 7600 Beach Street in Key Marie. After cruising by the complex a few times, he became familiar with the layout. Later, he found a motel to stay at, as close to Park Place as available. Right after checking in, he returned to Park Place and parked the pickup next to the curb across the street. It enabled him to watch some of the parking area in the garage, also the units across the street and the tennis courts.

His second day of surveillence produced results—Pamela Zachary, driving a blue Honda pulled out of the garage, stopped for traffic before turning left onto Beach Street. Serin followed her in the same pickup that he had stolen in Indianapolis. Pamela turned off Beach Street toward the ocean. She pulled into a parking lot that belonged to Overly's Bar & Grill on the north shore of the island.

Serin was glad that she was alone. He watched from a comfortable distance as she sat on a stool at the bar. She had downed her second glass of wine and appeared to be mesmerized by the surf crashing against a group of rocks that jutted out to sea. A man sat down next to her, probably in his thirties, and began forcing his attention on her.

Feeling confident that she would not recognize him, Serin sat on a barstool next to the young man. Serin was amused by the immature approach the man was using. Instead of working his way in with smooth talk, he began to touch her—lastly, putting an arm around her shoulder.

Pamela grabbed the young man's arm and pushed it away, "Hey, watch it," she snapped.

"Sorry," the guy slurred.

Wiping beer from his face, Serin smirked when Pamela told off the young punk. Serin's eyes locked on hers for a moment. Serin was pleased that she didn't recognize him—he needed that advantage. He was convinced that the stone was in her possession, likely hidden in her room at Park Place.

Serin became aware that Pamela was beginning to notice his interest in her confrontation with the young man. She put her fingers to her lips and looked at him. Quickly turning his head, he pulled on the brim of his cap, which was already pulled low over his eyes. Glancing at Pamela again, he was relieved that she was looking out the window at the surf. When the bartender set a bottle of beer on the bar in front of Serin, Pamela got off her stool and headed toward the door.

Serin took a couple of long gulps, set the bottle down and said to the bartender, "Cash me out."

Moving quickly out into the parking lot, he got there in time to see Pamela leaving in the blue Honda. He had no problem following. She was forced to drive under twenty-miles-per because a car driven by "a niner" was leading a caravan of vehicles. Niner's were usually northern snowbirds that drove their cars at a crawl.

Pamela turned off Beach Street and drove into the parking garage area at Park Place. Serin, who was following with the pickup, parked in a visitor spot and watched while she parked in the Unit 150 space. Remaining in the pickup truck, he saw her leave the car and disappear around the corner. Serin got out and followed. She must have gone up that stairway, he thought.

Serin was pleased with the results of his surveillance—he had learned exactly what she drove and where she parked. He walked back to the pickup truck and wrote down the license number of the blue Honda. Serin drove back out onto the street and returned to his motel.

———

PAMELA FELT SECURE PARKING THE CAR in one of the two stalls reserved for Unit 150. Once in her bedroom, she showered and got into her nightclothes. Her aunt was out for the evening with a male date. Pamela was relaxing on the couch in the living room when she remembered the gem. Returning to the bedroom, she fetched it from the medicine cabinet in the bathroom.

My God, it's huge, far bigger than any gem I've ever seen before, she thought. Tossing it up in the air, she caught it in one of her palms. *What do I do about this?* Putting aside her idea of showing it to Melissa, she made a decision to keep the gem a secret, at least until her memory returned.

Before falling asleep, she tossed and turned, feeling guilty about taking advantage of her aunt. If it weren't for the potential of the gem, I'd be gone to Sarasota tomorrow, she thought. She should know by now that I'm not a doll. Gad, I hate the way that woman snuggles up to me.

She was asleep by the time Melissa came home with her date.

10

PAMELA HAD MADE COFFEE and was sitting out on the balcony reading the paper when Melissa entered, yawning. Pamela lowered her cup and looked up at her aunt.

"How was your date?"

"We had a great time. Bill is such a nice man."

"Cool," Pamela replied.

Melissa got an empty cup from the cupboard above the counter and added, "Bill has great possibilities. We had gone to a dinner theater and a local version of *Pandora's Box*. I like Bill. He is such a breath of fresh air, especially at an honesty level—way ahead of that Dale Strong, who is out for my money. I should warn my friend Lucy Barrows about Dale."

Pamela and her aunt were the same height. They had similar blonde hair and narrow faces. Except for crow's feet wrinkles next to Melissa's eyes, a neutral observer would think they were sisters. Pamela let her hair grow long, almost down to the shoulders. Melissa's was cut shorter, even with the chin line.

"Anything new this morning?" she asked Pamela.

"No, not really, Melissa. I really appreciate what you are doing for me, but I'm going out today and check on some of the realtors in Sarasota. My job doesn't start for a couple of weeks, but I need to find a place to live."

"Oh, come on now, Pam, you can stay here with me as long as you need."

The two women remained on the balcony, sipping coffee and chatting. Later, Pamela made two phone calls and headed down to the garage. She unlocked her car, placed the key in the ignition and turned it. There wasn't any response. The battery was dead. Darn it, she thought, the insurance company loaned me a bummer.

Returning, she explained the problem to Melissa.

"Why don't you take my car? I'm not going anywhere today, just planning on spending the afternoon on the beach."

"Oh, you're so sweet...cool," replied Pamela. "When I get back, I'll call a service station for a jump start."

Melissa retrieved her car keys from her purse and handed them to Pam.

She placed her soft arm around Pamela's shoulder. "Have a fun day, Pamela. I sure will."

Pamela pulled away from Melissa. "Thanks."

She was scheduled to meet with a realtor in an hour. After the meeting, she planned to call Tom Hastings. The reason for her decision to contact him was to help refresh her memory of what had happened up north—he was there at the accident.

She really didn't dislike her aunt so much—just couldn't stand her snuggling to my body. Right now, she thought, I don't have any choice. It's a place to stay until I find out what the gem is worth. I've got a hunch it's worth a lot of money—probably more than my wildest dreams.

———

TOM WAS AWAKENED BY THE SOUND of heavy surf beating against the shoreline. While the coffee was brewing, he walked out onto the balcony. He watched a man and woman, hand in hand, working their way along the beach. They paused occasionally to examine deposits left by the retreating surf.

The sky met the water in almost a straight line in the north but faded into a haze to the south. Tom wondered if there was bad weather coming from the southern part of the gulf. He was looking forward to spending productive tanning time on the beach that afternoon.

A speedboat was approaching from the south. As it got closer, he could see it getting tossed about. Not much fun, Tom thought. The driver was standing and leaning forward. Flocks of gulls and pelicans scurried to make way for the noisy intruder.

He thought about Julie. She was stuck in an office building in St. Paul. Julie would soon be here, enjoying the surf and the beach. One of her favorite pastimes was scavenging the beach just after dawn, searching for newly washed-up shells and other treasures. She is a darn good tennis player, too, pushing me to the hilt most of the time.

Tom returned to the kitchen, swung a cabinet door open and grabbed a cup. Filling it with coffee, he returned to the balcony and sat down. Two boats were barely visible through the haze on the horizon. Down below, he noticed a man wearing a baseball cap standing on the sand, just out of reach of the surf. There was something about him that looked familiar—the cap, *he had seen that cap before.*

His phone rang. Probably Julie, he thought.

"Hello," he answered.

"Ah, are you Tom Hastings?"

"Yes, I am."

"I got your name from the police. I'm the person that you helped rescue back in southern Tennessee."

"Oh my gosh, when did you get out of the hospital? I'm happy to hear your voice. How are you doin'?"

"Actually, I wasn't hurt too badly. Quite the coincidence, but I am staying with my aunt at 150 Park Place. I think we're neighbors."

"Yes, that is a coincidence. Amazing!" Tom exclaimed.

"However, you were heading this direction when you left the road," he added.

Tom liked the sound of her voice, soft and smooth, a lot like Julie's.

"My memory of what happened, between the air terminal in Indianapolis and the helicopter ride to the hospital is missing. I'm having a hard time connecting things. You were there, at the accident...you helped me...I would like to thank you in person, if possible."

"Sure. How about meeting down in the courtyard by the pool?" asked Tom.

"That would be good, but there are usually a lot of people around. How about on the beach?"

"That would work," said Tom. "Ah...I had planned on having lunch at Steinbrook, a German restaurant at the Keys Mall, about two miles south of here. Perhaps you would you join me?"

"That sounds cool. I'll ask my aunt how to find the Keys Mall. What was the name of that...restaurant, again?"

"Steinbrook...Steinbrook, in Keys Mall, about in the middle."

"I've got some other stuff to do this morning, but I'll be there...do my best to find it."

"Great. I'll wear my straw hat. I'm a senior and wear glasses and have a mustache."

The next phone call Tom had was from his daughter, Kris. She had lived in Europe the past four years, finally settling down as an international airline flight attendant. When Kris found out her dad was going to be in Florida for a month, she manipulated her schedule to lay over in Miami for a few days.

Kris looks a lot like her mother did, Tom thought. Her sparkling brown eyes and long dark brown hair are the spitting image of Becky. Tom reminisced about the last time the three of them were out for dinner together at Mary Ann's. It was only two days later when a pair of plane hijackers took Becky's life.

I can still feel the warmness of Kris's hand when we walked down the aisle together at the funeral. Geez, that was an awful day, Tom thought remorsefully.

"Dad, I plan on taking some days off. I'm not sure when it will be, but as soon as I find out, I'll let you know. I would like to come and see you."

"Geez, that would be great, Kris. Just let me know. I have an extra bedroom."

Tom was excited hearing from his daughter. He hadn't seen her for a long time. It was last Thanksgiving, he thought. Yeah, she flew to Minneapolis and we had turkey at my Towers apartment. Then, we took in a movie. Her brother Brad couldn't make it. He spent the holiday at Terry's parent's place in Madison, Wisconsin. Amazing how Brad's wife resembles Kris, he thought.

11

TOM HAD PARKED HIS PONTIAC AND WALKED across the driving lane that paralleled the sidewalk. He headed for the Steinbrook restaurant at five minutes to 12:00. It was in the same strip mall as the hardware store, about eight units down. A senior gentleman reading a newspaper was sitting on the fancy bench next to the door. He looked up when Tom approached.

"Anything big in the news?" Tom asked.

The man looked up and didn't answer. Noticing an earring, Tom didn't press the conversation and entered the restaurant. Tom was from the old school and didn't like earrings on men.

A tall maitre d', speaking with a German accent, greeted him. He took a table in the corner that overlooked the sidewalk and parking lot. After ordering a glass of beer, he relaxed and looked around the room. The walls were decorated with large framed photographs of ocean liners. The tablecloths and other linens were red and white checkered. There was background music—a soft mixture of German vocals and violin.

Tom was delighted with the atmosphere. When the maitre d' approached, Tom explained that he was meeting a woman.

At two minutes past 12:00 noon, a blue Honda pulled into a vacant spot directly across from the entry door of the Steinbrook. The blonde woman that emerged was dressed in white shorts and a blue top. She looked average height, Tom thought. Her hair was long, brushing her shoulders. Her facial skin was pale—apparently not being in the sun much. The woman's lips were large and colored bright red. Large, blue-framed sunglasses covered most of the upper half of her face.

She paused and looked in all directions before attempting to cross the traffic lane. Tom was watching. She walked with a smooth swagger that was attractive, he thought. Entering, she looked around and appeared anxious. Tom stood and waved. Smiling and seeming relieved, she approached the table. Tom stood and extended his right hand. She grasped it and looked up into his eyes.

The inside of Tom's stomach melted as she continued to hold his hand. He thought about a friend of his back in Minnesota that had married a younger woman. It was working well for his friend, even though there were three teenagers. *I wonder if Pamela has children. This is not a good time to ask*, he thought.

"How can I ever thank you enough for what you did for me at the accident? You are so cool."

"You are welcome, but I didn't really do very much, just called 911 and went down the slope with another guy."

"What guy?"

"Oh, as I recall, his name was Ben Pierce. He pulled up behind me in a pickup truck after I stopped on the shoulder of the highway."

That's who it may have been on the beach wearing the baseball cap—Ben Pierce, Tom thought.

"The two of us went down the slope and found you in your car," Tom added. "Two highway patrolmen showed up and they called in a helicopter."

Pamela frowned and looked up at the wall behind Tom's head. Bringing up the thumb and forefinger of her left hand, she supported her chin. Tom noticed the long narrow fingers and lily-white hand. The blue stone on her ring finger looked impressive.

"I'm trying to remember, Mr. Hastings. The police tell me I was driving around a hundred-miles-per. I never drive that fast—unless, unless...someone was chasing me. Do you think I was going that fast?" Pamela asked.

"Well, I was doing about eighty-two. When I saw you come up behind me, I was afraid it might be a highway patrolman. When I saw the red, I knew it wasn't. You passed me quite easily...went by like a rocket."

"I'm so confused, Mr. Hastings. I keep seeing a shadow—someone I met at the airport in Indianapolis. Pickup truck, you mentioned a pickup truck."

"Yes, the guy that pulled up behind me on the shoulder of the road. He drove one of those...a pickup truck."

Pamela frowned again, staring out into space. Tom looked down at the tabletop and allowed her time to think.

"What did he look like, this Ben Pierce?"

"Ah...middle aged guy...about forty-five. He was wearing a baseball cap. About my height...no glasses...had a ponytail of blond hair...narrow face...lots of stubble."

"What was his voice like, Mr. Hastings?"

"Sort of raspy, like he needed to clear his throat. You can call me Tom, Pam."

Pam shook her head. "I can't remember meeting anyone looking like that...I don't like whiskers...they remind me of someone who I'd rather forget."

"Can I help you?" asked the waitress in a strong German accent.

Pamela jerked slightly and responded, "Oh, yes, I would like a cup of tea to start."

"How about you, sir, would you like another beer?"

"Ah, no, I'll have a cup of coffee."

"Very good, sir," responded the waitress and left.

When the coffee was poured, Tom took a sip and added, "Oh yes, an odd thing happened down the slope at your car. When I was checking you out in the front seat, this Ben Pierce guy was trying to get your trunk open. I remember glancing back there after feeling the car bounce a little—sort of like after someone rocks a car to get unstuck from a snow bank in Minnesota."

Pamela's eyes narrowed and her lips parted slightly. She didn't say anything, but Tom felt that his mention of the name Ben Pierce and the car trunk disturbed her. The waitress returned and they ordered lunch.

Pamela's demeanor changed. She took a long drink from a glass of water and looked out the window—a puzzled look on her face. She didn't ask any more questions and after their food arrived, they ate in silence.

Tom looked across the table occasionally, wondering why this woman had taken an interest in him. Was there more than the accident? She would be nice getting to know, he thought—attractive and pleasant.

After finishing her plate, Pamela said, "Well, I've got to leave. Thank you very much, Tom. Our talk helped. You are staying in the condo overlooking the beach, second floor, aren't you?"

"Yes, I am, Pam, and you're on first, overlooking the pool?"

"Ah, yes, I'm staying with my aunt, Melissa. Do you know her?"

"No, I don't. Is she renting or does she own?"

"She owns her unit. I will never be able to thank her enough for picking me up in Chattanooga."

Pamela reached in her purse for a billfold. Tom reached over, placed his hand on her wrist and said, "I'll take care of this, Pam. Just go ahead and leave if you wish."

Without saying another word, Pamela Zachary stood up, hoisted the purse strap over her shoulder and strode out of the restaurant.

She's really nice, thought Tom. She's got that look in her eyes—adventurous and alluring. You never know. Well, I can put those thoughts aside with Julie arriving on Saturday. Besides that, she's at least twenty years younger. Kris would frown on me giving up on Julie—She really likes that woman.

12

SERIN EXPECTED IT WAS GOING TO BE A LONG DAY. Parking his pickup in a public lot about a quarter mile from Park Place, he gathered his beach paraphernalia and headed toward the water.

Wearing shorts and sandals, he fit the profile of an average beach walker. Arriving at the front of Park Place he observed there were four people using the lounges out front. They didn't notice when he walked to the wrought iron gate. He gave the handle a twist, but it didn't budge. It was apparent the gate was there for security reasons. Quickly he returned to the beach. After remaining at water's edge for a few minutes, he returned to the lounges.

Selecting an empty one, he spread his gear out. Not being certain that he would recognize Pamela Zachary, he needed an opportunity to get into the Park Place complex courtyard. Leaving his things on the lounge, he returned to the gate, hoping to manipulate someone to let him in.

Finally an attractive smiling woman came by and opened the gate. "I left my key upstairs," Serin lied. She accommodated him further by unlocking the second gate allowing access to the condo units.

Going up one flight of stairs and into the outdoor corridor, he selected a location where he could watch the door of Unit 150. Serin pretended to be watching the surf while keeping his hands on the wrought iron railing.

At last, just after the lunch hour, the door of Unit 150 opened. A woman, who was wearing a large straw hat and extraordinarily large blue framed sunglasses, emerged. She didn't pay any attention to Serin while turning the corner to head down the stairs. Moments later he followed and watched her pass through the first gate, into the courtyard and through the second gate.

Once again, he had to wait for another resident to come along to open the gate and allow him to access to the beach.

His lucky day—the woman in the straw hat had taken up a position on a lounge only three spaces down from his. It had to be Pamela Zachary. *A million dollars*—Serin would kill for less than that. Vince always talked big. *Boys, I've got a deal for you*, is what he said and meant every word of it.

Ratcheting the back of the lounge up slightly, he positioned himself to watch Pamela unobtrusively. Like everyone else, he was wearing sunglasses. Pulling the beak of his cap low, Serin watched and waited. He paid close attention when two of the sunbathers picked up their belongings and left. Except for himself, there were two others and the Zachory woman remaining.

The pills that Serin had taken the night before for sleep hadn't lost their effect. He knew taking more than two was dangerous. It took six to get him to sleep. Lying on the lounge with the sun beating down on him, he couldn't help himself and reluctantly fell asleep.

An hour later, the pain at the top of his shoulders awakened him. Suffering from immediate feelings of panic, he was relieved to see the blonde woman still lying on the lounge. He had not intended to fall asleep. After sitting up he stretched and gently rubbed his shoulders.

The other two sunbathers had left. He was alone on the sand with Pamela Zachory. Scanning the beach, the nearest person was heading away from Park Place—*now was the time*.

Getting up off the lounge, he pulled the brim of his cap down even lower. Gathering his things together, he bunched them on the lounge. Reaching into a small bag he grabbed a knife. It's been a long time since I've used this, he thought. Yeah, it was about ten years ago, in Chicago—the handle feels different.

Calmly stepping over to where the blonde was lying with her eyes closed, he came up behind her—she was dozing. What a break, he thought.

Looking back at the condo complex, he didn't see anyone watching. There were only two walkers on the beach and they had just passed. The noisy surf easily masked the sound of the blade as it released from the handle. He put his left hand over the woman's mouth and pushed the blade directly into her heart. Her body convulsed for a few seconds and finally went limp.

Serin quickly wiped the blade using the woman's beach towel. After placing the knife into his pocket, he pressed the towel over the spurting blood and pushed the straw hat down over her face. Some of the blood had dripped over the woman's side forming a puddle in the sand. By pushing sand with his foot, he covered most of the reddish discoloration. After applying his towel the dripping had stopped. He quickly grabbed her purse and returned to his lounge.

Anxiously, he searched it. Not expecting to find the stone, he removed a set of keys that he was hoping would be there. Four people were approaching along the beach from the south. He waited for them to pass before returning to Pamela's lounge to return her purse.

Grabbing the rest of his beach items from his lounge, he used one of the keys to open the gate and enter the courtyard. Moving quickly, he opened the second gate and dashed up the stairs to Unit 150. Considering the possibility of someone coming by, he laid down his things half the distance between units, The large key turned the lock and the door opened.

Once inside the condo, he began his search. Starting in the main bedroom, he went through every dresser drawer. As Serin searched, he was careful to return items to their original place. He found no stone in the boxes on the shelf of the bedroom closet, either.

Serin had generously allowed himself an hour to find the stone. He felt that staying longer would be stretching his luck. Looking at his watch, he saw there was still plenty of time. The living room and kitchen searches did not produce the stone. Pushing open a door, he entered the second bedroom. There were empty suitcases in the closet. His heart skipped a beat when he spotted the carry-on bag. He wasn't certain, but it looked like the one in the trunk of the Chevy. The zippered side compartment was empty. The bottom of the bag contained a few miscellaneous items—no stone.

The medicine cabinet was a lot like the other one—the usual stuff inside. *This had to be Pamela Zachary's bedroom.* The other, bigger bedroom was her aunt's—the envelope in Pamela Zachary's carry-on bag had her name on it, he remembered. After searching all of the drawers in the second bedroom, he searched the closet. There were blankets and pillows on the shelves. The Guni was big—should be easy to spot, he thought.

Thoughts of panic and defeat were playing on Serin's mind as he sat on the living room sofa. His watch showed that he was beyond his planned limit of time—the hour was up. *Where in the hell did she hide the stone?* She may have taken it elsewhere, such as a safe deposit box in a bank. Naw, he thought. She wouldn't know its value.

Serin thought about her reaction when noticing him messing with the zipper of the carry-on bag at the airport. Surely, she would have wondered why. *What would she do with the stone after finding it?* Would she take it somewhere to find out its value? Eventually, yes, he thought. But, she was released from the hospital only yesterday.

The sound of a key turning in the door jerked his mind alert. Getting up off the couch quickly, he stepped out onto the balcony. Peeking around the edge of the drapes, he saw the face of the person that entered—it was Pamela Zachary. Serin felt a bomb go off in his stomach. *I've screwed up big time and killed the wrong dame.* Did I kill her aunt instead? Damn, did I botch this whole thing?

Serin thought of Vince Gulloti sitting behind his expensive desk in Atlanta, waiting for him to show up. If Vince knew what I just did, he'd kill me. Vince always went about things organized and rarely made a mistake.

Serin was determined to recover the stone. He had just seen Pamela go into her bedroom. Reaching into his pocket, he grabbed the knife and was about to press the issue—another killing wouldn't make any difference, he thought.

A knock on the door sent him back behind the drapes. "Anybody home?" a man's voice asked.

Serin saw Pamela emerge from the bedroom and respond to the person at the door. She talked to him for a moment and followed him out into the corridor.

Hastily, Serin moved to the door and peeked out. Great, he thought. They're gone. Exiting the condo, he double-stepped the stairs on the way down and left via the garage. Five minutes later, he was back in the pickup and on his way back to his motel. His only gain had been the key that opened the door to the gates and Unit 150. I'll be back and soon, he thought—real soon.

13

TOM RETURNED TO HIS CONDO RENTAL about 4:30 p.m. after picking up some supplies. He gazed out over the ocean and looked forward to getting into swim trunks and enjoying the beach.

Before heading down, he stepped out onto the balcony to check for the availability of a lounge. There were plenty of empty ones, he noticed. His curiosity was aroused when he saw a cluster of beach-clad people milling about. One of the women standing at the edge of the group was holding a hand to her face.

A uniformed police officer was leaning over one of the lounges, which appeared occupied. Towels were covering all of the person except for a tuft of blonde hair. Tom pulled up a chair next to the rail, sat down and anxiously watched. The cluster of people was growing in numbers, the most recent to join was Richard Schweitzer, one of Tom's new acquaintances. Richard broke away from the others and approached the officer. They talked. The officer pointed toward the lounge and shook his head.

A woman wearing a tan straw hat with a red band and wide brim had joined the cluster. After spending a few moments with the group, she hurried over to the police officer and Richard Schweitzer. There was something familiar about the way she moved, Tom thought. The officer took her by the arm and escorted her to the towel-covered lounge.

Tom could see him carefully lift the beach towel. The woman screamed and jerked her hand upward, causing the hat to fall off her head. Tom was startled. The straw-hatted woman was Pamela Zachary. Rising up from his chair, Tom stood and placed both hands on the rail. *I'm staying with my aunt* was what she had said at the restaurant.

After seeing Corrith Schweitzer place both arms around Pamela, Tom hastened back into his condo and headed down the stairs. Entering the courtyard, he could hear the sound of a siren in the distance.

Tom cautiously walked through the gate and over to the cluster of people.

"What happened?" he asked one of them.

"Someone has been murdered, right over there on that lounge."

Edging over to Richard Schweitzer who was standing next to his wife and the sobbing Pamela, Tom asked him, "What happened?"

"It's Pamela's aunt, she's dead—murdered," Richard responded.

Pamela turned, saw Tom and fell into his arms. "Oh, Tom, it's my aunt."

Tom held Pamela close and mumbled, "Oh my God, that's awful."

They remained close for at least a minute. There was something about her body language that puzzled him—she seemed so stiff. Her sobbing stopped when she pressed her mouth against his chest.

After they separated, Tom looked into her eyes—they were rigid and cold. If there were any tears earlier, they've dried up. Ann Plum moved up and took Pamela's hand.

In her high-pitched voice, Ann said, "So sorry. Your aunt was one of my best friends."

Tom backed away, startled by the voice of Ann Plum. It reminded him of a grade school teacher who had spanked him when he was eight years old.

———

VINCE GULLOTI, SIPPING A WHISKEY at Lowe's Bar and Grill in down town Atlanta, was becoming increasingly agitated by Serin's delay.

"Damn, if Serin double-crossed me, he's dead. I'll find that dimwit, if it takes me the rest of my life," he whispered.

It had been about five days since Serin called from Chattanooga. Finding him would be like looking for a needle in a haystack. Just have to wait until he shows up or the stone surfaces, he soberly thought. According to his contacts in Indianapolis, the police had not caught up with the dimwit.

The police had picked up Terrance, but they didn't have enough reason to detain him—he didn't have the stone. There was another potential problem for Vince. He had heard that the Saudi Prince, using his own agents, was privately searching for the stone. They likely will find Terrance. If they kill him, that would be okay, an extra million for me, he thought.

When Vince sold a car, he always needed to feel that the buyer was getting a good deal, one that was good for both the buyer and the seller. He thought long and hard before deciding to take on the Guni job. I could benefit immensely, he thought. So would the two setup guys in New York. Serin and Terrance would make more money than they knew what to do with. The Saudis would learn to be more careful flashing their expensive wares around.

The trail of the Guni through Serin to me wouldn't be easy for the Saudis, he thought. Vince made sure of that during the planning stage. Even if the Saudis caught up with Serin or Terrance, he felt secure— there was no live connection.

Vince had made some calls earlier in the day to contacts in Chattanooga. They had agreed to cooperate and maintain vigilance for the missing Serin.

———

BARB SMITH OF THE KEY MARIE'S POLICE DEPARTMENT was doing her nails when the 911 phone rang. She and her husband Tully were the only dispatchers that the department employed. The police department of Key Marie was accessible by phone from 7:00 in the morning until midnight.

Barb was pleased with Tully after he had agreed to take the early shift. Looking at her watch, she thought about him. I took the sleepy man's place a little over an hour ago at 2:30. Barb smiled and visualized Tully in bed, sound asleep.

The department was housed in a building a block off Beach Street.

Captain Ken McSorley, who usually worked about ten daylight hours a day, was the chief. He was a big man at a height of six-two and sported a generous midriff, bulging and projecting above his belt. Like the other staff members, he wore a brown uniform with a Royal Mounted Police type hat. He was in a patrol car with Officer Nate Bloomberg when the call came in.

"Park Place. Nate, do you know where that is?"

"Yeah, it's up north, right on Beach Street."

"Okay, we need to go there. According to Barb, there's a dead woman—possibly a murder."

———

NATE BLOOMBERG HAD JOINED THE FORCE TWO YEARS AGO. He passed the police academy finals at Tampa, first in his class. He was single and lived in an apartment on the mainland side of the island. Flicking on the siren and the flashers, he pulled out onto the street.

Nate had expected to have more authority when he joined the force. His boss, Chief McSorley, ran a tight ship, a very tight ship. Nate soon found out McSorley's officers couldn't do much more than help school kids across the street.

He had been totally embarrassed by the chief after arresting a young woman for speeding and driving without a driver's license. The chief tore up the citation when Nate brought her to the station. How was Nate to know the driver was the daughter of a city commissioner? It led Nate to believe that his boss played favorites, something he had been taught to avoid by his instructors at the police academy.

Nate didn't like the way McSorley talked to Barb, either. In Nate's mind, she was valuable and a nice employee. The chief treated her like dirt at times.

"Look at those idiots, crawling along about nine miles an hour. Jesus, Nate, can you get around them?"

"I'll try, Chief."

Nate saw an opening in the oncoming lane. He pulled into the lane and passed a bunch of cars. The first car that he met was forced to take the sidewalk.

"Serves 'em damn right," said the chief, "Will ya' look at that, someone with brains, they pulled off and stopped."

"Illinois plates," Nate added.

"Someone over there is waiting for us," Nate said after pulling into the parking area at Park Place.

The two officers exited the car quickly. The man in the parking lot approached. "I'm the manager, the one who called you. Follow me, I'll get you through the gates."

The manager escorted the two officers to the lounge where the victim lay. Nate saw the stab wound in the chest. It didn't take the chief long to diagnose the reason for the woman's death. Nate saw fear in his boss's eyes. Probably his first murder, he thought. I wonder if he knows what to do...sure looks insecure. Best I remain quiet and wait for him to say something.

———

SARGENT CLIFF JOHNSON AND OFFICER STEVE HARRIS had been patrolling the school zones. Though the traffic moved very slow along Beach Street, the city council insisted that the police be present when students were released from school each day.

"Hey Cliff, did you hear that?" said Steve. "That was the Chief. He and Nate are headed over to 7660 Beach. Someone has been killed."

"Shucks, it looks like things are under control here," answered Sargent Cliff Johnson anxiously. "Let's head over. We can probably be of a lot more help there than here."

———

PAMELA WAS DISTRAUGHT. After the ambulance left, the police disrupted her condo privacy.

The larger of the officers said, "I'm Police Chief McSorley. This is Officer Bloomberg. We need to check out Melissa Buntrock's condo. She was your aunt, I understand."

"Yes, she was," answered Pamela, her voice tailing off to a whisper.

"Just have a seat, this shouldn't take too long," added Chief McSorley.

Pamela saw two more officers come through the front door. The Chief looked at her and said, "Those two are Officer's Johnson and Harris."

While the officers were going through her aunt's bedroom, Pamela paced around the condo nervously. I had nothing to do with her murder, she kept thinking. The police mustn't know that the person who killed my aunt could have been after the gem. It could have been me out there on that lounge.

Pamela felt herself shaking with fear. She sat on the couch in the living room for a few minutes, then moved outdoors and sat in one of the deck chairs in the small alcove. An officer guarding the door occupied the other.

"Are you related to the victim?" Officer Nate asked.

"Yes, I am, as I told the other officers...ah, was...my aunt. I'm stunned...can't believe what's happened. Don't even know who to call."

"If you would like, when we get back to headquarters, there's a social worker we use. I could send her over."

"No thanks. I just remembered. I do have someone who I can contact. There is my other aunt, who lives in Atlanta. I'll call her. She'll know what to do. She's cool."

"Okay, ma'am, sorry about what happened."

See! They don't know what's going on...they know nothing about the gem. I'm not guilty of anything, she thought. I need to remain calm...tell no one. After all, I don't even fully know what happened.

An hour later, two officers exited the condo with Chief McSorley close behind. He turned and said, "Ma'am, we're all through inside. You can have it back. Thanks for your cooperation. But, before we leave, I need to ask you some questions."

Pamela took a deep breath and stood.

"Please sit down, ma'am. I'll make this as brief as possible," said Chief McSorley.

Five minutes later, Pamela watched them leave and hastened to her bathroom. Removing some of the cotton from the box, she was extremely relieved to see the over-sized green gem—fondling it, she felt her heart throbbing. Pamela sat down on the stool and lowered her head down between her hands.

I didn't kill Melissa. Someone else did. I didn't steal the gem. Someone gave it to me. I was put at great risk, now I need to benefit. It's mine.

Pamela thought about what had happened earlier after arriving back home following lunch with Tom Hastings. I felt uncomfortable in the condo. Little things seemed to be out of place. The manager had come and I stepped out for a couple of minutes to pick up a package that was in his office.

When I got back, there was this strange smell—someone had been there other than my aunt. The police officers who were searching the condo didn't smell like that.

The gem— was it connected to my aunt's murder? If so, could it be worth a lot of money? Showing it to the police would certainly mean losing it, especially if it's really valuable. This could be the opportunity of a lifetime, especially after screwing up my life so bad to this point. I need a new hiding place—time to think—and plan.

The key to Melissa's condo! Pamela dashed into her late aunt's bedroom where the purse was lying on the bed. She dumped out the contents. *No key! Whoever killed her took it.*

14

THE PHONE RANG IN UNIT 230. Tom answered and was surprised to hear the soft voice of Pamela Zachary.

"Tom, I hate to bother you, but I'm scared. The police just left and I'm all alone. This condo gives me the creeps with my aunt gone."

"Yeah, Pam, I feel for you. Must be quite a shock."

"I'm devastated," Pam answered, her voice breaking down.

"Oh my God, do you have anyone, a relative, someone to help you right now. This is awful."

"Yes, I've called Melissa's sister in Atlanta, my other aunt. She's coming down tomorrow. Meanwhile, I need someone to talk to. Are you free this evening?"

"Yes of course...why don't you come over and we can go out and get something to eat. How would that be?"

"Okay...just great. I'll be over in about half-an-hour."

Pamela was scared, but she felt good, she thought. First, my aunt is never going to hug me again. Secondly, I have someone to lean on. Tom Hastings seems like a nice man. Besides, he could come in handy.

——

AFTER HANGING UP, TOM WAS ON EDGE—not being sure what he was getting into. He thought about Julie coming on Saturday. Hopefully this mess—the murder—will be cleared up by then. Meanwhile, there shouldn't be any harm in helping out the distraught woman.

The gentle tap on the door a few minutes later generated a grain of fear in Tom. His mind flashed back to the past two years of being involved in a series of deaths—all murders. There were three in his country neighborhood in central Minnesota and four at his present home at the Towers in Minneapolis. Both killers were caught, convicted and sent to prison.

Surely my luck is changing, he thought. The young woman that was knocking on the door should have been killed back there in Tennessee. It was a miracle that she survived. She's coming over to thank me, just like the highway patrolman predicted. Or, does she have some other motive?

"Come on in, Pam, I'm having a beer. Would you like one or perhaps a glass of wine?" Tom offered even though he realized his guest had just lost her aunt—not to underestimate the trauma Pam suffered from the terrifying accident in Tennessee.

"Yes, I'll have one...a beer I mean. It'll probably help me relax. Don't bother with a glass."

Tom gestured for Pam to sit on the couch in the living room. She was dressed in denim shorts and a white blouse. Returning from the kitchen with a beer and napkin, he handed her the bottle.

"Thanks so much, this is really going to help me relax. It's been a tough day."

Sitting in an armchair next to the couch, Tom watched as Pamela downed about a third of the beer on the first lift.

"I know you're going through a tough time, but you need to take care of yourself. Do you need to eat?"

"You're probably right. My appetite is non-existent right now, but I should have something"

"I can't help you out right here, at my apartment, but I've heard of a good place not far from here, Overly's. They've got good food, someone said. Do you feel up to it?"

"Okay. I know it's best for me."

———

SERIN KNEW HE WAS RUNNING OUT OF TIME. Sooner or later, Vince was going to find out he was not in Chattanooga and would come looking for him. Vince has contacts all over. He paid big bucks for information—no use trying to hide.

Not finding the stone in Pamela Zachary's condo was frustrating and devastating for Serin. Could she have stored it some other place— maybe a safety deposit box? Damn, he should have taken the purse, perhaps a key to the bank box—but then, it wasn't hers, anyhow. It belonged to her aunt.

Serin was glad Pamela Zachary was still alive. He could force her to talk. A knife pushing into the skin on her neck should do the trick.

After parking, Serin entered Overly's Bar & Grill, taking a seat at the far and darker end of the bar. Three beers later, his heart jumped into his throat. He saw Pamela Zachary enter the bar and grill, or at least someone who looked like her. She was with a guy. Jesus, he realized, it's the same guy from down on the slope at the accident in Tennessee. Serin searched his mind for a name— Hastings. That's it. What the hell is going on here? *What kind of game is that old bozo playing with me?*

15

"THERE'S A BOOTH OVER IN THE CORNER. Should we grab it?" asked Tom.

"That'll be fine," answered Pamela.

"What'll you two have?" asked a shorts-clad waiter.

"I'll have a Bud. How about you, Pam?" asked Tom.

"Yes, that'll be fine."

"Would you bring us an appetizer menu?" asked Tom.

"Sure will."

A minute later, two Budweiser's and the appetizer menus were delivered to their booth.

"Tom, I really appreciate this, spending time with me until my aunt comes."

"So, when was it that you mentioned earlier...your aunt coming?" asked Tom.

"Tomorrow. She lives in Atlanta. That's going to take a load off my mind, arrangements and all that. I don't have a clue on how to handle it."

"Complications like this have a habit of working out. Try not to worry."

"You know, Tom, I'm sort of an outcast from my family. That is...I ran away from home at age sixteen. What a stupid thing to do! On a motorcycle yet—those long dark curls of his were everything, so I thought."

Tom listened as Pamela continued. "Two months later, I was forced to call my dad from a gas station in West Virginia. The rotten guy dumped me. Dad came and got me. He wasn't very happy about what I did. When the pregnancy test came in positive a few months later, he really hit the roof.

"So, I was sent away to a girls boarding school. After the baby was adopted, I finished high school, grew up and returned to the real world. Got a job in Richmond and met some new people. I met another guy several years later. We were supposed to be married, but he died of a drug overdose. Can you beat that?"

"That's quite the story. What brings you here to the Keys?" asked Tom.

"I needed a change. My job was barely keeping my head above water, financially that is. The job market in Florida sounded inviting and because of the efforts of my dad, I have a job waiting for me in Sarasota."

Tom drank three beers while Pam had two. They ate two plates of appetizers. The bill came and Pam made an effort to take it, but Tom insisted on paying the tab.

While Tom was signing the credit card slip, Pam said, "Tom, I appreciate all you've done for me so far, but there's one more favor that I would like to ask."

"What's that?" asked Tom.

"I need a place to sleep tonight. Being alone in 150 would just be too uncomfortable for me. Would you...could you let me use your spare bedroom? Only one night would be necessary. I'll be out tomorrow when my aunt gets here."

"Sure, I'll be glad to help you out," replied Tom.

"I'm so relieved and grateful. Thanks so much."

———

SERIN WAS WATCHING TOM AND PAMELA. He felt intrigued that the two appeared to be enjoying each other. Maybe the they are in cahoots. Maybe it wasn't a coincidence that he was the first to show up when her car went over the side, thought Serin.

His hope was that Pamela Zachary would be home by herself tonight since he had the key to the condo. Then he had a troubling thought. Would they have noticed her aunt's key missing by now?

Pamela glanced in his direction and Serin jerked his head back to face the back of the bar. He was glad that Hastings was sitting on the other side. That man might recognize me. Got to be careful.

The bar and grill had gotten crowded. The standing room in the bar area was full of people. Hardly anyone noticed Tom escort Pamela toward the exit door, except the man with the baseball cap. His beak was still pulled low over his eyes. After the couple exited the building, Serin got off the stool and followed. He saw them drive off in a maroon Pontiac—same car as the one on the highway in Tennessee, Serin remembered.

Serin followed until the Pontiac drove into the main level parking lot at Park Place. He drove past half-a-block and pulled into one of the visiting parking spaces two buildings down. Walking back toward Park Place, he looked for the maroon Pontiac. He found it readily, noticing that it was parked in one of Unit 230's spaces.

Returning outside, he watched with excitement as the lights in Unit 150 came on. Reaching into his pocket, he felt the keys that he had lifted from the purse of the woman on the lounge. Four in the morning will work, he thought.

16

TOM HAD ESCORTED PAMELA TO UNIT 150 after returning from Overly's.

"Would you like me to wait?" He asked.

"No, It'll only take me a couple of minutes."

Tom waited until he was sure that Pam was safe and said, "I'll leave the front door unlocked."

"Okay, thanks, be up in minutes," replied Pam.

After Tom returned to his condo, he dialed Julie's number.

"Hello. It's good to hear from you, Tom. How are things down there?"

"Well, Julie, it seems as if I'm a marked man. There was a woman murdered here yesterday, on a lounge down on the beach."

"That's incredible, especially after what's happened up north at your country home, and the Towers in Minneapolis."

"Well, let's hope it doesn't involve me or spill over into your visit," said Tom.

"Did you go to that Yankees game in Tampa on Tuesday?"

"Yeah, I sure did, quite the thrill. I got a couple of tickets for Sunday. Would you like to go?"

"Sure would."

Tom was careful not to make any mention of establishing a friendship with the niece of the murdered woman. Julie may not have liked the idea of Pamela spending the night in his spare bedroom. He was looking forward to Julie's visit. He and Julie would both enjoy spending time on the beach and exploring the restaurants in the area.

After another ten minutes of conversation, Julie said, "It's time for me to go to bed. Big day tomorrow."

They exchanged goodnights, Tom hung up the phone. He went to the fridge and opened a beer. He knew that allowing Pamela to stay at his condo could spell trouble. On the other hand, he was alone and didn't make any close friends at Park Place, yet.

Tom thought about the times he and Julie spent together in Minneapolis and at his home. They had met on the Internet and contrary to many opinions, relationships that originate in that manner can work. Tom felt wary of his new friend at first, but as the months went by, their friendship grew.

Tom thoughts wandered to Pamela. Does she want to spend the night in my condo because of her aunt, or is she interested in me? I remember the warm feeling experienced when holding her out on the beach. Her aunt has just been found dead and Pam showed no tears. I'll see how it plays out.

He heard a noise and looked up. "Oh, there you are. Your bedroom is in there, through that door," he said and pointed. "It has its own bathroom. Make yourself at home. I'm going to try to find a movie on television."

Pamela smiled and disappeared through the door into the bedroom. Ten minutes later, Pamela emerged in a nightgown and robe.

"Now, that looks comfy. If you need something from the kitchen, help yourself. Please, don't pay any attention to me. I'm likely to fall asleep watching the movie."

"Thanks so much, Tom. I need a good nights sleep so much. As a matter of fact, I'll probably hit the sack real soon," responded Pamela.

Tom had shut off the television in the living room and had gone to bed. Sleep was close when he heard a noise. Someone was shouting. Sitting up, he concluded it was coming from across the courtyard. He staggered to the window and pushed back a panel of drape. The window across the courtyard was open exposing the interior part of a room. Two people were shouting at each other.

The woman picked up a book and threw it. The man ducked and the book hit a flower vase, knocking it to the floor. Tom was searching for names. Oh yes, Marv and Ann Plum—they seemed like a nice couple at the cocktail party. Marv advanced a couple of steps toward Ann and pointed his finger. Tom was amazed at the size of his hands.

The Ann stormed out of the room. Marv man sat down on the couch and brought a glass up to his mouth.

Hmm, a marital spat—none of my business, thought Tom. He slipped back under the covers.

———

BEFORE GOING TO BED, Pamela looked around Tom's spare bedroom. She needed a new place to hide the gem. In the closet, she noticed three shoeboxes stored on an upper shelf. She took the boxes down. The bottom box was partially full of colorful kitchen knickknacks. Perfect, she thought and placed the gem under the items and put the boxes back.

She got under the covers and listened to the surf pound the sand. She tossed and turned for over an hour. The gem is the most important thing in my life, she thought. Any guilt feelings that surfaced were quickly put aside. We're all in this life for ourselves. Why should I worry about my dead aunt...or Tom Hastings for that matter? He's big enough to take care of himself.

———

MARVIN PLUM OPENED A BEER AND PLOPPED DOWN in an easy chair. I hope that bitch has gone to bed, he thought. Time to relax. He took a long drink from the bottle and let out a deep breath.

Richard is sure lucky. He's got a real doll for a wife. Marv smiled when thinking about the good times they had in high school—on the football team. Well, mostly good, except when I ran a fumble the wrong way and scored for the other team.

At least for once, I got most of the attention. Usually it was Richard surrounded by all the girls and fans. Oh, he was a darn good quarterback. Marv smiled thinking about Richard throwing his helmet against the wall in the locker room after they had lost.

It was our only loss during our senior year. We lost the game because I screwed up...in the finals of the state regional tournament. Marv remembered looking up at the scoreboard. We were leading by only one point and there was less than one minute to play.

Marv burped and laughed out loud. Yeah, the girls didn't surround poor Richard after that game. They could call me "Wrong-way Plum," all they wanted. I got a lot of attention after that one. Funny thing, but I wasn't even embarrassed...I was happy for a change.

He thought about his father, a construction worker who spent his evenings on the couch coddling with a six-pack of beer. He was disgusted with me after blowing the big game, but I was glad.

Dad was never the same after that. The verbal abuse that he had experienced at the local pub after the game was intolerable. From that day forward, dad did all his beer drinking at home. Maybe I did him a favor...us all a favor, my mother and I.

Marv did get a football scholarship from the local college, but dropped out after being caught drinking during orientation. Later, he got a job with the same construction firm that his dad worked for.

Richard didn't have to worry. His dad owned and operated a large, successful manufacturing plant on the outskirts of the city. He didn't even play football in college. Instead, he graduated with honors with a degree in structural engineering. After college, Richard married Corrith Sanderson, daughter of the mayor of Peoria.

Marv thought about where he had met Ann. It was in a bar that he had frequented often. He wasn't sure if he was actually in love, but they got married anyhow. His bride was the daughter of Simon Beckert, who amassed a fortune in the gold market.

Ann's father and mother had divorced when she was six years old. She chose to live with her father, but his attempt at raising her failed miserably. She was spoiled to the hilt, thought Marv.

Their marriage was in trouble from the very first day. Marv continued to hang around bars and eventually lost his job. Ann was working as a receptionist for a local legal firm. If she hadn't hounded me about getting a job every day, it would have been easier. I can't believe I settled for that job with the city utilities department—collecting garbage.

It's a good thing that Ann maintained a friendship with Corrith Schweitzer. She's the one who helped us find this place in Florida. Hell, no use me working after Ann's father died. She inherited it all.

―――

SERIN WOKE AND LOOKED AT HIS WATCH. Jesus, it's 3:45—got to get over to Park Place. Getting out of bed, he poured himself a straight shot of whiskey to clear his mind. His plan was to attack the Zachary woman in her bedroom and force her to talk. She knew where the stone was, he thought. If she doesn't tell me, I'll kill her. But then, I was going to kill her anyhow after I got my hands on the Guni. She'll sing when feeling the blade going into her neck. They always do.

Getting into the pickup, the motor grunted when he turned the key. Jesus, the battery is going down, he thought. This stupid pickup probably needs a new one, but I don't have the money or the time to steal another vehicle right now. He tried the ignition again and Serin felt immensely relieved when the engine turned and started. Soon, I will have lots of money and soon. Screw the battery, I'll buy a sports car after I get paid.

Parking on Beach Street across from Park Place, he made sure his gloves were on and the knife was in his pocket. Pulling the brim of his cap down over his forehead, he walked briskly across the street and into the Park Place parking garage. He smiled—there wasn't anyone around.

Using the key he got from the dead woman's purse, he opened the wrought iron gate and walked up the one flight of stairs. Smoothly, he placed the key in the lock of Unit 150, turned it and heard the click.

Entering the condo, he closed the door gently and stood still, waiting for a few minutes allowing his eyes to adjust. Serin knew which door accessed the spare bedroom, where Pamela Zachary slept. The door was partially open and he peeked in without using a flashlight. He could see from the light filtering in through the window that the bed was empty. *She has to be in the other bedroom.*

On his way to the master bedroom, his shoe caught the leg of a chair. Stumbling, he recovered but not before the chair fell against a lamp making a noise. Serin held his breath for a few moments and remained still, listening for the sound of anyone stirring. All was quiet. Pushing the bedroom door fully open, he entered. Expecting to hear breathing, he was puzzled when hearing none.

"Jesus," he muttered. "There's no one in here."

After closing the blinds, he snapped on the light. The bed was made just as it was the last time he had been there. Returning to the spare bedroom, he was sure that's where the Zachary broad slept. Entering the bathroom, his eyes fixed on a bluish box sitting on the glass shelf under the mirror. A few pieces of large tufts of cotton were lying inches away. He picked up the box and looked inside. The hollow space was just about the right size.

Flinging the box against the shower stall, he knew where Pamela Zachary had originally hidden the stone. A major screw up on my part, he thought disgustingly. "Where the hell did she take it?" he whispered out loud.

She was with that Hastings guy last night. *Could it be she's with him right now?* Serin, confused and disgusted, left Unit 150. He walked down the stairs and out into the parking area. Heading back to his pickup, he was about to cross the street when a police car drove by.

17

WHEN SERIN GOT BACK INTO THE PICKUP, he turned the ignition key and heard an irritating clicking sound. That damn battery...it's really dead now, he thought. I don't like the idea of walking the ten blocks back to my motel with that police car cruising back and forth.

Slinking down on the bench seat, he decided to wait until after daylight when there would be other people around. Besides, the thunderclaps he had just heard were getting closer. Stealing another vehicle at this place and time was too risky, he thought. I'll negotiate a jump-start from someone in the morning.

Serin had nodded off to sleep when the headlights from a vehicle lit up the sun visor and the area above the windshield. He turned his head to look through the rear window and saw that the light wasn't coming from headlights but rather the spotlight of a police car, parked directly behind.

——

NATE BLOOMBERG WAS ON PATROL. His usual beat didn't include the condo units on Beach Street, but because of the murder, he had driven by there at least six times. The time on his wristwatch read 5:00 a.m. when he spotted a man coming from the parking garage of Park Place condominiums.

Nate drove past the man, noticing he was wearing a baseball cap. Probably no big deal, someone spent the night with a girl friend, he thought and smiled. In his rear view mirror, he saw the man cross the street and open the door of a pickup.

Continuing on Beach Street northward for four blocks, Nate turned his car around and headed back south. He remembered what Chief McSorley said yesterday—*keep an eye on Park Place*. Cruising along slowly, he came abreast of Park Place and noticed that the pickup was still there. In spite of the dimness of light, he saw some movement within the cab. Because he had no reason to investigate the pickup, Nate continued driving southward on Beach Street.

Again looking at his watch, Nate noticed there was less than an hour left of his beat—about fifty minutes. He was really looking forward to going to bed. Very seldom anything of any significance ever happened in Key Marie. Most of the residents were retirees. The rest of them were young working parents and their kids. No one in the police department had ever fired a shot since he was on the force.

His biggest challenge to date had been wrestling with a drunk, who insisted on knocking on the door of his ex-wife's apartment. The guy got a lucky punch in and it took two weeks for the black marks around Nate's eye to disappear. He cringed when thinking of all the ribbing he took from his fellow officers. Nate looked westward and could see a thunderstorm approaching. Flashes of lightning lit up the sky. That'll make sleeping good, he thought.

Nate rotated the handle of the spotlight to focus it on the license plate—Indiana. He called the Department of Highway Safety and Motor Vehicles to check on the number.

After a two-minute pause, a voice came on and said, "That vehicle, a 1996 Dodge pickup truck, was reported stolen at Indianapolis International Airport this past weekend."

Nate felt the tension. He looked at his watch. There was still half-an-hour left on his beat, he realized. Thoughts of seeing earlier movements in the truck entered his mind. Some one could be in that cab. Reluctantly, he opened the police car door, grabbed his flashlight and lowered his feet to the pavement. After a couple of steps he stopped and unbuttoned his holster strap.

Shining the flashlight beam through the driver's side window exposed the brim of a baseball cap and the lower part of a person.

Nate rapped the edge of the flashlight on the driver's side window, keeping his fingers on his gun.

"Hey, you in there, would you step out, please?"

A man rolled down the window and asked, "Anything wrong officer? I'm just picking up a little snooze."

Nate Bloomberg was scared but excited. Confronting a stolen vehicle driver was a first for him.

He raised his gun and said, "Get out of the truck, right now.... Keep your hands in sight...Now!"

Crouching slightly, Nate felt the trigger with his finger. The man sat up and opened the door. As he was getting out, Nate saw the barrel of the gun—his body froze. All he could do was stare at the barrel. His final thought was, what will the chief think? Nate could feel himself falling backwards into a black hole.

———

FROM MIDNIGHT TO 6:00 IN THE MORNING, the Key Marie Police Department's 911 calls get routed to the Florida Highway Patrol. The dispatcher in Tampa took the call just before 6:00 a.m.

"Something's wrong here. There was a gunshot. Across the street from Park Place parking lot, there's a police car. It's running...the doors open and nothing seems to be happening."

"Address and name please, " the dispatcher requested.

"This is Richard Schweitzer, Unit 280, at 7660 Beach Street in Key Marie."

"Thank you," responded the dispatcher after writing down the information. "Does anyone appear to be hurt?"

Not that I can see....Oh, wait just a minute...let me have a closer look. Samhill, there's someone lying on the pavement."

The dispatcher looked up the address on the map and made an instant decision. He rang the number of Key Marie Police Chief, Ken McSorley. Then he contacted the nearest ambulance service.

———

SERIN LOOKED UP AND SAW LIGHTS in a window that was overlooking the street. The officer who he had just shot was lying on the pavement and illuminated with the spotlight. *I've got to get out of here and fast.* Running away from the scene, he crossed the street and sidewalk while making for a shadowed area on someone's lawn.

He gasped when slipping on the grass and twisting his ankle. Limping along, he looked for an opening between buildings, wanting to get down to the beach where it was dark. A series of fences were blocking access to the beach.

At last he found an opening between two buildings. While limping through, the pain in his ankle had become excruciating. Stopping at water's edge, he allowed the surf to bathe the throbbing ankle. Stumbling along for another fifteen minutes, he felt overwhelming relief to see the beachside lights of his motel. "Carrackow! Carrackow!" The loud cackling sound of a blue heron that he had surprised added to Serin's misery.

At close to 6:30 a.m. he was exhausted after sliding under the covers of his bed. So much for the pickup, he thought. I'll have to find another vehicle, probably at the strip mall. Maybe I should just get the hell out of here. This is not going well. If that officer dies, it could be the chair for me. In Serin's dream, after finally falling asleep, he was trying to push a wheelbarrow. The cargo, a huge green stone, was too heavy. The lone front wheel wouldn't roll.

18

"GET OUT OF THE SACK, CLIFF, Nate's in trouble. I'll pick you up in five minutes."

Chief McSorley backed out of his garage and into a garbage can causing the cover to roll onto the street. He pushed the fuel pedal to the floor and screeched up the street, turning the corner on two wheels. Cliff was waiting by the curb when McSorley arrived.

"Should we use the siren?" asked Cliff.

"Ah, heck...I just didn't have time. Yes!"

Cliff pushed the lever. He felt excited when hearing the wail.

Chief McSorley and Sargent Johnson could see lights flashing as they approached Park Place fifteen minutes later. "That's an ambulance. I'm afraid of the worst. Nate could be shot," said the Chief anxiously.

Chief McSorley jammed the shift into park and pushed the door open. He vaulted out of the car and headed over to the fallen officer.

"Jesus help us. Is he alive?" The Chief asked of one of the attendants.

"Yes sir. He is. Breathing is normal. Pulse reads okay."

Cliff had joined the chief next to Nate's side.

Chief McSorley had never experienced a downed officer before, much less investigated a murder. My God, he thought, now I've got both within a couple of days. I was planning to visit here later in the day and set up some interviews. The Chief looked up at Park Place and took a deep breath. Hell, I'm doing my job.

He looked up at Cliff and didn't care for the look of doubt in the officer's face. I could call in the state guys, but guys like Cliff would think less of me. I'm supposed to be in charge here. *I am in charge here.*

"Nate, can you hear me?" the chief asked while watching the attendant open the officer's jacket. McSorley became queasy spotting blood under Nate's left armpit.

Nate did not answer but began to groan.

Taking a deep breath, the Chief raised his head and whispered, "Lord, let this young man live."

The groans got louder and Nate stirred, raising hope for the Chief that Nate would survive.

"The wound is a good distance from the heart and the bleeding appears to have stopped," said one of the attendants.

"Thanks, fellas," said the Chief while watching them push the gurney into the ambulance.

TOM LOOKED TOWARD THE SPARE BEDROOM after hearing a noise. Pamela came through the door dressed in a robe. He noticed that her hair was a mess and she was wringing her hands, not a pretty sight. After pouring a coffee, she asked him, "Did you hear all that ruckus out there last night, just before daylight?"

Tom sipped coffee, looked up at her and said, "No, didn't hear a thing...what ruckus? Didn't you sleep well?"

"Yes and no. I was doing well until a flash of lightning—a real blast. The thunder was so loud that it rattled the window. "

"All weather is good, really," Tom responded while thinking about the caption under his photograph in the Minneapolis Tribune last April. He was in-line skating on a paved trail around Lake Calhoun and it was snowing hard. A Star Tribune photographer was attracted, took a series of pictures and conducted a short interview, which led to the caption.

"Then there was another loud noise. I don't think that one was lightning. It sounded different, like perhaps a gunshot. Minutes later, there were sirens. The wailing stopped after it got close," said Pamela.

"Hmm, wonder what happened. I must have slept through it all," responded Tom.

He walked out onto the balcony and took another sip of coffee. There were four people down there and they seemed to be engaged in intense discussion. He recognized the Schweitzer's. The other two were Grady Prichard and his wife, Helen. There was something about their demeanor that aroused his curiosity.

Returning to the kitchen, he said to Pamela, "I'm getting dressed and heading down to the beach. There are some people on the beach who will likely know what the ruckus was about last night."

"Would it be okay if I went with you? I'd like to hear what happened, too."

"Sure, I'll be going down within five minutes," replied Tom.

Tom watched Pamela hurry to her bedroom. He went to his bedroom and came out dressed minutes later.

She emerged in a few minutes looking tense. Tom said, "Wow, that didn't take long."

Something is really bothering that girl besides losing her aunt,

Tom thought. When I talk to her, it's as if she wants to tell me something...perhaps about the reason for her accident.

I wonder what the people down there on the beach are talking about. It must have something to do with the siren that Pam heard early this morning.

They hustled out the door and down the two sets of stairs that led to the first gate and the courtyard. Two people were standing on the walkway that leads to the second gate. Tom realized he had met them before but didn't remember their names.

The tall blonde turned and said, "Oh, hello there, Mr. Hastings. We met down here the other day. I'm Lucy Barrows. This is my friend Dale. Your friend is?"

"Good to see you again....Ah, this is my neighbor, Pamela. She is staying in her aunt's condo," responded Tom. He felt a little uncomfortable at Lucy Barrow's insinuation—Pamela and him, more than friends.

"Oh, you're not the one—number 150." Lucy's eyes widened as she asked, "Melissa was your aunt?" while touching her lower lip with an extraordinarily long fingernail.

"Yes, Melissa Buntrock was my aunt," said Pamela. Her voice trailed off, slightly stammering. She dropped her chin and looked at the ground.

"Oh, you poor dear," responded Lucy.

Dale narrowed his beady eyes and added, "I'm going to block my door besides locking at night. This is getting a little too close. First the murder and now a shooting."

"Shooting! What shooting?" exclaimed Tom.

"Haven't you heard? One of Key Marie's young officers was shot about 6:00 this morning," answered Dale.

Lucy added, "There's a pickup with Indiana plates out in the street with police tape around it. Apparently it has something to do with the shooting."

"I heard the pickup truck was stolen and whoever was driving it shot the officer. Poor boy, he's in the hospital. Going to be okay, I hear," added Dale.

———

PAM WANTED TO SCREAM, but her throat went dry and she couldn't even speak. *Pickup from Indiana!* When she heard that, memory fragments of seeing such a truck in her rearview mirror in Tennessee returned. *That truck was following me.* The man in it was after the gem and now he's found me! Desperately, she grabbed Tom's hand.

"Are you okay, Pam?" asked Tom.

Dale added, "Do you know Richard Schweitzer? He saw the shooter...had a look at his face."

"Yeah, I met Richard earlier this week, the cocktail party in the courtyard," answered Tom. "I want to talk to Richard. Do you want to come along, Pam?"

Pam's mind was miles away, attempting to remember something that happened at the airport in Indianapolis. She didn't respond to Tom's question.

"Pam, are you okay?" Tom repeated, frowning.

Pam recovered her day dream and said, "Oh yeah, Tom, I'm okay. You asked me something?"

"Yup, I'm going out to the beach to find Richard. Do you want to come?"

Lucy was staring at Pamela and asked, "You don't look so good. Is there something wrong?"

Pamela looked at Dale. He was staring at her.

Dale turned away and said, "I'm going over there to check it out."

———

TOM SLIPPED HIS KEY INTO THE GATE LOCK and pushed it open. He held it allowing Pam to pass. Dale and Lucy followed. They strolled over to the beach to join the Schweitzers. Grady and Helen Prichard had separated from them and wandered over to the surf.

Corrith turned as Tom and Pamela approached. She said, "Good morning folks. Oh, Pamela, I feel so bad about what's happened."

"Hi, Tom. Yes, Pamela, your aunt was a classy lady. We're all going to miss her," added Richard.

Tom felt a lump forming in his throat while thinking about his dead wife. He watched Corrith raise her eyebrows. At that moment, Tom feared the dark cloud of death that had followed him from New Dresden to Minneapolis was overhead. He looked up at the sky.

————

PAMELA HAD NOT BEEN RESPONDING to Richard's inquiries. Tom diverted attention away from Pamela by asking Richard, "I hear you saw something out in the street last night, a policeman got shot?"

"Well, I didn't see the shooting, but I saw the guy who did it. About 5:30 this morning. I was headed for the bathroom and heard what sounded like a car backfiring outside. I looked out the window that faces the street and saw this cop car. For just a moment the spotlight was on a face, ugly, lots of facial hair. The man wearing a baseball cap was standing on the pavement. We didn't find out until later that a policeman was down, shot in the shoulder I heard."

Corrith interrupted. "Richard, you need to tell the police right away...about what you saw."

"Well, Corrith, as you know it was I who called in the shooting. I gave them my name and phone number. They'll be around...asking questions. I'm sure I'll get my turn at bat...probably the leadoff hitter."

"What was the color of his hair?" Pamela's crackling voice asked.

"Blond, everything seemed light, hair, eyes and skin."

"Was he short or tall?"

"Couldn't tell the height from up above. How the samhill could I?"

Grady Prichard and his wife Helen meandered back to the group.

Grady said, "Hello, Hastings, that's your name, isn't it? We met at the party earlier this week."

"Yeah, I remember. Your wife's name is Helen."

"You have a good memory."

"Please call me Tom."

"Does anyone know what's going on here? We've had this condo for years. Nothing like this has ever happened before. What are we to do?" asked Helen, her voice quivering with concern.

Corrith put an arm around Helen's shoulder. "It's going to be all right. None of us are the cause of whatever is happening. The police will catch whoever is behind the murder and shooting. You can count on that."

Pamela felt intermittent waves of needles jabbing the walls of her stomach. She feared the worst—the gem that she was hiding in Tom's closet could be the reason for her aunt's murder and the shooting of the police officer...also for the misery that Helen and others were experiencing.

Pamela tapped Tom on the shoulder and whispered, "I need to get back to my aunt's condo. Could I leave my overnight things at your place for now?"

"Sure, I'll go back with you. See you people all later." Suspicious eyes followed Pamela and Tom as they left the beach together.

19

"THANKS SO MUCH, TOM, FOR LETTING ME STAY HERE," Pamela said. "I'm going back to 150 and see if there are any messages. Hopefully, my other aunt will arrive today. Otherwise, I don't have the smarts to decide on what to do with Melissa...what's left of her...her remains."

Pamela returned to Tom's spare bedroom and closed the door. She entered the closet and slipped out the bottom shoebox. Opening it, she felt elated when seeing the gem. *This could be the answer to the rest of my life.* After returning it into the shoebox and placing it back on the shelf, she reentered the living room where Tom was sitting, reading a newspaper.

"Tom, I'm on my way now. Thanks again for letting me stay here last night."

"No problem, Pam. If you have any difficulties over there, let me know."

When Pamela entered Unit 150, she knew something was different. There was that smell again. She stood just inside the open door for a few moments. The phone's answering machine was beeping. She left the front door open and advanced to the phone.

After pressing the PLAY button, she listened. It was her aunt calling from Atlanta. "Hello, Pamela dear. I have some distressing news about myself—it's a recurring emphysema problem. It means going to the hospital for a few days. Meanwhile, I've contacted a mortuary and made arrangements for Melissa's remains.

"They are bringing my poor sister back to Atlanta for burial. You are welcome to come to the prayer service. After that's over with, I would like you to please remain in Melissa's condo until I can get down there...perhaps in a week...hopefully sooner. You take care of yourself, Pamela. Do ya' hear?"

"Yes. I hear," whispered Pamela as she closed the front door.

Pamela walked into the kitchen and opened the refrigerator. She removed a bottle of beer and took a seat outside on the balcony. Her mind was on the gem. It was safe for the time being in Tom's condo. He is going to be here all month. If Julie, his friend from Saint Paul shows up, she might become a problem.

Setting the beer down on the kitchen counter, she sauntered into her bedroom and continued into the bathroom. She gasped when spotting the box of cotton balls on the bathroom floor. The man at the airport...the accident...the man wearing the baseball cap...the pickup truck... the gem...her aunt's murder...the smell. *My memory is returning.*

Should I call the police? She thought. I could tell them everything. Ah, hell. My life has been a financial failure thus far. I need to turn that gem into money—lots of money.

How can I fathom spending the rest of my life working for peanuts? She thought. I still have a couple of weeks—that crummy job in Sarasota isn't available for another two weeks. Money isn't a problem right now. There's over two thousand dollars in my checking account. Thank God!

She thought about her credit cards. Two of them were maxed, but a third one just opened had a limit of three thousand dollars. That credit card plus the cash in my checking account, she thought, can keep me afloat until I turn that sparkling rock into cash—a ton of cash. Who around here could help me do that?

That Dale guy who I met down in the courtyard might be just the person, she thought. Pamela remembered overhearing a conversation that Dale was having with Ann Plum. They were talking about some big money deal that he'd gotten away with. Yes, tomorrow, I will contact him. Meanwhile, the locks needed to be changed. Melissa's key was missing and she was quite certain who had it—the man wearing the baseball cap—*the one who shot the police officer.*

Flipping through the yellow pages, Pamela found three locksmiths listed. She called the Anderson firm and set up an appointment for 2:00 that afternoon.

———

SERIN WOKE UP WITH A HEADACHE and was not looking forward to the day. It must be close to noon, he thought. I've failed to recover that crummy stone and it's killing me. I have no transportation.

The pickup truck he stole in Indianapolis was now in police hands. It was sure to attract the FBI. Any day the motel management is going to discover that the credit card I used when registering was stolen. My need for money and a vehicle has never been greater.

One of his eyes opened and with it the hope of another attempt to recover the stone. The secret to its location was centered on the guy I saw at the accident site, Tom Hastings, Serin thought. The key that I stole from the woman's purse next to the lounge is still in my pocket. It will get me into the condo complex. A knock on the door with a gun threat to Hastings may hit the jackpot.

The pain in his right ankle aggravated the headache. Moving his leg back and forth against the sheet told him the ankle was swollen. If he could make it on foot to the strip mall, he should be able to steal another vehicle to drive to Park Place. There were lots of careless seniors coming and going all day long.

The tightness in his ankle let up after getting out of bed and walking around the room. Encouraged, he dressed and considered a walk to the mall to steal a vehicle and hopefully a credit card. He felt starved and needed something to eat before executing any new strategy. There was a sports store in the mall. He needed a different hat after remembering the window overlooking the street at Park Place. Serin had looked up and saw a man looking down at him right after he shot the cop.

After getting dressed, he headed for the door but stopped dead when hearing a knock. Must be the maid, he thought. Opening the door, his heart stopped.

"Well, if it isn't my favorite delivery boy?" mocked a sneering Vince Gulloti while waving a pistol in Serin's face.

20

POLICE CHIEF MCSORLEY HAD JUST RETURNED from the hospital. He was elated that Nate was going to be all right. The bullet went right through his shoulder. *Bullet*...it must still be out there, out on the street. He dreaded the thought of investigating the woman's murder and the Nate shooting. It wasn't his thing.

Tully Smith knocked on the chief's door and opened it slightly. "Tampa's on the phone, Ken, line three."

"Hello, McSorley, this is Masters-Tampa. Sounds like you have some problems out there."

"Yeah, Masters, a murder and one of my boys was shot. He's going to be okay, though. We got lucky there."

"I've got good news for you. Because the pickup truck was registered out of state, we've called in the FBI. They should be in touch with you today. Meanwhile, don't let anyone touch the truck. You can count on seeing a team of technicians down there later in the morning."

"I like the sound of that. I'm going down there myself in a few minutes to talk to the manager and set up some interviews."

"Fine, but mainly the truck needs to be secure. Have a good

day, we'll talk later."

———

FBI AGENT COREY DOWNER WAS SIPPING COFFEE and munching a bagel in his Tampa office. His door was open when Sam Klaptin, his boss, entered.

"Hi, Corey, guess we're headed to Key Marie. This is likely a nickel-dime situation, but we've been asked to check it out."

"What's the deal?" asked Agent Downer.

"A local police officer was shot by a guy driving a stolen pickup truck. It was stolen at the Indianapolis Airport about a week ago. The officer was following up after calling about the license. Perhaps it's a coincidence, but right across the street there's a condo complex. A woman resident was murdered on the beach the day before. Whoever did her in also searched her condo—for what I don't have a clue. That's what we need to find out."

"Ah, it's a great day for a drive. When are we leaving?"

"No big hurry. The state guys are on their way now to check out the condo. That'll keep them busy most of the afternoon. Let's plan on leaving after lunch."

"Okay, Sam. I'll be ready."

Sam Klaptin was not in a very good mood. His attorney had just called and the divorce settlement wasn't going well. Sam was not anxious to leave town. He was depressed.

He reached back and pressed his fingers against his lower back. Ever since his marital problems began, some months ago, he was racked with constant pain. It was difficult for Sam to get out of a car.

The thick, dark-brown hair that he enjoyed combing for so many years was thinning and graying at the temples. During he college days, he stood six-foot-one. The last time he was in for a physical, the nurse wrote down five-foot-eleven. He had lost two inches, probably because his back was slightly stooped.

Sam removed his hand from his back and planted it on Corey's desk. The long fingers were slightly wrinkled. They were just the right lengths to grasp and spin a baseball—he had the most wins of any pitcher in his high school's baseball history.

He smiled slightly when observing Corey's family picture that was perched on the desk—a pretty wife and two teenage boys. His soft brown eyes narrowed while thinking about his daughter and how she would deal with the divorce.

"I'll see you about 1:15," Sam said and left the room.

———

CHIEF MCSORLEY AND SARGENT CLIFF JOHNSON arrived at 7660 Beach Street at 10:00 a.m. They parked their car in a visitor space.

"Doesn't look like the technicians have arrived yet," stated Cliff.

"Naw, they'll be here in about half-an-hour. Let's go talk to the manager. No point in touching the pickup," answered the chief. At that moment, he thought about the bullet. *How would it look for me if I were the one who found it?* The State guys and the FBI would be impressed.

———

HALDOR NEILSON HAD MANAGED PARK PLACE for the past fifteen years. None of the visitors or residents had ever even been threatened before. He shuddered seeing the police car pull up and park in front of his office. Two officers got out and walked across the street. They stopped short of the pickup, which had police tape wrapped all the way around.

Haldor recognized Chief Ken McSorley. The two officers appeared to be searching the pavement and the approach to Park Place. He continued to watch and saw one of them bend over and pick up something. The officers returned to the pickup truck and stood there for a few minutes before coming back to the Park Place parking lot. Haldor heard the anticipated knock.

Haldor Neilson was born and raised in a small town in Michigan. He worked in his father's drug store during high school years. After enrolling at Michigan State University in East Lansing, he had planned to become a teacher. His father died during his sophomore year and he was forced to return home and manage the drug store.

He married Tonia Nelson, who eventually convinced him to sell the drug store and move to Florida. Haldor and his wife decided to pursue a career in real estate management. He landed a job at Park Place and Tonia signed on with a competing condo complex in the northern part of the island.

Haldor enjoyed landscaping work and that was one of the reasons why Park Place always looked so tidy. He was often seen working with the employees who tended to the plant beds and lawns.

Life was boring for Haldor. Even though he liked yard work, he was tiring of the continual bickering he had to put up with from some of his tenants. Every week he bought a lottery ticket. One of these days, I'm going to get lucky, he thought. It's depressing to think that my wife and I will manage condo complexes for the rest of our lives.

Haldor always wore shorts. His light brown hair in a fifties style crew cut was sheared well above the ears. His body was trim compared to the police chief.

"Hello, Chief, come on in. You too, sir."

"Ah...you're Haldor, right?"

"Right. How ya' doin'?"

"I'm Police Chief McSorley and this is Sargent Johnson. As you probably guessed, we are here about the shooting last night and also the killin' two days ago."

"Man alive, this whole business has rattled my tenants, not to mention me. I'll help all I can. Since I live elsewhere, I can't tell you much about what happened in the street last night."

"We appreciate your cooperation, Mr. Neilson. Right now, I'm mainly interested in a list of occupants that overlook the beach area and Beach Street."

"Sure, that's easy, have a seat and I'll print a list."

"Could you mark down their unit and phone numbers?"

"No problem. I can do that. Shouldn't take long."

Haldor clicked the OK icon and the printer produced a list of all the tenants. He marked those who overlooked the areas, which the chief had mentioned.

"Thanks, we appreciate it. Oh, by the way, the state criminal bureau and the FBI are going to assist in the investigation. Technicians from Tampa could arrive at any minute. Two FBI agents will be here this afternoon."

"Yeah, I've already been notified by the state. Unit 150 is ready for them. The FBI...why are they involved?"

"The pickup truck parked on the curb was stolen in Indianapolis. The driver shot one of my men and may have murdered your tenant.

"Park Place may be in the middle of something big. We're not sure what, just yet. If you see any strangers hanging around, give me a call. Thanks." Haldor stood behind his desk, his mind agape as the two officers left his office.

21

A LETTERED VAN PULLED into the visitor's parking stall at Park Place five minutes after the two policemen left—Florida State Police.

Haldor was standing outside the door and knew the technicians had arrived. He walked over to their vehicle, greeted them and pointed out the location of Unit 150. Haldor had left a message with Pamela Zachary about the pending arrival of the technicians. She had made no objections and talked to him about changing locks. The technicians decided to do the pickup truck first.

He was down on his knees pulling weeds from a flowerbed when he noticed the technicians leave the pickup and begin walking toward him. He stood up. "It's unlocked, fellas. Unit 150, that's where you want to go, isn't it?"

One of the technicians lifted his clipboard and said, "Yup. That's the one we're interested in—Melissa Buntrock, it says here."

Haldor didn't like Melissa Buntrock. She was one of his most irritating clients. "This isn't right...that's not right...when are you going to get this done?" She was a real pain in the butt. Now she was gone and that sexy niece of hers was staying there—a marked improvement.

Haldor thought about his marriage. No Kids—he always wanted a son. Adopt one, their friends would say. Tonia didn't like the idea—cost too much money, she always said.

The technicians only spent about half the time in unit 150 as they did on the pickup truck. "Thanks a lot, Mr. Neilson. You made our job a lot easier."

"No problem," replied Haldor as he stood and watched the technicians get into their van.

———

COREY DOWNER HAD GUIDED THE CAR OFF an exit on Interstate 75. He made a right turn and accessed the highway that led to Key Marie. Sam Klaptin, sitting next to him, was reading bulletins that he'd fetched from his briefcase.

"Hmm, listen to this, Corey. Our Indianapolis office has received information that a rock worth 30 million dollars or more was stolen from a New York hotel suite and may be headed for Atlanta...a Guni gem, they called it."

"Wasn't that pickup over at Park Place stolen in Indianapolis?" asked Corey.

"Yeah, at the airport, I hear. Gads, do you suppose there's a connection between the rock and the guy who shot the officer?" asked Agent Sam Klaptin. "Hmm...maybe the woman that was murdered across the street had something to do with it, too."

Sam added, "That's probably why we're being sent to Key Marie, Corey. Furthermore, the Saudis have been putting pressure on our office in Washington. Prince Omar Vallif has experienced major embarrassment losing his birthday present. He wants this to be quiet and has requested a free hand to recover the rock."

———

CHIEF MCSORLEY LOOKED AT THE CLOCK on the opposite wall from the desk in his office. According to the information we received earlier in the day, the FBI agents would be arriving soon. The big city boys are going to have to wait, he thought. I'm a busy guy.

"Give me a call when they show up," he instructed Tully Smith, the dispatcher on duty. "Make them comfortable and ask them to wait." The chief chuckled. I'd better go out the back, he thought. Time for a cup of coffee.

The chief hadn't been out of the office for more than ten minutes when Tully reported that the agents were entering the police station.

"Look sir, we need to talk to your chief. Get him back here as quick as you can," Agent Sam instructed Tully.

"I've called his car. He should be here soon."

Chief McSorley made sure the agents waited at least half-an-hour before he entered the waiting area, coming from his office.

"Come on in, fellas. I'm Chief Ken McSorley. Welcome to Key Marie."

The introductions and greetings were cool, probably because the agents weren't happy about the wait. After ushering his guests into his office, Chief McSorley summarized the events. The murder occurred on the beach at about 4:30 p.m. on Wednesday. The next morning, one of his officers was shot across the street at 5:30 a.m. He handed them a copy of the list of the occupants of Park Place who overlooked the street. After giving them directions to Park Place, the chief gave them the keys to the pickup truck and said, "Help yourselves, I've got tons of things to do."

————

"THAT GUY IS RUNNING A CHURCH SOCIAL. He doesn't have a clue," snorted Sam when they were driving up Beach Street looking for Park Place.

"There it is," said Ben.

He stopped their car, a gray Oldsmobile, in a visitor slot.

"Let's take a look at that truck and then we'll talk to the manager," said Sam.

"Sure smells in here," said Corey after sitting down in the driver's seat of the pickup.

22

PAMELA WAS PLEASED WITH THE WORK that the Anderson locksmith had done on the front door. The entire lock system was replaced with a modern deadbolt.

"Cool job, mister," she said as the locksmith replaced the tools in his bag.

Twice that day, visitors interrupted her. First it was the state police technicians from Tampa. They were in the condo for close to an hour. Later, condo manager Haldor brought over two FBI agents that asked a lot of questions. Gosh, you would think I was a suspect, she thought.

Pamela was amazed that all the out-of-town police knew about her accident in Tennessee. She had been using her advantage, a medical report verifying her loss of memory, to impede most of the questions. The officer named Corey looked deep into her eyes as if searching for something. Pamela wondered if they knew about the gem.

———

TOM HASTINGS WAS SUNNING ON A LOUNGE when Haldor came through the gate.

"Tom, how ya' doin'?"

"Could be better. I'm okay, but the murder and shooting have me a little nervous," he replied.

"I've got to ask you a favor. The FBI are here and investigating the Melissa Buntrock murder. They've asked to interview everyone in the condo that has either a street or a beach view. Could you help me out?"

"Sure, when do they want to see me?"

"How about in fifteen minutes?"

"Okay, I've had enough sun for one day, anyway."

Tom returned to his condo and waited. In twenty minutes, he heard a loud rap outside. He left the couch and advanced to the door.

"Sorry to bother you, Mr. Hastings. I'm Sam Klaptin and this is my partner, Corey Downer. We're from the FBI, investigating the murder of your neighbor and the shooting out in the street. We would like to talk to you."

"Sure, come on in and have a seat." Tom directed the two visitors to the couch.

Sam began, "We would like to know the nature of your relationship with Pamela Zachary. How well do you know her? Where did you meet her?"

"It's a weird story. I first saw her in the Smoky Mountains. She went off the road, down a steep slope and crashed her car into a tree. We found her, still in the car—the seatbelt and airbag had saved her life.

"Pamela called me a few days ago from Unit 150. She was staying with her aunt, who picked her up from the hospital in Chattanooga. I was one of two witnesses who saw her car go down the slope."

Corey asked, "You use the word 'We'. You must mean the other witness. Could you give us a name?"

"Ah, it was a guy by the name of Ben Pierce."

"What does he look like?" asked Sam.

"He was wearing a baseball cap, hair long and blond—ponytail...yeah, he had one of those girl things in his hair."

"Was he a small man, medium or large?" asked Corey.

"Medium, a little smaller than me."

Sam asked next, "What type of vehicle was he driving?"

"A pickup truck."

"You didn't notice the plates, did you?" asked Corey.

"No, I didn't."

"How about the model—Chevy, Ford or Dodge?"

"No, I'm afraid I didn't notice. All I can remember is the small red Chevy that went through the rail."

"Ah, Mr. Hastings, what happened when you arrived at Park Place? Did you have any contact with Miss Zachary?" asked agent Klaptin.

"Yes, one of the patrolmen at the accident gave her my name and phone number and she called me."

"Where did she call you from?"

"Well, I think it was from her aunt's condo."

"Was she the one? The aunt that was murdered?"

"Yes, she was...the one and the same."

"Have you ever met Miss Zachary's aunt previously?"

"No, I hadn't."

Klaptin asked, "Could I use your bathroom?"

"Of course, it's behind that door."

Klaptin went into the bathroom and Downer continued with the questioning. "Mr. Hastings, did she, Miss Zachary, ever talk about a gem—a very rare, expensive gem—one worth in the millions?"

"No, she sure didn't. What's that all about?"

"We're not sure. It may have nothing to do with this case. How many times did you meet with Miss Zachary?"

"Ah...twice. Once at lunch and another time at Overly's Bar & Grill."

"What do you remember was the main topic of conversation?"

"Mostly about what happened in Tennessee and her recovery of memory."

A raspy cough and a couple of wheezing sounds came from behind the bathroom door. Corey looked over there, an expression of concern on his face. The door opened and Klaptin returned, looking rather pale.

"Sam, I'm done. Do you have any more questions for Mr. Hastings?"

"No," he said while sitting down and picking up his notebook.

Both agents paused and worked on their notes. The room was dead quiet for a few minutes, except for the sounds of pen points scribbling on paper.

Tom was thinking about the night Pamela spent at his condo. Her reason for staying over seemed logical to him. Since they didn't ask, he decided not to bring it up.

"Well, Mr. Hastings, that's about it. We appreciate your cooperation. If you ever hear from Ben Pierce, please call us," said

Sam as he waved his card. He left it by the phone on the kitchen counter, and the two agents left.

———

THE PHONE RANG. Julie was on the line. "Tom, I'm so sorry. Something has come up. I won't be able to come tomorrow. Instead, I've shifted my schedule by a week. Would next Saturday be okay?"

"Sure, Julie, but I'm disappointed you can't make it tomorrow. I was looking forward to our visit. It's rather lonely for me out here, all alone, but I understand."

"Have you made any new friends?"

"Yes. I've made some tennis friends, but I would rather have you on the court."

"Uh-wee, that's so nice."

"You're makin' me melt, young lady," responded Tom.

"How's the murder case going? Anything new?"

"I had a couple of FBI agents here earlier. They were really interested in the young woman who was in the car accident in the Smoky Mountains."

"Well, I can understand that. She's the niece of the murdered woman, isn't she?"

"Yup, she sure is. Makes you wonder if there is a connection. Oh, well. That's for the cops to work out."

"I've got to go, Tom. My daughter's calling."

23

TOM DROVE TO OVERLY'S BAR & GRILL on Friday evening. He was still disappointed that Julie was not coming tomorrow. Two entertainers were drawing a large crowd on the outdoor patio. The guitarist was singing, while his accompanist drummer was gently working the surface of a snare drum.

Tom stood and listened for a few minutes before taking a position on a barstool inside. He had ordered a beer and was reviewing the menu when a tap on his shoulder caused him to turn. He came face to face with Pamela Zachary.

"Hi there, Tom. Do you mind if I join you?"

"Oh, no, of course not. Grab a stool."

"Tom, were the agents at your place, too? They sure worked me over...asked me a ton of questions."

"Yes, Pam, they were in my condo for about half-an-hour—they asked me a lot, too."

"Did they ask anything about the guy and the pickup truck at my accident?"

"Ah...yeah, they did."

The bartender set a beer down for Pamela and interrupted, "Another beer, sir?"

"Yeah, the same."

"Tom, you were on the highway that day. You talked to the man that drove a pickup truck. Do you think it was the same one? The one that's parked out in the street—with the police tape all around it."

"Geez, Pam, I didn't pay much attention to the pickup parked behind my car on the highway. What a coincidence that would be if it was."

"If the police catch the guy who shot the police officer, we should know—if the pickup was in Tennessee, too," said Pamela.

"The chance is remote. I would be amazed," added Tom.

Tom and Pamela were at the bar for another hour. He put his hand on her shoulder and said, "Well, it's time for me to get home. Been a long day."

"Thanks for visiting with me. I'm going to hang out for a bit. Have a nice night."

When Tom was walking to his car in the parking lot, he sensed that Pamela Zachary was deeply involved in more than an accident. She must have something that someone wants—*she has secrets.*

Why is the FBI so interested in her? Maybe she was running away from something—or someone. I could be putting myself in danger hanging around her, he thought. I wish Julie were here. Then this wouldn't be happening.

———

VINCE GULLOTI AND HIS HENCHMAN, Emil Buteo, took Serin for a car ride ending at a wharf located on a point extending from Key Marie toward the mainland. Emil worked part-time as a taxicab driver in Atlanta. He was more than happy to accept an offer of easy money—a couple thousand. Vince had always treated him fair. He was glad that he wasn't in Serin's shoes at the moment. Emil's wallet was padded with ten one-hundred-dollar bills. Another ten would follow when they got back to Atlanta.

The pleading eyes of Serin didn't stop Vince from pushing him off the pier onto the dock where the boat was anchored. Reluctantly, Serin stepped onto the boat's deck and entered the cabin, guided by Emil's hand. When they all got into the cabin, Vince pushed Serin down onto a couch.

"Okay, Serin, where the hell is the stone?"

Beads of perspiration broke out on Serin's forehead while he was explaining the incident at the Indianapolis Airport and the ensuing car accident. Vince paced around the small cabin. Emil stood in front of the door.

"Now, Serin, I'm going to give you one last chance to come clean. So, let's spit it out—where is the stone? Last chance."

"I tell you, she has it or they both have it. I sure as hell don't. It wasn't my fault the cops were waiting in Indianapolis. I thought I did darn good to get out of there."

"You lied to me."

"You gotta believe me. If I hadn't dumped the rock in the bag, the Saudis would have it back by now. Give me a break."

Vince put his hands on his hips and paced the small cabin. "Take us out to sea, Emil."

Serin stood up. His voice stammered. "I'm getting out of here. I'm not going to feed the fish."

Vince turned. His gun was pointed at Serin's chest. "Sit back down or you're a dead man."

"Oh, come on. Give me a break!"

"Emil, take'er out," shouted Vince.

The cabin cruiser slowly backed away from the pier on that pleasant Saturday morning. After it cleared the line of vessels, the stern dipped and it headed out to sea.

———

THE UNIQUE SENIOR GENTLEMAN who Tom had watched the day after arriving was standing at water's edge. There was no mistake about the shaggy, grayish beard—it was like seeing Santa Claus. The gentleman was wearing the same straw hat and a pair of shorts as he did other times.

When Tom sat down in a chair on the balcony, he saw the man pointing out to sea with his cane. The man took a few slow steps, stopped and pointed again. There was a bulky looking object out there, rising and falling with the surf.

Probably a dead dolphin, Tom thought, returning to the newspaper. The next time Tom looked up, the man wasn't alone. A man and woman had joined him—it looked like Corrith and Richard Schweitzer. The object in the sea had drifted in a bit closer, though it was still too far out to see what it was.

Returning with a full cup, Tom's attention was drawn once more to the water's edge by a scream. Corrith was pointing at the object in the water and totally losing her composure. Richard grabbed his wife and held her face against his chest, muffling the screams. The sudden noise and activity drew a number of people to the beach.

The group now included the manager, Haldor. Whatever was washing ashore was no dead fish. Grabbing his binoculars, Tom focused on the object. My luck isn't changing, he thought. Of all the places in Florida that I choose to visit, it has to be the one where a dead body washes ashore.

Haldor left the group and walked hastily toward his office. The people that were gathered down below backed away as the body got closer. It would attach to the wet sand at times, only to be reclaimed by the surf. Minutes passed and the people watched in horror as the body finally stuck and remained in the sand. With each wave, the ocean water flowed over the body and receded by trickling back around the head and feet.

Tom stayed on the balcony and wasn't surprised when the sound of a siren penetrated the atmosphere. The noise got louder and louder, peeking as it drew even with the building, dwindling to nothing when the police car pulled up. A minute later Police Chief McSorley and another officer trotted out onto the sand. Richard Schweitzer accompanied the two officers as they approached the body. Young officer Steve Harris reached out and grabbed the hand of the victim.

He dragged it away from the reaches of the surf. Minutes later, a pair of medics carrying equipment arrived. Richard stood near as the officer helped two medics pick up the body and place it onto a gurney. Chief McSorley raised his arms at the remaining bystanders and Tom could hear him say, "It's all over folks. Please go home."

24

VINCE GULLOTI WAS REASONABLY CONVINCED that Serin had told him the truth. Disposing of him was necessary, regardless. The scum-bag had withheld information that would have been useful in recovery of the stone—you don't lie to a Gulloti and get away with it.

Vince did get two names from Serin—Pamela Zachary and Tom Hastings. Their addresses were basically the same, except for unit numbers. The secret of the whereabouts of the stone was with either one or both of them he reasoned, and shook his head angrily. That nitwit had mistaken Melissa Buntrock for Pamela Zachary. Then he blew it later by getting stranded in a pickup, a stolen one at that!

Serin's attempt to recover the stone had failed. Killing the wrong woman and shooting a cop were stupid things to do. Diplomacy, if done right, would work better than force, Vince thought.

He rented two rooms at a motel called Cyprus Gardens on Cyprus Lane, a distance of about six miles south of Park Place. One room for his associate, Emil, and the other that would be used as his office. Though his business in Atlanta included a reliable car lot manager, Vince needed to stay in touch.

"Emil, I want you to hang around here, take any messages. If you need something to eat or drink, there's a couple of eating places in that strip mall, a couple of blocks away."

"Okay, boss."

Vince drove to the strip mall, stopping in front of a beach clothing store near the south end. Making a mental note of its location, he drove up the service lane to the other end of the mall where a liquor store was part of a large grocery.

After purchasing a couple of bottles of whiskey, he drove back and parked near the beach clothing store. Clumsily brushing through a few racks, he made several selections and laid them on the checkout counter. After signing the credit card, he carried the shopping bag to his car. He was especially fond of the wide brim straw hat he had just bought. Vince reached up with his arms and placed both fists against his ears. Adam...that's who I am going to be...must remember that, he thought.

Adam had called Haldor, the manager of Park Place on Saturday morning before he and Emil took Serin for a boat ride. The manager was pleased that someone was interested in renting the available unit for a month.

Half-an-hour later Adam was touring the unit. He hung around and was among the cluster of spectators that watched Serin's body wash ashore. Adam was pleased with how he and Emil accurately calculated the direction of the wind and the time it would take it to reach the beach. Serin's body washing ashore would certainly send a message to the tenants of Park Place, particularly to Pamela Zachary—perhaps Tom Hastings as well.

———

HALDOR WAS RATTLED BECAUSE THE DEAD BODY had washed up on his beach, but all the rental units were accounted for because the new person, Adam Stokes, had agreed to rent that morning. Negative publicity about the drowning, plus the shooting of the policeman could have kept away potential tenants.

The next day, on Sunday morning, Haldor was pleased that the rental deal was finalized. Adam Stokes would be coming over tomorrow to move in—he had just signed an agreement and paid cash up front. Ya' can't beat that, he thought.

After making a call to his cleaning staff, he picked up a newspaper and focused on an article about the body washing up on the beach. The victim was Ben Pierce, a male about forty-five years of age. Cause of death was listed as drowning.

Uneasiness was tensing up Haldor's stomach. First, the murder of the woman in Unit 150 and the next day a policeman was shot. Now a body washes up on his beachfront. He assumed and hoped the most recent incident was a coincidence. Some of the owners are surely going to have questions at the next board meeting. Haldor had a growing concern that the hostile events were all related to the new woman, Pamela Zachary. After all, it was her aunt that was murdered.

Haldor was hoping that the Buntrock condo would sell—new owners would be a breath of fresh air. The lateness of the season meant that Pamela could very well live there until summer. He really didn't want her around to tempt him, he thought. He was happily married.

His thoughts dwelled on the questions asked by the two FBI agents. They were more interested in Pamela Zachary than anyone else. Haldor's intuition told him that the drowning was somehow related to Melissa Buntrock and Pamela Zachary. He wasn't sure, but the nature of the questions—there was a hint.

———

TOM CHOSE TO HAVE COFFEE on the beach Sunday morning. After getting settled on a lounge, he saw Ann Plum standing in almost the exact spot where the body had washed ashore. She just stood there, hands on hips, and looked out to sea. Then she bent over and picked up something. She leaned to the side and flung it toward the water. It must have been a stone as Tom saw it skip four times.

Ann did the same thing with another stone, this time it skipped only twice. Quite the arm for a female, thought Tom. Ann turned and headed for the gate. She saw Tom, stopped and said, "You look comfortable."

Tom lifted his head in response to the high-pitched voice. "You've got a good arm, Ann. I bet you pitched softball in your early days."

"You're right, Hastings. I hear you're a good tennis player."

"Oh, I can hold my own."

"You do a lot more than hold your own," she said and headed for the gate, meeting Richard Schweitzer, who had just come through.

"Good morning, Tom. It's quite the excitement we're having around here, huh?"

"Yeah, that's for sure, Richard. I could do without all of it. I came down here to relax. Anyhow, there's some good news. I hear the policeman is going to live."

"Yes, that's what I heard too. What blows me away is that the man who shot the police officer was the same as the body that washed ashore."

"What do you mean, the same?" asked Tom anxiously, putting down the coffee cup and shifting to a higher position on the lounge.

"According to Haldor, the body was identified as a man by the name of Ben Pierce—that's the same one who shot the officer."

Tom was startled. His head began ringing and an alarm went off— Ben Pierce was the guy that he met on Interstate 75 and went down the slope with to help Pam. *The pickup truck across the street belonged to him? He shot the officer? He washes ashore, dead? Where does Pamela Zachary fit into all this?*

"Richard, I met that man on the highway north of Chattanooga."

Richard's interest perked up and he asked, "Now, what's that all about? What the samhill happened?"

"It was Ben Pierce and I who went down the slope together to find the car that had gone through the barrier. We found Pamela Zachary alive—the same woman that is now staying in Unit 150, the murdered woman's condo."

Richard blew a blast of air from his mouth and said, "Whew, this is getting complicated. You're telling me that this Ben Pierce was involved in Pamela Zachary's rescue. Her aunt gets murdered on the beach, then Pierce shoots an officer across the street from where Pamela Zachary is living and finally the same Ben Pierce washes ashore, dead."

"Richard, it makes sense that Pierce must have been following Pamela. For whatever reason, I don't have a clue. What does she have that he wanted?" asked Tom.

"Beats the hell out of me. That's what the FBI is supposed to find out," responded Richard. "Why don't you ask Pamela?"

"She claims to have no memory of what happened. Did Pierce kill Pamela's aunt by mistake? Did he think it was Pamela out there on the lounge? They do resemble each other," added Tom.

"I don't know, Tom, but staying close to that woman, Pamela, might be dangerous. Better be careful,"

While thinking about the murder of his former neighbor in the lake country of Minnesota, Tom knew this was not going to have a simple solution, FBI or no FBI. Some pieces of the puzzle were missing— *where does Pamela fit*? She and Ben Pierce have been in it all the way— until he gets killed. Drowning, *or was it murder*?

25

RETURNING TO HIS CONDO, Tom was considering leaving Park Place and returning to his home in Minneapolis. There was something deep and sinister about the recent tragic events. He could leave and go home, but how would he explain that to Julie? She was looking forward to a couple of weeks on the beach.

Tom's daughter, Kris, was also planning on spending some time with her dad. Thoughts of going home to Minneapolis prematurely were quickly put aside. Tom's challenge for the moment was Pam. He rang her number, ignoring Richard Schweitzer's warning. "Good morning, Pam, would you like to take a stroll to Beach Café? They've got great pancakes."

"Cool, Tom, beats what I've got in the fridge. I'll be put together in five minutes. Meet you out on the beach?"

"Sure, see you then."

Pamela emerged in short shorts, a loose blouse and a wide brimmed straw hat. "How far is this place, Beach Café?" asked Pamela.

"Almost a mile," responded Tom, pointing southward.

They walked in silence for the first few minutes until Tom asked her, "Pam, are you aware that the dead body that washed ashore yesterday belonged to the same guy who accompanied me down to your car when you went off the highway?"

"Yes, I talked to Richard Schweitzer earlier. He said you told him."

"Does that scare you at all? About Ben Pierce, I mean?"

"It does make me wonder, but my memory of what happened at Indianapolis and up to the accident is still vague. Perhaps Ben was stalking me. I really don't know, and really don't care," she said.

After arriving at the Beach Café, they stood in line and put in orders for pancakes and sausage. Tom found an empty outdoor table and they proceeded with breakfast. Tom looked toward the surf and saw four pelicans glide into the water. One of them dipped its' head into the water and came up with a fish.

Tom's eyes locked on those of a man sitting about six tables away. Before looking away, he noticed another man at the table. Instinct advised him that evil lurked there—the wide, narrow, black mustache paralleled the front brim of the man's straw hat. The other man was hatless, his black hair slicked straight back.

"I'm starting a job in Sarasota in a week and am trying to decide whether to stay in my aunt's condo or get my own place," said Pamela.

"Even though Sarasota isn't that far away, the slow traffic could get frustrating," Tom replied, glancing back at the two men.

"Yes, but I would leave early in the morning, before the locals clog the streets," Pamela responded.

Tom nodded and took another glance at the two men. They had gotten up and were strolling down the walkway leading away from Beach Café. He could see their backs. One of them was wearing long pants. The slicked-back hair looked longer, almost down to his shoulders. The other man, slightly shorter and wearing a straw hat, was dressed in beach attire.

Tom and Pamela were walking the beach on the way back when a dark object appeared in the water a distance of about a football field away.

"What's that?" asked Pamela anxiously.

Tom stopped and looked out to sea. "A dolphin. Not another body, I hope."

"It is a dolphin," said Pamela laughing.

The gate of Park Place loomed ahead. Tom stopped before turning up the slight slope and asked, "Pam, is there something you aren't telling me? Why was Ben Pierce following you? Do you have something he wants, or what?"

"Tom, I don't remember. I really don't."

Tom looked into her eyes—she turned away. He began to doubt her answer. *A very rare, expensive gem—one worth in the millions—* that's what the FBI agents said, he remembered. Does the gem have something to do with the murder of Pam's aunt and the shooting of the police officer?

26

PAMELA WAS TORN BETWEEN CHOICES for a place to hide the gem after returning to her aunt's condo. She was considering leaving it in Tom's closet for the time being. The knowledge that Tom was going to be at Park Place for another three weeks favored that possibility. On the downside was Tom's girlfriend, Julie, arriving on Saturday—it would be more difficult to retrieve the gem if needed.

Since she didn't have a local bank account, renting a safe deposit box didn't appeal. Her thought about approaching Dale Strong regarding disposal of the gem was still a possibility. She didn't know the man, but her instincts and observations favored contacting him.

The man, Ben Pierce, who had pursued her from the airport in Indianapolis, was dead. Was it an accident? She asked herself. He was obviously the one who deposited the gem into my carry-on. Unless his death was a drowning accident, someone else is after it.

Instead of fear, Pamela felt enlightened by the potential value of the gem. Her original thoughts a few days ago were to offer it to a buyer for one million dollars. The price had just gone up—now, she had more like five million dollars in mind. She was positive that her aunt Melissa died by mistake. It was all because of the gem.

It could have been me out there in the lounge, dead with a knife wound in my chest, she thought. Whoever is after the gem is likely going to come after me. I'm going to have to make a move with the gem and fast—no time to feel sorry for myself.

She thought about teenage years and how her father built a wall between her and what she wanted to do—go out with her friends—do drugs and smoke cigarettes.

Her mother bought a pretty dress for her to wear to her first communion—she was proud as pie. Her dad didn't say anything except, "Just don't screw up."

When Pamela thought about her mother, she felt guilty for what she was doing regarding the gem. When she thought about her father, she didn't feel sorry about anything.

Should I invite Tom Hastings into all this? No, he would likely call in the cops, even if I offered him a big cut.

Making sure the dead bolt was engaged, she relaxed and watched television until bedtime. Before falling asleep, she considered phoning Tom and asking him out for lunch tomorrow. He was an interesting man and very observant. She noticed him glancing at the two men at Beach Café earlier that morning. His stare as they were leaving was purposeful. *But why, who were they?*

––––––

ADAM STOKES ENTERED THE OFFICE at Park Place mid-morning on Monday. Haldor handed him a duplicate of the form signed on Saturday and also a copy of the receipt. He had paid with cash up front earlier even though Haldor didn't ask for money at that time. Adam made sure that the condo didn't go to anyone else.

"Here's two sets of keys. I hope you enjoy your month," said a smiling Haldor.

"I will. Thanks for helping me out," replied Adam.

After moving into Unit 112, Adam walked out on the balcony overlooking Beach Street. Both tennis courts across the street were being used. He watched for a few minutes wondering if one of the players was Tom Hastings. Shouldn't take long to find out who's who and what's going on, he thought.

Taking the stairs down to the parking area, he guided his car out and headed for the strip mall to stock up on food and booze. After setting the boxes and bags in his trunk, Adam grabbed the newspaper from one of the bags and walked into Steinbrook Restaurant. After being seated at a table, he noticed two familiar people, Tom Hastings and Pamela Zachary.

They were seated at the other end of the room. Adam was certain that one or both of them knew where the stone was. He had decided to delay meeting them until he learned more from Haldor and other residents of Park Place, especially that Dale guy—he likely had connections—knew what was going on. After being seated, he deliberately didn't look in their direction. Instead he focused on the pedestrian traffic outside the window.

Glancing over at their table, Adam noticed the woman was gesturing toward him, sort of like she did at the Beach Café. They were watching me then and they're watching me now, he concluded.

A few minutes later, he headed for the restroom in the rear. Adam stopped at their table and said, "Hello. You two live at Park Place, don't you? I'm Adam Stokes, just moved in yesterday."

Tom looked up at a smiling Adam and wasn't sure how to take the intrusion. "I'm Tom Hastings. This is Pamela." There was no effort by Tom to shake hands—his right hand was clutching a fork.

Pamela said, "Hi, what part of the complex are you in?"

"Unit 112, next to Beach Street."

"We'll see you around," responded Tom as he used his fork to lift a chunk of potato.

"Yeah, see you around, too," Adam said and headed for the restroom.

When Adam returned, Pamela and Tom were gone. Part of Adam's plan was to spend time on the beach every day. Wearing sunglasses and a straw hat would fit him right in with the crowd. He would watch and listen. Later he would work on establishing friendships by attending the cocktail parties in the courtyard. He knew that getting close to Pamela Zachary and Tom Hastings could lead him to what he was after, the Guni.

———

DALE STRONG LIT UP ANOTHER CIGARETTE and took a sip from the glass of whiskey that sat on a small table next to his lounge. His condo unit was across the street, overlooking the tennis courts. Thoughts drifted back to how he acquired it after settling with his adversaries in New York ten years ago.

The opposing lawyers didn't have a clue as to how he managed to possess the papers and titles. Smiling, he could still visualize the judge banging the gavel down and ruling in his favor.

The money that he made on that deal was almost gone, causing him great concern. He needed a new financial plan to provide cash flow that his lifestyle demanded. Teaming up with Lucy Barrows would help, but he would have to put up with her perpetual laugh.

The Sunday morning tennis players were out in full force. He recognized the Schweitzers on court one. Getting close to Richard was difficult, if not impossible, Dale thought.

Dale knew the Schweitzer's had tons of money, but getting some of it was not on the table, at least for now. His thoughts drifted to the newcomer that checked in that morning. He was dressed like a dude but there was something about his air that needed checking out. He looked cocky—too confident, a player. Dale recognized the type.

The poolside cocktail hour that evening could produce more information. Dale was hoping Adam Stokes would show up. Another interesting person was Pamela Zachary. She appeared out of nowhere and could be involved in the Ben Pierce death. Her aunt murdered out on the beach the day after her arrival certainly meant something. A man by the name of Ben Pierce shot the cop—later the same man washed up dead on the beach. That must have been a payoff, but for what? Someone else had to be involved. I'll keep my eyes and ears open, he thought.

Dale dozed off attempting to read the Sunday morning newspaper.

27

SUNSET WAS APPROACHING, sending warm golden rays into the open end of the courtyard at Park Place. Most of the beachside chairs next to the pool were occupied. The other party people were standing and mingling. It was Sunday evening and the poolside cocktail hour was under way.

"There's that new person," said Corrith to Lucy Barrows and Helen Prichard.

"Wow, a good looker—wonder if he's married?" Lucy's eyes gleamed.

Helen added, "Look at those furrows in the forehead. They give him away. He's a worrier."

Adam sauntered into the pool area and encountered Richard and Dale standing on the shady side of the pool.

"Hello there. You're new. I'm Richard Schweitzer and this is Dale Strong."

"I'm Adam Stokes."

The three men chatted for about five minutes until Richard said, "Uh-oh, duty calls. Good meeting you, Stokes."

"So, where do you hail from?" asked Dale.

"Atlanta," replied Adam.

"What do you do in Atlanta?" continued Dale.

"Financial services."

"As in investments?" asked Dale.

"Yeah, you might say that. What do you do?"

"I'm retired. Moved here from New York ten years ago and haven't looked back."

Ann Plum sauntered over. "Good evening, gentlemen. Is our world better now?"

"Not really," responded Dale.

Adam glanced toward the open end of the courtyard and saw Tom Hastings arrive. The broad, Pamela was not with him he noticed.

"Who's that?" Adam asked.

"Oh, he's new—renting for only this month. Tom Hastings is his name, I think."

"Is he here alone?" asked Adam.

"Dunno, for sure, but he and that Pamela Zachary sure hang around together a lot."

"It's a pleasure to meet you, Dale. I'm going to mingle a little."

Tom was having a conversation with Corrith and Lucy when Adam approached him.

Lucy turned, smiled and said, "Well, hello, you're new aren't you?"

"Yes, moved in this morning. Adam Stokes here."

"I'm Lucy Barrows. This is Corrith Schweitzer and Tom Hastings."

Lucy and Adam exchanged warm pleasantries.

———

ON THE OTHER SIDE OF THE POOL, Dale was talking to Pamela.

"Dale, there is this piece of property that I would like to turn into cash. It has to be done at street level, no publicity. Do you perhaps know anyone?" asked Pamela.

"Property! What do you mean by property?"

"Well, it's actually a valuable gem. If I get close to what I am asking, I'm willing to pay ten percent."

"Do you have a name for the gem? What do you think its worth?"

"No, I don't have a name, but it may be worth close to a million. That's where I need help, to establish a value."

"Tell you what, Pamela, let's get together for lunch. You bring the gem along, and I'll have a look. I do know of a person who will evaluate it privately—cost some bucks, though."

"I don't have any money up front—any compensation has to be on contingency."

"I think that could be arranged," said Dale, his chin elevated. "Give me your phone number and I'll see what I can do."

"Hello, we meet again," were the words Tom heard as he was about to return to his condo.

"You're new here, just arrived, haven't you?" Tom asked.

"Yes, I have. Have you been here long?"

"No, about a week. I'm only staying for the rest of the month."

"Where are you from, Hastings?"

"Minneapolis. How about you?"

"Atlanta. Where did you have the privilege of meeting Miss Zachary?"

Tom didn't care for the question. "She's a friend of my daughters."

"Go to school together, your daughter and Pamela?" Adam asked.

"No, friends from work," said Tom continuing with his lie.

He was quite certain Adam was one of the two men he saw at Beach Café the previous morning—the mustache, a dead ringer. Tom rotated and observed his right wrist. The handshake—he experienced a weird feeling shaking hands with Adam. Why is he so polite? Tom thought.

Tom was walking up the steps on the way back to his condo when he heard Pamela behind him.

"Tom, could I ask you another favor?"

"Sure, what is it?"

"I'm missing a personal item. I probably left it in your spare bathroom or closet. Could I come in and have a look?"

"Sure, of course. Do you need it right now?"

"In a few minutes. I need to make a call first."

28

PAMELA HAD HUNG UP THE PHONE. The meeting was all set for Tuesday at a place called Jasper's, on the pier, a few miles south of Park Place. Dale would be there at 5:00 along with his contact.

After leaving her condo and walking up the stairs, she knocked on the door of Unit 230.

"Hi, Tom, thanks a lot for letting me in. It won't take long."

"No problem, Pam, help yourself," answered Tom, smiling.

Pam was in the spare bedroom for only a minute. She returned and found Tom sitting on the couch in the living room, sipping a cup of coffee.

"Did you find what you were looking for?" asked Tom.

"Sure did. My that coffee smells good."

"Help yourself. You know where the cups are."

Pamela returned from the kitchen with a cup and took a seat on the armchair in the corner.

"When is your friend coming? I thought she was due last Saturday."

"Julie was delayed for a week. She will be here this coming Saturday."

"Oh, that will be nice. Have you known her long?"

"About four years, we met on the Internet."

"You're kidding. Maybe I should try that."

"It's easy, Pam...almost too easy. You have to be careful, though, screen out the fly-by-nights."

"How do you do that?"

"Read their lines carefully, look for inconsistencies and discrepancies. Sooner or later, they give themselves away. Don't rush into meeting someone until you have communicated for at least a month, better yet, three months."

"Thanks for all the advice and the coffee. When I start my new job, maybe I'll give the Internet a try."

"Good luck with your new job. It's coming up pretty soon, isn't it?"

"Yes, next Monday. I've got to go now."

———

JASPER'S BAR & GRILL WAS AN OLD WOODEN BUILDING attached to the pier, which was a part of the largest wharf in Key Marie. The door was made up of boards, grayed with age, and a splattering of peeling green paint. An outdoor patio extended out over the water on the bay side of the building. Gulls circled constantly, taking advantage of scraps of food discarded by people eating outdoors in the patio area.

Inside, a long bar took up the entire length of the far wall. Scattered about the walls were pictures of pirates and fishing schooners. Rustic tables and chairs populated the wooden floor.

Pamela had parked in the pier's parking lot and her heart began beating fast as she approached the door to Jasper's. A small diamond shaped window appeared miniscule within the massiveness of the outer wooden wall. She put her fingers through the large rusty handle, pressed the latch and pulled the door open.

In spite of a bright sunny day, the interior of the bar and grill appeared dark. Pamela drew the eyes of most everyone in the room as she entered. Shading her eyes with her right hand, she scanned the room, looking for two men, one of them Dale.

Pamela was relieved to see a raised hand. She recognized Dale, who was sitting at a table in the far corner with another man.

Dale stood. "Pamela! Glad you could make it. Have a seat," said Dale, clearing his throat. "This is the man I told you about. Meet Bruno."

Pamela sat down and nodded at Dale's visitor.

Bruno was a stocky man, not a hair on his head. He had large ears and a round face. He was wearing a black turtleneck. After staring at Pamela, he looked toward the bar and snapped his fingers. When he sat down, he appeared to spread out beyond the confines of the chair.

A bar waitress came by and asked, "Anything for you, ma'am?"

"No thanks."

"How about you, sir?"

Bruno held up his hand. "I'll have a Coke."

The waitress left.

Dale asked, "Did you bring it?"

"First, I'd like to know more about your friend."

"Look, Pam, Bruno is an old hand at this. He can be trusted and will give you an honest evaluation. Since you want this all to be confidential, he has to remain anonymous."

Pamela looked at Bruno and tightened her lips. "Well, okay."

Pamela reached into her pocket and brought out the gem, holding it cupped in the palm of her right hand.

"Jesus, that looks like the Guni. I can't believe it. How in the heavens did you ever get hold of that?" asked Bruno, his eyes dancing with excitement. "Ah, never mind, can I examine it please?"

Pamela extended her hand to Bruno. He carefully picked up the gem and held it to the light after glancing around, making sure they weren't being watched.

He rolled it around in his fingers for a few seconds and pulled it back toward his chest. "What would you do if I got up and walked out?" he asked Pamela.

"See those two men sitting over by the door. They are my insurance."

"I see. You plan well, my dear." Smiling wide, he handed it back to Pamela. She grasped the gem with both hands and returned it to her pocket.

Bruno put both hands on the table, leaned forward and said, "The Guni is worth a lot of money, but the risk of attempting to market it is huge. Latest I heard was that a certain Arab prince has some of his top agents looking for it. Two of them are in Florida."

Pamela looked at him anxiously and said, "Well, how much will you give me for it?"

"Four million, tops. That includes your friend's share."

Pamela could feel her heart moving into her throat. For her, it was a chance in a lifetime. Her quick calculation netted her three million-six hundred thousand.

"When can you have the money?" she asked.

"It'll take about a week, say next Monday. We meet right here at five, same time. I'll have the money...you have the rock...we'll both be satisfied."

"I'll be here," Pamela responded.

"I want you both to remain at the table as I am leaving. It's important for me to walk out alone," whispered Bruno.

"Gottcha'," said Dale. "Well, Pamela, looks like we have a deal. I will expect the four hundred thousand immediately, before we leave the building after you get the money."

"Dale, you'll be right here...with me. You'll get your money. This place gives me the creeps."

"Ah, but it will be so profitable," responded Dale, smiling.

29

PAMELA DIDN'T TRUST DALE. In the future, she didn't want to meet with the two men alone. Not knowing many people in the Keys area, the only person that came to her mind was Tom Hastings. She decided to ask him to come with her to Jasper's. Her fear was that he would figure out why and go to the police.

Driving back to Park Place, Pamela thought about finding a different safe place for the gem until Monday—there wasn't any good alternative. Changing the lock of the condo increased her confidence, but the gem was too important for her future to chance losing it.

Pamela decided she would return the gem to its hiding place in the closet in Tom's condo. She needed to approach Tom today.

She noticed some people in the courtyard after returning, but Tom wasn't one of them. She went up the steps and walked over to Unit 230. The door was partially open.

She knocked and sang out, "Anyone home?"

"Hi, Pam, what's up?" asked Tom. He put a hand up against the wall, leaning slightly to face Pamela.

"Tom, are you free this evening? I would like to take you out for dinner for helping me out so much."

"Oh really. That's an offer I can't turn down. I was pondering what to do this evening. You have just solved my dilemma."

"Great, I'll pick you up in an hour. How's that?"

"Perfect, see you then."

———

PAMELA PEEKED UP AND DOWN THE CORRIDOR before leaving her condo. She had the Guni in her purse, wrapped in tissue paper. Moving quickly up the steps, she felt anxious to get it back into its original hiding place. She was at the top step when meeting Richard Schweitzer.

"Hi, Pamela, looks like you're going out for the evening. You look great."

"Thanks, Richard. I'm taking Tom Hastings out for dinner. He's been a real help to me."

"Have a good time," responded Richard as he bounded down the steps.

Tom's door was open. Blazes, anyone could walk in here anytime, she thought. Maybe I'm doing the wrong thing by hiding the gem here.

She rapped her knuckles on the opened door and announced, "Hi, Tom, I'm here."

"Hi, Pam, I'm ready to go—are you driving?"

"Yes, I am, but I need to visit the bathroom."

"Help yourself," Tom said, gesturing his arm toward the spare bathroom door.

The second door in the bathroom provided a gateway to the closet and an opportunity to return the gem to the bottom shoe box on the shelf.

Overly's Bar & Grill was crowded when Tom and Pamela arrived. The young man writing down names at the outdoor station said the wait would be about fifteen minutes.

"Let's head over to the bar, Pam. Looks like a couple of barstools are open."

"I'll have a Bud," Tom told the bartender. "How about you, Pam?"

"The same, thank you. Why don't you start a tab? This is my treat, you know."

"Ah, naw, I'll pay cash for the beers. No big deal," answered Tom.

"So what's on your mind, Pam?" asked Tom.

"What makes you think there's something on my mind?"

"You have that look, a plan? Well, if it's none of my business, let's talk about something else."

"There is something, Tom, but you've already done so much for me."

"What is it, Pam?"

"I have a business deal with a couple of men next Monday at the wharf. There really isn't a problem, but I don't care to go alone. I was wondering..."

"You want me to go with you?" Tom responded, smiling.

"Yes, that's exactly it."

"What kind of business are you getting into? Is there some risk?"

"There'll be no risk for you. I've decided to sell some of my aunt's jewelry. It will look better for me if I have a man along."

Tom looked at the wall beyond her. "Next Monday, huh? Let me think about it."

He looked back at Pamela and read the disappointment on her face. "You probably know that my friend Julie will be here by then. I'm going to have to turn you down. Sorry."

Pamela did not respond.

"I would like to help you, but can't this time."

Pamela smiled. "Tom, thanks for considering it."

They were approached and escorted to a booth by the maitre' d. A waitress followed.

"Do you like wine, Tom?" she asked.

"Yeah, sure do."

Pamela ordered a bottle of wine. She wasn't about to give up. Perhaps a little coaxing, she thought. Pamela also needed to consider what the presence of Julie would do to her strategy of storing the gem in Tom's condo.

The thought of two doors in the bathroom brought a smile to her face. If she needed access, simply using the bathroom would work— unless there was someone in the bedroom. Pam wasn't sure if Julie was going to use the second bedroom.

When the bottle arrived, Pam grabbed it and poured, filling both glasses.

One glass led to another and eventually Pamela and Tom got the giggles.

"I haven't laughed this much in a long time," said Tom.

"I haven't either. You're nice company, Tom. I enjoy visiting with you," responded Pamela.

Tom had his arm around her shoulder when they left Overly's. You know, Pam, perhaps I could go along with you on Monday. It won't take long will it?"

"No, not very long."

———

DALE HAD BEEN LOOKING OUT OVER THE STREET from his unit when he saw Pamela's blue Honda turn onto Beach Street. He noticed she had a passenger, Tom Hastings. Wonder what those two are up to, he thought.

He had been pleased with the meeting. Bruno had come through as he had hoped—at least it appeared that way. Four hundred thousand dollars would go a long way in satisfying his financial needs for the rest of the year, and hopefully then some. Frowning, he wished he'd quoted 20 percent instead of 10.

Bruno had been evasive when I questioned him about the Guni at Jasper's, he thought. I did hear him say something about an Arabic Prince. I wonder who would have more information—it could create an opportunity to make more money. The person who came to his mind was the newest tenant, Adam Stokes. Dale made a mental note to feel him out on the subject the next time they talked.

———

DALE'S ANXIETY WITH THE GUNI was the reason he had phoned Adam Stokes. He hoped to learn more about the gem. Adam seemed more than happy to join him at Overly's Bar & Grill for a drink after Dale mentioned the word, "property." Dale had volunteered to drive, so they met in the Park Place garage.

After arriving and getting seated at Overly's, Dale noticed that Adam's attention was frequently drawn toward the bar. Dale's position prevented him from seeing whom Adam was watching. A trip to the men's room satisfied his curiosity—it was Tom Hastings and Pamela Zachary. *Why should Adam be so interested in those two?*

When Dale returned, he sat and looked Adam in the eyes, "Have you ever heard of a rare and valuable gem called the Guni?" Adam's eyes narrowed and his glances toward the bar stopped. "Ah, what was that...a gem...called what?" asked Adam.

"Guni, a real big gem that was mined in Pakistan. It was stolen from a Saudi Prince in New York. I was wondering if you ever heard of it."

Adam responded, "Ah, seems to me there was something in the papers about it being stolen. Why do you ask? What do you know about it?"

Dale's stoic facial expression deepened—the sudden aggressive interest by Adam took him by surprise. Perhaps I better back off a little, he thought.

"Ah, I heard some people talking about it. Apparently, it's worth some money."

"People talking around here?" asked Adam.

"Ah yeah, in the Keys."

"Key Marie?" asked a stern Adam.

"Naw, south of here, a couple of islands down," answered Dale as he tightened his lips together.

30

WEDNESDAY, MID-MORING, Tom was playing tennis across the street with the Schweitzers and Lucy Barrow. He partnered with Corrith during the first set which ended in their favor, six-four. Richard blew an easy overhead that would have tied the set.

"Holy mackerel, you guys are real tough," said Richard and laughed. "If it wasn't for my partner holding me up, the set wouldn't have even been close."

"You are so flattering, Richard," responded a gleeful Lucy. She laughed and Tom shook his head.

The tennis match ended and the four players walked back across Beach Street to Park Place.

As Richard was turning his key in the lock of the iron gate, Lucy asked Tom, "Would you like to come over for some wine this evening? I'm having some people over."

They had passed through the iron gate and met Ann Plum in the courtyard. Tom delayed his answer as Ann interrupted loudly, "The fun people approach."

Lucy's outburst of laughter sent Ann hastily walking toward the other side of the courtyard.

"Ah, sure, that sounds fine. What time?" Tom responded.

"Five. We can watch the sunset from my balcony. Gosh sakes, that Ann can get so moody."

"Okay, see you then," replied Tom.

He wasn't sure about Lucy's intentions. She was a big flirt and may have had other things in mind—no way, with that laugh. Not too bad a tennis player, Tom thought. Her laugh is an aberration that chases people away. She's not going to be pleased when Julie comes and replaces her in the foursome. When I talked to Julie the previous evening, she mentioned looking foward to playing tennis.

———

WATCHING FROM HIS WINDOW was Vince Gulloti. He constantly had to remind himself that his name at Park Place was Adam Stokes. Information gotten from Dale yesterday added to his suspicions that the Guni was here at Park Place. Either Tom Hastings or Pamela Zachary had possession and they might be in the process of selling it.

Vince thought about the strong-arm tactics that Serin used attempting to get the stone back. Those tactics failed and Vince was determined to use diplomacy and talk to the right people at Park Place. Pamela Zachary was his prime objective. She usually spent time on the beach early afternoon.

Adam's arms were laden with beach accessories as he made his way through the courtyard, passed the gate and walked out onto the beach. The sun was hot and there were several people stretched out on the lounges. Stopping, he surveyed the group attempting to determine if Pamela was one of them.

Standing there he thought of Serin and how easy it would have been to make a people identification mistake. The women on the lounges all looked alike with their straw hats and sunglasses—the color of hair was the main difference. It didn't matter now—Serin was gone, a blip in history. Striding down to the water, Adam continued to observe the lounges. After walking back up, he selected one available next to a blonde woman.

"Hi there, Adam. Going to get some sun?" asked Lucy Barrows as she reached up and lifted her sunglasses.

"Good afternoon, Miss Barrows. How are you today?"

"Just fine, Mr. Stokes."

The woman next to Lucy lifted her sunglasses, too. It was Pamela. Adam settled into the lounge and hoped that Lucy would leave before Pamela did. A few minutes later, he got his wish.

"See you folks at five. Oh, Adam, would you like to join us?" Lucy asked. "I'm having a few people over."

"Five, huh? Count me in," responded Adam.

"So, how are things with you?" Adam asked Pamela as he elevated to a sitting position.

"Couldn't be much better than this," she replied.

"I heard you had a tragedy a couple of weeks ago, your aunt?"

"Yes, Adam, my dear aunt was murdered right here on the beach, in one of these lounges."

"Who would do a thing like that?" asked Adam.

Pamela tightened her lips together and appeared irritated. "It's all in the hands of the police and the FBI. Why are you asking me all these questions?" responded Pamela angrily.

"Sorry," Adam replied. "I apologize."

That broad has the stone and is likely in the process of selling it, he thought. She is extremely defensive. Dale Strong and Tom Hastings are involved to the hilt. The timing of a cocktail party at Lucy's condo this evening is perfect.

ADAM CALLED VORDI IN ATLANTA. "Who do you know in the area of Key Marie who would be capable of brokering the Guni?"

"Bruno."

31

RHOUL MASSIF AND BERN TALLIN checked into a motel on Key Marie Island on Wednesday afternoon. Earlier that day, their conversation with a man by the name of Vordi in Atlanta led them to that island.

The wide smile on Vordi's face had disappeared when Bern grabbed him from behind and pressed the point of a blade into the skin of his neck.

Vordi's face had reddened. His eyes showed terror for a few moments. Calming he'd said, "Gentlemen, I am a business man. You have to understand that. I have heard about your Guni, but it has never been in my possession, nor has it even been offered. You have to believe me."

Vordi was shaking when the two men left his office. The big one, Massif, was someone he never wanted to face again.

If Vince Gulloti calls, I'll have to offer less, he thought. Then, I'll visit my friend Martinez in Mexico for a year or so—they'll never find me.

———

LATER THAT AFTERNOON, after the two Saudis had settled in, Bern spent over half-an-hour on the phone. Rhoul was lying on one of the beds staring at the ceiling.

His master, the Prince, wanted the Guni back at all costs. Even if it meant *killing* to get it back—Rhoul understood that they were to use diplomacy first. The Prince was willing to spend as much as two million dollars in ransom. What's the obvious first step? *Find out who has it,* meen—*who?*

———

LUCY BARROWS TOUCHED UP HER HAIR—she was ready for her cocktail party. Hurrying to the door, responding to the first knock, she stood face to face with Adam Stokes.

"Good evening, Miss Barrows, remember me? I'm Adam Stokes."

"Why, yes. So glad that you could come," replied Lucy, smiling.

He noticed her smile fade. Looking back over his shoulder, he saw a man and woman approaching.

"Come on in, folks. Have you met Mr. Stokes?" asked Lucy.

"I don't believe so," answered Marv.

"Adam, these are my friends Marv and Ann Plum."

She sure doesn't seem too happy to see those two, he thought.

While visiting with Marv and Ann, Adam saw Dale Strong arrive next and put his arm around Lucy. Adam kept glancing toward Lucy and saw her push Dale's arm away. He turned away from Ann's loud voice. I don't hear a damn word she's saying and really don't care. She's not a player.

Adam walked away from the Plums and felt the sting of Ann's glare. He walked over to Lucy. He noticed that Ann Plum had left her husband standing alone and joined Dale, who quickly lost his smile and looked across the room. Lucy's atrocious laugh was more that he could bear, Adam thought. "Excuse me, Lucy, I need some food," said Adam and walked away.

He joined his new acquaintance Marv at the dining room table where Marv was picking at the appetizers. I've got to hang in here until either Hastings or Zachory show up, he said to himself. Talking to either of the Plums or Lucy is a waste of my time, he thought. Dale's the only important person here right now.

Oh no, here she comes again, Adam feared as he noticed Lucy heading his way. He braced for her arrival, but was pleasantly surprised when her attention was diverted to the door where Pamela

Zachory had just made her entrance.

"Welcome," he heard Lucy say to Pamela. At that moment Tom Hastings came through the door. Now, I can get somewhere, Adam thought anxiously.

When he saw Lucy tie up Hastings, his wish was granted. Pamela Zachory headed for the appetizers. *Here she comes.*

"Good evening, Miss Zachory. We met at the restaurant at the mall. Remember? I talked to you on the beach yesterday."

"Oh yes. You stopped by our table. Your name...I don't quite remember."

"Stokes...Adam Stokes. You were with Tom Hastings, were you not?"

"Yes, we were having lunch."

Adam waited until Pamela dipped into the appetizers before asking. "How long do you plan on staying in your aunt's condo? What company are you going to work for in Sarasota?"

He noticed Pamela's irritation with his questions. She picked up her small paper plate and headed back toward the people in the center of the room. She joined Hastings, who appeared to be involved in a boring conversation with Lucy. Adam took note how Hastings welcomed the intrusion by Pamela.

Richard and Corrith Schweitzer made their appearance. They moved around, greeting everyone, except Adam who was still at the table eating appetizers. Adam saw that Tom was alone for a moment. Setting down his little plate, he joined him.

"I hear you're expecting some company," Adam said.

"Yeah, I am."

"A lady, I hear."

"Yes."

"She going to stay long?"

"A week, perhaps...why?"

"Just wondering. I see you and Pamela together a lot."

TOM GAVE ADAM A CLASSIC INQUISITIVE LOOK. Why is he asking me all these questions, he thought. Some of them are darn personal. "Excuse me Adam, I have to move on."

He saw Pamela standing alone and quickly moved to her side. Tom and Pamela discussed a possible visit to Overly's Bar & Grill after the cocktail party.

"Let's blow this joint," Tom told Pamela a few minutes later when they had another private moment.

"I'm all for that," she responded.

Tom and Pamela left separately, but she joined him at his condo where they had a good laugh talking about Lucy Barrow and her ridiculous cackle.

Just before they left for Overly's, Tom got a phone call from Julie.

"Tom, I'm so sorry but there's another problem."

"What, Julie, now what?"

"My daughter in Colorado—she's in the hospital. I have to go there—there is no choice. Oh, how I would much rather go to Florida."

Tom was very disappointed and he appreciated Pam's company that evening at Overly's, more than ever.

"What kind of questions?" asked Tom when Pamela complained about Adam.

"What I was doing in Indianapolis? What do I remember from the accident? What my future plans are? My God, he really dug."

Tom frowned and was trying to think what Adam talked to him about. Oh yeah. It was about Julie and me seeing Pam a lot. Quite the coincidence that he shows up about the time that Ben Pierce washed ashore. He made a mental note to volunteer that information to the FBI agents when they returned.

32

TOM RECEIVED A WELCOME SURPRISING PHONE CALL later that evening after returning from Overly's—his daughter, Kris. He had been hoping to hear from her because she had talked about visiting him during their most recent conversation. Kris had already landed in Miami and would be free for the weekend. Tom encouraged her to visit as soon as she could.

"I'll be there the day after tomorrow, Dad," she had said.

After hanging up, Tom thought about their separation a few years ago. Kris had befriended the wrong crowd during college days. Those were difficult years for me. I'll always be grateful that she recovered and is living a responsible and healthy life. Her mother's tragic death in a plane crash brought us even closer together. It will be good to see her again.

He had difficulty going to sleep that night. Not because his daughter was coming to visit, but because Julie wasn't coming and he missed her. He was going to be alone the rest of the month. Kris was going to visit for only a short time. He thought about Pamela.

A straw hat kept popping up in his thoughts. He remembered the dark-looking face under the hat and the narrow black mustache, which appeared to have been created using a magic marker.

Why was Adam Stokes asking Pam and me all those questions? Tom wasn't certain but Adam could have been one of the two men that watched he and Pamela at the Beach Café. He would have been the man wearing the straw hat sitting at the same table as the evil-looking one—the slicked back hair. Tom remembered the uneasiness and strong feelings of discomfort about being watched by them.

———

BRUNO WAS IN HIS OFFICE ON THURSDAY AFTERNOON. He had just returned from a late lunch. The arrangements for Monday were finalized. The money was going to be delivered to him at a tennis clubhouse on Sunday, at 6:00 p.m. sharp. His locker was going to serve as a home for four million dollars, just for one day. It was a short drive from the tennis club to the wharf.

He became instantly concerned when overhearing his secretary's voice in the next room, "You can't go in there."

Rhoul Massif and Bern Tallin entered his private office. Bruno stood up and asked, "To whom do I owe the pleasure of this visit?"

"We represent Prince Vallif of Saudi Arabia. I'll get right to the point. Rumors have it that you know where the Guni is," the tallest man said.

"Gentlemen, yes, I have heard of the Guni—a very valuable treasure, but I am not that fortunate to possess it, nor do I know where it is."

The small beads of perspiration that appeared on his forehead caused Bruno to feel uncomfortable, very uncomfortable. Those dark eyes have noticed, he thought. *They know I'm lying.*

Massif handed him a card. "My phone number is there. If you hear where the Guni is, you will phone me. Not doing so could be very dangerous...even fatal."

"*Ma'assalama,*" Rhoul said as he and Bern stood by the desk, glaring down at Bruno. "Goodbye to you."

The Saudis left the office and bowed to Bruno's secretary in the next room.

Bruno's hands were quivering. The Guni would be in his possession the very next day. The visit by the two Saudis complicated his plan. Still, six million would tide him over for the next ten years. The squeeze was on—Vordi had dropped the original price from twenty million to ten million. Now Bruno knew why.

He poured a glass of whiskey and took it out on the small porch connected to his office. Thoughts of the Saudis showing up when he was finalizing the purchase from Pamela Zachary paralyzed his mind.

Bruno felt instant relief when the first splash of whiskey hit his stomach.

———

FBI AGENT SAM KLAPTIN HAD JUST GOTTEN OFF THE PHONE. His partner, Corey Downer, was running a file over his fingernails.

"Corey, the plot thickens. According to our office in Miami, agents of the Saudi Prince Omar Vallif have arrived in Key Marie. Their names are Rhoul Massif and Bern Tallin. They've already checked into Motel Surfside. It was on Wednesday."

"Phew, that should be interesting. I sure wouldn't want to be the one with the Guni in my pocket," responded Corey.

"The two Saudis are here legally and we can't touch them unless they commit a crime. There's more—they visited a dealer, Bruno. Ever heard of him?"

"Yeah, I remember his name being brought up more than once in some of our recent criminal reports," Corey Downer said as he set the nail file down on the small table.

"I've put a tail on this Bruno guy. It's possible that whoever has the rock will contact him, if they haven't already."

"Good idea, Sam. So, do you think there may be someone else in the hunt other than the Saudis?" asked Corey.

"Sure looks that way, at least one party—maybe more. The Guni is a hot item. I think the Saudis are willing to deal."

Sam picked up a sheet that the fax machine had just generated. "Hey, look at this release. That Tom Hastings guy was involved in a case where one of our agents died in Minnesota two to three years ago. Remember Allan Burnside?"

"Do I remember him. Allan was a classmate of mine. I went to the funeral in Michigan. So, what's that about? Is Tom Hastings being here a coincidence perhaps, or are we missing something?"

"Actually, according to this report, Hastings was part of the solution, not the problem. He helped capture Burnside's killer. Ah, yeah, Corey, I think whoever killed Pierce is also after the Guni—

big time...I don't think Hastings is one of them."

"Speaking of Ben Pierce, did you see what his real name was?"

"Yeah, Serin—just Serin. Oh, and this report from McSorley's office—it places Pierce at the Key Marie wharf last Friday. That's the last time he was seen alive by anyone that we are in touch with. So, if we find out who took Pierce for a boat ride, we should be close to a solution."

"You know, Sam, I think Pamela Zachary lied to us when we asked her if she knew anything about the Guni. She may be hiding behind this medical memory thing. I don't think Hastings is lying, though."

Sam was glad that his partner, Corey, was thinking this case through. My heart just isn't in it, Sam thought.

"Yup, you're probably right. I think we better make another visit to Park Place...put Zachory on the spot."

———

ADAM STOKES CHANGED INTO BEACH CLOTHES and took up a position on the beach after lunch on Friday afternoon. He positioned a lounge so he could view both gates—the one that separated the units and garage from the courtyard, and the other that secured the courtyard from the beach.

His straw hat was tilted down, but not enough to block his view. The book that he held in his hands had remained on the same page since he had arrived. He was hoping that Pamela Zachary would show up.

After waiting for an hour, he became intrigued with the appearance of two men of apparent Arabian visage. They were walking rapidly, coming from the south, reaching the beach directly in front of Park Place.

After glancing at the building and the lounges out front, the two Arabs walked to the edge of the water and gazed out to sea. Adam watched with interest as they meandered along the beach, back and forth, but never out of sight of Park Place.

The gate to the courtyard opened and Pamela Zachary made an

appearance. Pausing and looking around, she slowly advanced toward the lounges. The swimsuit she wore could only be viewed by peeking, as it was mostly covered with a colorful beach shirt. Her dark glasses and wide brimmed hat suggested she was going to stay awhile. The two darker-skinned men standing at the edge of the water watched as Pamela selected a lounge isolated from the rest.

She spread out her things, took off the shirt and stretched out on the lounge. Adam put his book down and sat up. The gate opened again and Tom Hastings strode to the cluster of lounges. He dragged one near to where Pamela lay. She removed her sunglasses and smiled.

Adam picked up his book.

"Good day to you, Tom. What's new?" asked Pamela.

"My daughter is coming today."

"Your daughter! Is she going to stay with you?"

"Yup, sure is, for a few days."

Adam set his book down again. The surf was reasonably quiet that afternoon and he was digesting the conversation, hoping to gain information about the Guni.

"I would like to meet your daughter, Tom," Pamela said.

"Why don't you stop by later. I'm going shopping after I leave here. Gotta get some wine and something to munch on. How about 6:00 or so?"

"Cool. I'll do that, thanks."

Pamela remained on the beach after Tom gathered his things and left. Adam looked toward the beach and focused on the two Saudis. He looked back at Pamela. She had her eyes closed. One of the Saudis gestured toward her with one of his hands.

Adam watched the two dark-skinned men like a hawk the next half-hour. Every minute that passed intensified his urge—to get the Arabs away from Park Place. As time went by, there wasn't any doubt in his mind that the dark-skinned men were agents of the Prince. They were here on a surveillance mission—to study the most likely persons to possess the Guni, Pamela Zachary and Tom Hastings. Adam hastily returned to his condo unit.

BARBARA WAS WORKING AT THE DISPATCHER'S STATION at police headquarters in Key Marie on a Friday afternoon. Calm turned into alarm when she received an anonymous phone call. A man had said there were two mid-eastern terrorists on the beach at Park Place, 7660 Beach Street.

"Hello, who is this?" she eagerly asked.

She heard a click—whoever it was hung up. Her boss, Police Chief McSorley, was working the streets with Nate Bloomberg that day. She felt sorry for Nate, but was happy that he was recovering from his wound. She didn't want him to get involved in another shooting, but the threatening phone call overcame her sympathy. She reached Chief McSorley on the first ring.

———

"TERRORISTS!" EXCLAIMED THE CHIEF after hearing Barbara attempt to relay the anonymous phone message.

Barbara's hands were shaking and her voice developed a tremor.

"Okay, Barb, you've done your job. We'll check it out...ah... you better give Steve a call. Have him meet us there, at Park Place, as soon as he can. Understand?"

"Yes! I'll get hold of him right away."

It took Chief McSorley and Officer Bloomberg only six minutes to pull into the visitor's parking lot at Park Place. Since he didn't have a key to the gate, he knocked heavily on.the manager's door. No one answered. Frustrated, he walked over to the gate and rattled it. There were two ladies sunning by the pool.

"Ladies, this is the police, please open this gate. It's an emergency."

The chief paced around impatiently, while one of the women rummaged through her purse for a key.

"Gosh sakes, " she blurted, hastening to the gate.

"Now, I want you to open that one, too," McSorley told the woman.

After the second gate was open, the chief pulled out his gun and told Nate, "Come on, Nate, let's take 'um."

Chief McSorley led the way onto the beach and he yelled, "Hey, you two over there. Put your hands up over your heads and don't move."

The two Saudis appeared surprised and confused. Rhoul pointed a finger toward his chest.

"Yeah, you—and the other guy, too," responded the chief.

Obeying the police chief's command, they raised their arms and elbows, placing hands on their heads.

"What's the problem, officer? There must be some mistake," Rhoul said.

"I want you both down on the ground, on your bellies. Now!"

Reluctantly the two Saudis lay down.

"Put your arms behind your back. Okay, Nate, cuff 'em."

As Adam had hoped, the incident drew a large group of onlookers, huddled together in clusters and scared to death. He was watching the gate, awaiting the arrival of Tom Hastings.

Minutes later, Hastings came through the gate and joined the onlookers. At that moment while the Saudis were still down on the sand, Adam quickly moved through the gate and dashed up the stairs. His wish was realized when discovering Unit 230 unlocked. There was only a screen door and it readily opened. Staying calm and cool he began searching the condo, looking in all the unusual places.

Bingo, there it was in the shoebox, the Guni—he had found it within five minutes. Placing things back as neatly as possible, he left the unit. On the way back to his rental unit, he passed through the courtyard. The Saudis, followed by the officers, were approaching the gate. Adam quickly moved beyond the pool and took the short flight of stairs that led to his unit.

———

THE POLICE ACTIVITY ON THE BEACH HAD DRAWN A CROWD. Richard Schweitzer was standing next to Lucy. Her face was contorted with fear. Tom Hastings was a couple of steps away, his hand on Pamela Zachary's shoulder. Marv Plum was off to the left, his arms extended from his body as if he was going to attack the Saudis. Dale Strong was approaching from the gate, his mouth partially open. He moved aside to allow the police to escort their prisoners through the gate.

Ann Plum had been watching from her balcony. She had seen the new tenant, Adam Stokes, leave the group and move through the gate into the courtyard. Haldor was watching from the other end of the pool, leaning on a garden rake.

"Well, that takes care of that," said Richard. "What next?"

"I've got to get back, my daughter will be arriving any minute," Tom responded.

Pamela followed Tom toward the gate, "What time should I come over?" she asked.

"How about 6:30? Hopefully what just happened will not interrupt anything."

"Okay, see you then."

33

KRIS HASTINGS ARRIVED AT PARK PLACE in a rental car on Friday late in the afternoon, after driving all the way from Miami. Her dad was overwhelmed to see his little girl again. He hugged her for what seemed like minutes. After going down to the garage to bring her baggage up, they sat in the living room and talked for over two hours.

At 6:30 there was a gentle tap on the door.

"Come in, Pam, I want you to meet my daughter, Kris."

The women shook hands while Tom headed for the kitchen.

"Beer okay, Pam?" he asked.

"Sure, fine."

Tom's half-full beer was on the coffee table when he handed a bottle to Pamela, who sat down on the couch, next to Kris. As he watched the two women visiting, he noticed that they were about the same height and had similar hair color. The big difference was in their eyes. Kris's were a sparkling blue, while Pamela's were dark brown.

The mood in Tom's car later that evening was jovial. He drove onto Beach Street and headed for Overly's. The restaurant was crowded as usual. While they were being escorted to a booth, Tom spotted Richard and Corrith Schweitzer. After pausing for a couple of minutes and introducing his daughter, they were seated and began studying the menu.

The evening moved along amidst an abundance of laughter. The Schweitzers stopped by as they were leaving.

"Holy buckets, I'm so relieved that the police have arrested those men. We sure don't need any terrorists around," said Corrith.

Richard said, "I'm not so sure that the two Arabs were terrorists. The police chief may have jumped the gun."

"Why do you say that?" asked Tom.

"Tully Smith, over at the police department, told a guy who I know. The Arabs had proper papers and did not possess anything that resembled a weapon. One call to their embassy and FBI agents showed up within an hour. The red-faced chief was forced to let 'em go."

Because of Pamela's presence, Tom didn't talk about what he was thinking. *First, Pam's aunt gets murdered on the beach...then the policeman gets shot across the street...then the guy who shot the policeman washes ashore, dead...then two alleged terrorists get arrested at Park Place.*

Tom noticed Pamela fidgeting with her glass. Two of her fingers were moving up and down the side of the glass. She was squirming in her seat.

"Well, guys, should we head home?" Tom asked Kris and Pamela.

Pamela anxiously responded, "Yes, Tom, I need to get home. I'm really tired."

———

VINCE GULLOTI COULDN'T BELIEVE HIS LUCKY STROKE. He had returned safely to his condo with the stone. His role of playing Adam Stokes had ended. Carefully, he wrapped the stone in tissue paper and placed it into a plastic freezer bag. Tucking it into his front pocket, he gathered the rest of his belongings and placed them on the bed. After packing them into two suitcases, he grabbed a glass from the kitchen and partially filled it with whiskey.

Sitting on the couch, he thought of Vordi—it was time to give him a call and set up an appointment. Vince picked up the phone. Vordi didn't seem excited when Vince told him he had possession of the Guni.

"It's worth only five million now, Vince. The fires of hell are surrounding that stone."

Vince was expecting at least ten and was taken aback by Vordi's offer. He responded, "Damn, Vordi, you know it's worth a lot more than that. Besides the two Saudis have been taken into custody."

"Yeah, they have, but they won't be there very long. The Saudi Prince had made a deal with the FBI, right after the heist."

"I'm going to sit on this for a while," responded Vince firmly.

"Okay, but it may be worth less tomorrow."

There was a pause. "Oh, okay...you gotta deal. I'll bring it back to Atlanta tonight and take the five."

"Good, you are wise. I'll be in the office at 10:00."

Vince stretched out on the couch. He owed his New York connection a million-and-a-half. Terrance would demand a million when he got out of jail. Perhaps Terrance would end up same as Serin, he thought. That left three-and-a-half million for him. It'll have to do and I better get going, he thought. After writing out a note for the manager, he carried his two suitcases onto the elevator. After placing them in the trunk, he made a final jaunt upstairs to pick up some remaining items.

On the way down he touched the bulge in his pocket and felt elated—he was only minutes away from getting on the highway back to Atlanta. Down in the garage, he opened the back door and dumped the items on the back seat. After slamming the door shut, he opened the driver's side door. "Outta here," he whispered and smiled, his black mustache narrowing.

Adam's smile disappeared in a moment—his mouth dropped open and his eyes closed—his brain experienced a huge blinding flash of light and retreated into darkness as he fell to the concrete floor. The person behind him dropped the heavy-duty tire iron to the floor and began searching his clothes.

―――

HEADLIGHTS FROM TOM'S CAR FLASHED AGAINST THE BACK WALL of the garage when they returned from Overly's. Shutting off the engine, the three exited and slammed the doors closed. When Tom pressed the button on the ignition pad, the door locks clicked and the horn sounded.

Kris asked, "Do you hear something?"

They stopped to listen and Pamela added, "Yes, it sounds like a moan."

Tom advanced toward the sound and exclaimed, "Geez, there's someone down there! On the floor, look!"

He got closer and said, "It's Adam Stokes."

Adam was lying on his back and his eyes were closed. Some of his hair was soaked in blood that had already dried. One of his arms was crumpled underneath his body—the other was stretched outward.

"He's been hurt! We better get some help."

"The poor man," said Kris.

Tom dashed up the two sets of stairs and entered his condo. He rang 911. After explaining the situation to Tully Smith, he hustled back down the steps and rejoined Kris and Pamela. Kris was leaning over Adam Stokes's body. Tom noticed the right side pocket of Adam's trousers was inside out.

"He's breathing, Dad, and his pulse is good."

"Good news. Best not touch him. The police and ambulance will be here shortly."

Tom picked up a piece of paper that was lying next to Adam's body. There was some writing, but too dark to read. He put it in his pocket. It could be evidence or possibly just a shopping list, he thought.

―――

SARGENT CLIFF JOHNSON AND OFFICER NATE BLOOMBERG pulled into the parking area within five minutes— their car's rooftop lights were flashing red and blue colors and the siren tailed off.

"Over here," yelled Tom when the officers exited their car.

Sargent Johnson knelt by Adam's body and did a preliminary examination.

"He's alive. Let's hope the ambulance gets here quick. Nate, would you get the names and phone numbers of those people?"

Tom, Kris and Pamela stood and watched the ambulance arrive and tend to Adam Stokes. It didn't take them long to place the victim on a gurney and push it into the ambulance.

They returned to Unit 230. Tom and Kris sat on the couch, while Pamela plunked down on the easy chair and listened intently to Kris and Tom's discussion.

"What do you suppose happened to the poor man?" asked Kris.

"Looks like someone wrapped him over the head. Did you see all that blood soaked into his hair?" answered her dad. "Geez, he's only been here a few days. Monday of this week—that's the day he moved in."

"Dad, when I leaned over his body his shaving lotion intrigued me. I have smelled it before—very recently. Just now, I remembered. It was in my room—your spare bedroom."

"What are you inferring, daughter, that Adam Stokes was in your bedroom?"

"Dad, was the door locked when you were down on the beach this afternoon?"

"Well, yes and no. It was locked when I was down on the lounge. I probably didn't lock it when checking out the activity—the two Arabs being taken in by the police. But I was down there for only a short time."

"Was Adam Stokes down there at the same time?"

"Ah, not sure. Let's see, Richard and Corrith were there. Dale Strong...the Plums were there...at least Marv was. For once, Lucy Barrows wasn't laughing...she was there."

Pamela excused herself and headed for the bathroom. She closed the door and quickly went through the second door accessing the bedroom. Clicking on the closet light, she looked up at the shoeboxes. She paused, realizing they had been moved. Short of panicking, she grabbed the bottom box and opened it. The sinking feeling she experienced at that moment was immense. Throwing the box on the floor, she looked into the other two. *The gem was gone.*

———

"DAD, PAM HAS BEEN GONE FOR A LONG TIME. I wonder if she's okay."

"Why don't you check it out?"

Kris got off the couch and walked over to the bathroom door.

"Pam, are you okay?" asked Kris as she gently knocked.

Getting no answer, she opened it slightly and noticed that Pam wasn't in the bathroom. Moving through the other door, she entered her bedroom. Pamela was standing in the doorway of the closet holding a shoebox.

"What are you doing?" Kris asked loudly.

Tom heard his daughter's alarming voice. He got up off the chair, entered the bedroom and clicked on the light switch. "What's going on?" he asked.

Pamela had tears in her eyes and said, "I owe you an explanation. Could we sit down?"

34

"WELL, LET'S HEAR IT—what were you doing in the closet?" Tom asked Pamela.

"I had some expensive jewelry. After my aunt...what happened to her...I didn't trust her condo. The front door key was missing. Remember, Tom, when I stayed here one night?"

"Yeah, I remember, Pam."

"I stashed the jewelry in a shoe box in the closet. I went in there to fetch it, just now. It wasn't there. My jewelry is gone. I find it very embarrassing, to ask you Tom, if you know anything—about my jewelry, I mean?"

"Pam, I haven't even been in that closet since I moved here. Furthermore, I wish you had told me you were storing some of your things here."

Pamela's eyes were darting about the room and said with a nervous stutter, "I didn't want to bother you. I'm beat and gotta go."

Tom stood there, startled as Pamela left the bedroom, grabbed her purse from the table and headed for the door.

Walking out into the foyer, he said, "Wait, Pam, if your jewelry is gone, what do you think happened? Do you have personal insurance?"

"I don't know, Tom. I don't know."

"Does your missing jewelry change what you asked me to do on Monday, to accompany you to Jasper's?"

"Not sure, Tom. Goodnight."

Tom stood near the door and watched her leave. He went back to the living room and sat down.

"Kris, this is weird! Is Pam telling the truth? If she is, I've been burglarized."

"That gets us back to that crucial period of time when your front door wasn't locked," said a pacing Kris. "The smell of the cologne— and you're not sure if Adam Stokes was down on the beach. You better check your things and see if anything else is missing."

Tom rose from the couch and walked into his bedroom. He rummaged around for a couple of minutes and returned. "Nothing missing that I know of. My billfold is okay—car keys are here. Really, there's nothing else worth stealing."

He reached into his pocket and drew out the piece of paper he had picked up in the garage earlier.

"Dad, there's something whacko going on here. Maybe you should talk to the police," said Kris from the living room.

After glancing at the writing on the scrap of paper, Tom laid it on the dresser top and joined Kris in the living room. "What would I tell them? *I think some jewelry has been stolen but don't know if there was any...."*

"I don't think Pamela is leveling with you. Something is going on here...in this complex...in your condo. This isn't normal," said Kris.

"Well, I don't think talking to Police Chief McSorley is going to get me anywhere."

"How about the FBI? You did say they interviewed you, didn't you?"

"Yeah, but only because this condo unit overlooks the beach."

"Maybe it's also because you hang around her, Pamela, so much."

Tom turned and glared at his daughter.

———

AGENT SAM KLAPTIN WAS IN CHIEF MCSORLEY'S OFFICE on Saturday morning. He was standing and had both palms on the desk. The chief was sitting behind his desk, red-faced. He didn't like to be overruled. Sam used Federal authority to back his insistence that the two Saudis be released. McSorley was scrutinizing the paper that was lying on the desk. His eyes were peering through narrow reading glasses well down on his nose. He looked past Agent Klaptin and saw the other agent, Corey Downer, smirking while looking at the achievement plaques on the wall.

The chief got off the leather swivel chair, also put both his palms on the desk and looked straight at Sam. "Well, okay, but I'm off the hook. The complaint we got couldn't be ignored, in light of 911. Furthermore, you'll have to explain this to the manager over at Park Place."

"The Saudis have a car coming down from Tampa to pick them up. The car should be here within an hour. They both need to be released by then—with an apology. Is that clear?"

"As of right now...this moment, it's your problem," answered the chief sarcastically.

Agent Klaptin turned to his partner and said, "Come on, let's get out of here."

After the agents left, the police chief went out to his car where Officer Pete Glanner was waiting.

"How did it go, Chief?"

"We've been hooked by the Fed's—we're being forced into letting the Saudis go. You would think they would be more humble after screwing up so bad in New York."

"What do you make of the guy we found over at Park Place last night? He sure doesn't seem very cooperative."

"Yeah, Pete. What concerns me the most is that his ID just didn't fit in—anywhere. I checked Atlanta and no one has ever heard of Adam Stokes."

"Maybe the ID is a fake. How about getting some fingerprints?"

"Without reasonable cause, we could run into trouble doing that."

"Maybe we should have reported the incident to the FBI guys."

"Ah, the heck with 'em."

35

PAMELA COULDN'T SLEEP ON FRIDAY NIGHT. Thoughts of losing the gem wouldn't go away. She continued to search her mind on who may have sneaked into Tom's bedroom closet during the Saudis' incident on the beach. The Schweitzers were out there all that time. *How about Dale?* She couldn't remember seeing him around. *The new guy, Adam Stokes*—where was he? She looked straight ahead, mouth partially open—face frozen in a deep frown. *"Was it Adam Stokes?"* She asked out loud.

Why was he lying on the floor of the garage? *Someone hit him and knocked him down.* Did that have something to do with the gem? Ah, what the hell, she thought. Why don't I just get out of here, start my job in Sarasota and forget about all this? At least I'm alive and well. She dreaded calling Dale to call off the Monday meeting.

———

WHEN ADAM STOKES AWOKE, he was lying in a hospital bed. Other than a person in the next bed, there wasn't anyone else in the room. Sitting up, his head rocked with pain. By tilting his head down for brief periods of time, the pain lessened. His blurred vision managed to focus on two wood-grained, bi-fold doors—the closet, he assumed. Reaching up with his fingers, he could feel a lump on the back of his head, just above the right ear.

Then he remembered—the Guni. Someone had hit me over the head. Whoever did it took the stone. I didn't see anyone, he thought and didn't hear anything. Adam's head jerked left slightly when he heard a rustling noise. He looked into the curious eyes of his roommate.

The raspy voice coming from that awful-looking face said to him, "Welcome, friend."

Adam didn't say a word. He swung out of the bed and opened the drawer of the night table. Relieved that his billfold and keys were lying there, he scooped them up and headed for the bi-fold doors. Grabbing his clothes in the other hand, he approached the bathroom. Part way, he hesitated and braced himself on the wall with his arm. Adam recovered from the dizziness and staggered through the doorway into the bathroom.

No one even looked at him as he rapidly walked up the long corridor, his left hand covering the blood smear on his shirt. The stocky nurse coming down the corridor even smiled when their eyes met. Finding the exit, he took the stairs down to the lobby where he slipped into a booth and punched a series of numbers on a phone.

"Emil, get your butt up here and make it quick. I'm in the lobby of...Blake Medical Center. Wait, I'll be outside in the parking lot."

"Where is this joint?"

"Ah, shoot—oh, wait...here it is...2020 59th Street West. Get out here and be quick about it."

A security guard gave him a curious look as he went through the automatic door and out into the circular driveway. Just beyond the far corner of the parking area, he saw a bench—a bus stop. He hustled over and sat down, occasionally looking back toward the hospital entrance.

It seemed like forever before Emil showed up with the van, Adam thought.

"What the hell took you so long, Emil?"

"Got lost...never been here before...give me a break. What the heck are you doing here, anyhow?"

"Never mind, take me to Park Place. I need to get my car. It has my suitcases and other things."

Adam kept a hand shading his eyes all the way up Beach Street. He removed it as Emil guided the blue van into the parking area, pulling up into a visitor space.

"Aren't you going to your car, boss?" asked Emil.

Adam was watching two women who were standing and talking. "When those two broads get the heck out of here."

———

CORRITH SCHWEITZER AND LUCY BARROWS were having a conversation in the garage. Lucy's trunk was open and she was lifting out plastic bags of groceries, setting them down on the concrete floor.

"Corrith, I see Adam Stokes car is still here...right over there, that white one. Someone hit him over the head last night and left him lying there. I hear he's in the hospital."

"Here, let me help you with one of those," said Corrith. The two women walked toward the elevator.

"Ah, they're gone...at last. Stay here with the vàn, Emil, until I drive out and then follow me back to the motel."

Adam's head was throbbing. After starting his car, he backed out. The wheels of his car squealed as he turned onto Beach Street. Looking in the rear view mirror, he saw the blue van was right behind.

Arriving back at the motel, he told Emil, "I'm headed for my office room. See to it that I am not disturbed until you hear from me...got it?"

"Yeah, boss."

Vince desperately needed some down time, aspirin and sleep.

———

TULLY SMITH WAS MUNCHING ON A HAM SANDWICH that his wife, Barb, prepared that morning. She had worked the late shift yesterday, getting home shortly after midnight. Because Tully's culinary skills were lacking, she made both their lunches every work day.

"Key Marie Police Department," Tully said with his mouth half full of food.

"This is the Blake Medical Center Hospital. I'm Administrator Biglow. The patient you brought over on Friday night has disappeared—probably left on his own accord."

"What's the patient's name?" asked Tully.

"Adam Stokes. His address was listed as Park Place, Unit 112, 7660 Beach Street."

"Okay, thanks for calling. I'll let the chief know."

"Chief, I just got a call from the hospital. Adam Stokes has disappeared."

"What...when?"

"Don't know for sure. They just now became aware that he was gone. According to the caller, he was there, in bed, earlier in the morning."

"Thanks, Tully."

"Over and out."

"What's that all about, Chief?"

"Damn, Nate, that Stokes guy has disappeared. Remember, he's the one who was found unconscious in the garage over at Park Place last night. Apparently, he's left the hospital without officially being dismissed."

"Is there a law against that?" asked Nate.

"Well, not really. However, skipping on a bill is. Turn these wheels around and drive back to headquarters, Nate, as much as I hate to, I'm going to call the FBI. Wait! Head over to Park Place first. Let's check and see if his car is still there."

———

WHEN THE POLICE CAR DROVE into the Park Place parking lot, Haldor was outside, helping the maintenance crew plant some bushes. He looked up and watched as two officers got out. Haldor recognized Chief McSorley, who waved and beckoned for him to come over.

"Neilson, we need to check out Adam Stokes's car—also his condo unit. If you're wondering, we don't have a court order. We only want to peak in to see if he's there."

Haldor went into his office and came out with a ring of keys. He led the two officers along the row of vehicles in the garage.

"It's gone—the white car that Adam Stokes drove is gone. It should have been right there, in stall 12. Man alive, it was there the last time I walked by."

"How long ago was that?"

"About an hour ago."

"Damn-it, the Stokes guy came back to get his car—or one of his buddies—or whoever clobbered him. Now, can we peak into his condo unit?"

"Sure, follow me."

Haldor led the officers to Unit 112. It was located on the first floor of the north wing.

Before he used the key, Chief McSorley said, "Would you knock and check if he's there?"

Haldor knocked a couple of times—no answer.

"Okay, Haldor, would you unlock it?"

The key turned in the lock. Haldor turned the door handle and pulled the door open.

"We're not going in there without a court order, but would you step in and sort of check things out?"

Haldor entered and walked around the unit, including the bedroom. When he returned, he said, "All his stuff is gone. Sure left a mess in the kitchen."

"Nate, would you go down to the car and get the yellow tape. We're going to seal this sucker. Haldor, I don't want anyone in and out of here, understand? If that elusive Stokes comes back, give us a call."

———

WHEN CHIEF MCSORLEY ARRIVED BACK AT HIS OFFICE, he called Agent Sam Klaptin of the FBI and told him about the incident in the garage the night before, adding the news about the mysterious disappearance of the victim from the hospital.

"Thanks, McSorley. We'll get a court order to search the condo. Meanwhile, please seal it off and don't have anyone touch anything. You did the right thing by calling me."

After hanging up, the chief said, "Well, Nate, those FBI guys aren't so bad after all."

———

VINCE GULLOTI AWOKE FROM HIS SLEEP and was feeling much better than he did in the hospital. He got off the bed and headed outside. Using a key, he opened the door to their other room.

Emil was stretched out on an easy chair. The television was on with no sound. He was asleep.

Vince walked over to him and whacked him on the shoulder. "Wake up, Emil, we've got work to do. Help me get all my things out of the car. Then, I want you to follow me to the mall. I'm dumping this crate."

Vince parked the white sedan in a tight spot of the grocery store parking lot. Knowing that the grocery was opened twenty-four hours, he reasoned his car would go unnoticed, at least for a day or two.

After Vince got into the van, Emil asked, "Where we goin', boss?"

"Take a left, then another at the stoplight."

Minutes later, Vince said, "Now take a right and stay on Beach Street."

"Damn, this traffic is slow. There it is—see that sign, Park Place?"

"Yup, I do."

"I want you to drive by, turn around at the next block and park in that lot over there."

When the van came to a stop, Vince told Emil, "Tomorrow, bright and early, we're coming down here. They know me here. I have to stay out of sight. You're going to be my eyes."

"When this Hastings guy comes out with his daughter, we're going to follow them—understand?"

"Yeah, I get ya'."

36

PAMELA RUBBED THE SLEEP FROM HER EYES on Sunday morning. She was severely depressed. Her hopes and dreams of a financial future vanished when the gem disappeared. There is no way to get it back, she thought. But wait...there is a possibility...the Saudis. They might listen to me if I offered to help them...to find it...in exchange for reward money.

She lay in bed, wondering how to reach the Saudis. They might be in jail. Perhaps Dale could help. No, the police would be my best bet.

Barbara answered the phone at police headquarters and heard, "Hello, this is Marie Mundane. I'm a cousin of the two Saudi gentlemen that you are holding. Are they still there?"

"Why no, they've been released."

"It is imperative that I contact them...international reasons. Could you give me the address where they're staying?"

Barbara knew it was against the rules to give out that type of information. However, in this case the FBI forced the release of the Saudis. She had overheard the chief scolding the agents, *"Oh, the heck with 'em,"* he had said. Barb felt information about the Saudis was public. Compromising a vague set of rules, Barb said, "Ah, its Midway Motel in Key Marie, Unit 109.

———

RHOUL MASSIF LISTENED PATIENTLY to Pamela Zachary's story. His partner, Bern Tallin, was sitting on a stuffed chair watching the news on television. After Pamela stopped talking, she put her head down and placed her palms on her cheeks. She began to sob.

"Miss Pamela, you should have turned over the Guni to authorities, immediately, you know that?" responded Rhoul. "There could be some consolation if you told us all you know about the people that live at Park Place. We are especially interested in knowing which tenants were present when the police committed that...despicable act...against us."

Pamela spent the next few minutes in deep thought, periodically generating a name. Rhoul patiently sat at a desk, writing each name down on a sheet of paper.

"That's all I can remember. Perhaps later, there will be more."

"You have done well, Miss Zachary. I want you to report back to me...each day. Who's doing what...anything that looks suspicious...any conversations pertaining to the assault on Adam Stokes. If the FBI contacts you, tell them the whole truth. In exchange, if we get the Guni back, you would receive one-quarter of a million dollars as a reward."

After leaving, Pamela had dreadful thoughts about returning to Park Place. Yet she didn't have any choice. She was now working for the Saudis.

———

KRIS HASTINGS AND HER DAD WENT TO CHURCH on Sunday morning. The quaint wooden structure was located near the southern end of the island. The parking lot surface was gravel, perhaps demonstrating an example of parish priorities.

The priest smiled during the entire ten minutes of the sermon. His message was simple and clear. "Feed those that are hungry and you will be rewarded."

Tom became nostalgic, sitting next to Kris, remembering when they went to church as a family. His wife was an avid churchgoer. She dressed both Brad and Kris in their best clothes. They never missed a Sunday.

String music radiating from the violins of two teenagers filled the air. "Beautiful, absolutely beautiful," whispered Kris.

"Worth a ten spot," responded her dad, while searching his billfold.

The bill dropped quietly into the basket and Tom smiled. He remembered their priest many years ago saying, "I want a quiet collection today."

The organ player was sitting up perfectly straight and working her hands across the keyboard, generating a spirited ending to the service.

After leaving church, they drove across a bridge heading south on the Keys Highway. Several blocks of shops, including many clothing stores, dominated that part of the island. Tom was driving and found a spot around a corner where there were no storefronts.

"I saw a restaurant back there, just around the corner. Are you hungry, Kris? How about some breakfast?"

"Sounds like a winner, Dad. I'm starved."

They didn't notice the light blue van that circled a couple of times after they entered the restaurant.

After eating breakfast, they began walking the sidewalks. Kris was window-shopping. She needed some clothes.

"Dad, look at that dress. That place looks worth checking out."

"Why don't you go in and look around. I'll be out here on that bench." Tom pointed.

He had some brochures along and spent time looking through them while Kris was in the store. Approximately half-an-hour went by. Kris had not emerged. Man, she must be trying on a bunch of 'em, he thought. Tom sat there and people-watched for about another half-an-hour. Better check this out, he said to himself.

Tom entered the dress shop and didn't see anyone. Moving farther up the aisle between displays, he saw a tall woman clerk.

"Can I help you?" she asked.

"Yeah, my daughter is in here. She must be in the dressing room."

"There is no one in here."

"But she came in here close to an hour ago. I saw her go in. She has to be here."

"Sorry sir, there is no one. Come back here and see for yourself."

The tall woman talked with an exaggerated German accent. She's mistaken, Tom thought. He walked back with the woman and she opened the doors to both dressing rooms.

"See for yourself, sir, there's no one in there."

"Sorry to bother you, but she must have gone to another shop. Was there anyone in here—a woman, fairly tall, light hair, sunglasses, slim?" he asked.

"No, not today."

He walked back outside and looked up and down the sidewalk. Kris wasn't anywhere, so he returned to the bench and decided to wait it out. More time passed—his concern was growing bigger by the minute.

Walking into the shop next door, he asked the clerk if she would call the police.

"What for? What's happened?"

"This may sound silly, but my daughter has disappeared."

The clerk did not hesitate. She called 911 and handed the phone to Tom.

"Key Marie Police Department," the voice said.

"Hello, I'm Tom Hastings, staying at Park Place in Key Marie. My daughter has disappeared. I'm at...Nora's Specialties."

"Now, where exactly is that?"

"It's on Harrington Street, where all the shops are, in the southern part of Key Marie, ah...1500 is the number on the door."

"Okay, I'll send a squad car down there. Should be there in a few minutes."

Tom hung up the phone and said to the clerk, "Thanks a lot for the use of your phone."

"No problem...hope you find your daughter."

Tom walked back out onto the sidewalk. He glanced at the show window of Terry's, the clothing store that Kris had gone into. He looked at the dress that attracted his daughter—no mistake. That was the store she entered. The sign on the door read *Closed*. Huh? There's something strange going on here. He paced nervously up and down the sidewalk, awaiting a police car.

———

NATE BLOOMBERG WAS CRUISING SLOWLY down Keys Highway when he got the call. He flicked the siren switch and made a U-turn over to the south lane, tires screeching. He kept the siren and the flashing lights on until he got within a block of Terry's. Shutting them off, he pulled into a no-parking approach.

Getting out of the car, he recognized the man standing in front of Terry's. Nate wasn't sure of the man's name, but the face was familiar. He'd seen him at Park Place. Nate raised his right hand and felt the tender area below the left armpit—he remembered Park Place.

"What's your problem, sir?"

"Officer, over an hour ago, close to 2:00 p.m., my daughter, Kris, went in there to shop. She didn't come out. I went in to investigate and the woman told me no one came in. Damn, I saw her go in—she did go in there."

"What's your name, sir?"

"Tom Hastings. Don't you remember me from Park Place condos?"

Nate nodded and walked over to the door. He knocked, lightly at first, then heavier and heavier.

"No one's answering, Mr. Hastings. Let me call for help. We'll get in there and check it out."

———

TOM WAS GETTING FRANTIC—minutes were rolling by. Kris could be miles away from here by now. *Hurry, officer, hurry!*

In minutes another squad car came up the street. Sargent Cliff Johnson flicked down the window and pulled up, double-parking at the curb. "What's up, Nate?"

"This man claims his daughter went in there. She never came out."

"I'll drive around back," Tom heard the Sargent say. "Would you call headquarters and find out who owns this joint. We need to get in there and right now," the Sargent told Nate.

"Okay, will do."

Nate's phone rang within three to four minutes. "Yeah

...yeah...okay."

After pressing the off button, Officer Nate Bloomberg turned to Tom and said, "The owner doesn't answer. A locksmith is on the way. Let's head around back— that's where the locksmith is going to meet us. You can get in the car with me."

Tom got in the squad car and Nate drove around the block and up an alley, parking behind the other squad car. Minutes later, a yellow van arrived. The sign on the door read, *Bob's Locks*. The short, curly-hair locksmith had the back door open within minutes. "Need anything else?" he asked.

"No, thanks," replied Sargent Johnson.

"Okay, sign right here."

The two officers, followed by Tom, entered a small foyer.

"Listen, I hear something," said Nate.

Nate hastily opened a door that led to a narrow corridor. Following the noise, he entered a second door and snapped on the light. On the floor lay a woman. She was bound and gagged.

The officer rushed to her side and removed the gag. The woman took several deep breaths—her face was reddened and wet with perspiration.

"Oh, thank heavens, I was afraid they would come back."

"They?" asked the Sargent.

"Yes, two men and a woman. They were awful. Could I have a drink?"

"Did you hear the woman talk?" Tom anxiously asked the woman.

"Why no, come to think of it, she had something over her face."

Tom was totally frustrated. He couldn't believe what had happened. His daughter may have been kidnapped. *Why?* She came to see her dad for an innocent visit and they went to church—went shopping. He got a sunken feeling visualizing a gag over her mouth. She did nothing to deserve what's happened. *Is it because of me?*

37

CHIEF MCSORLEY EXPLAINED TO TOM, "Kidnapping is a federal offense. Why don't you go home and the FBI agents will get in touch with you? It should be soon."

The chief was glad this case was going to be out of his hands. He was embarrassed by the Saudi incident—he had had enough of Park Place and all the people that lived there.

———

TOM HAD A TERRIBLE SUNDAY EVENING, pacing around and not being able to sleep. Walking out onto the deck, he noticed the drapes weren't pulled in a window directly across the courtyard. The room was lit up and Tom could see straight in. Two people in robes were apparently arguing. Returning inside, he grabbed his binoculars.

He recognized the shape of the man—very large chest with huge arms. Marv, that's what his name was. The woman with the shrill voice—what's her name? Ann...yes, that's it—Marv and Ann. They've done this before.

As the couple continued to wrangle away at each other, their voices got louder and their shouts were beginning to radiate across the courtyard. Not my problem, Tom thought—even if they kill each other. I've got plenty of other things to think about. My daughter's life is at stake. Tom was glad his former wife wasn't here to experience the trauma. She would have had a very difficult time—much more than I am having, he thought.

THE PHONE RANG. Tom answered anxiously. It was Sam Klaptin from the FBI.

"We're on our way to your condo, Mr. Hastings. We should be there in five minutes. Would you meet us down in the parking lot? I don't remember exactly how to get to your unit."

Tom was relieved to hear that the FBI had been informed and they were going to be involved. A few minutes later, he met agents Sam Klaptin and Corey Downer down in the visitor's parking area.

The three men walked the stairs to Tom's condo. After inviting the agents to sit on the couch, Tom told the agents the story of how his daughter had disappeared.

Agent Klaptin stood up and walked to the sliding glass doors. After looking out for a moment, he turned. "Mr. Hastings, I feel for you, but your daughter has not officially been kidnapped. Until we hear from her or the alleged kidnappers, we cannot do much. However, we will install a wiretap and monitor all phone conversations in your condo, with your permission of course. A technician from Tampa is on his way.

"Meanwhile, I want to hear more about Adam Stokes. We have a story on file that you, your daughter and Pamela Zachary discovered his unconscious body Friday night in the parking lot."

"Yes, that's true. He was out cold. His hair was soaked with blood."

Agent Klaptin continued, "For your information, Adam Stokes left the hospital earlier this morning—he was not officially dismissed and his whereabouts are currently unknown. Furthermore, his real name is not Adam Stokes. We checked his credentials and they were all phony. We strongly suspect that he was living at Park Place for one reason, and one reason only."

"What was that?" asked Tom.

"To recover the Guni."

"What the heck is the Guni?" asked Tom.

"It's a rare, almost priceless gem mined in Kashmir several years ago. It was stolen from an Arab prince in New York about a month ago. It left a trail to Indianapolis, to the Smoky Mountains and eventually all the way to Key Marie."

"What do you mean by priceless?"

"It's probably worth close to fifty million dollars in the regular market," the agent responded.

"Whew! You've got to be kidding," exclaimed Tom.

"Not at all, Mr. Hastings. Some pieces of the puzzle are coming together. Pamela Zachary got possession of the Guni by mischance in Indianapolis. Ben Pierce, also know as Serin, in a desperate move to evade authorities at the airport, deposited the Guni in her carry-on bag.

"After failing to get it back in the parking lot, he followed her to Key Marie and killed her aunt, Melissa Buntrock, mistakenly thinking she was Pamela. After searching her aunt's condo, he failed to find the Guni. The reason was because Pamela hid it in your condo."

The room became silent. Tom stared at the agent. "What? My condo!" His mind felt as if metal balls were rebounding off the inside of his cranial walls. "Oh, so that's why she was playing the bathroom game."

"What game was that?" asked agent Klaptin.

"The bathroom has a second door...it accesses the bedroom...the closet. I was wondering why she contacted me so often. When she came over to my condo, she always used the bathroom."

"It all fits," responded the agent. "We think it was Adam Stokes who called the police to report the two terrorists on the beach. It was a phony diversion, of course. The Saudis are anxiously working with us to get the Guni back. Your door was open during the Saudis arrests, is that correct?"

"Yes, just for a few minutes."

"Well, that's apparently all it took. Stokes entered and found the Guni. Since all his belongings were missing from his rental unit, we assume his intention was to sceedaddle. He may have been putting his stuff in his car when someone bopped him on the head. Whoever it was took the Guni."

"I remember Adam Stokes at a poolside cocktail party. He asked Pamela a lot of questions," responded Tom.

"It all makes sense, he was after the rock. Somehow he got lucky when searching your condo. By tomorrow, we should know who this Adam Stokes guy is—that is, if he has a record. There were all kinds of prints in the car. Strangely enough, we found the Stokes car abandoned in the mall parking lot, near here," added agent Klaptin and nodded at his partner.

"Mr. Hastings, I have to ask you a tough question," said agent Corey Downer.

"Sure, shoot."

"Are you the one who knocked Adam down and took the Guni? Now, look me right in the eye. This is very, very important."

Tom was stunned, turning away for a moment. His head became erect and his eyes looked straight into the agent's, "No, Mr. Downer, I did not hit Adam Stokes. I do not have the...Guni."

"We believe you, but listen to this—whoever kidnapped your daughter thinks that you have it, the Guni."

"Geez, but I don't. What am I going to do?"

"Sit tight—wait for a call. It will come."

Agent Klaptin's cell phone rang. "Oh, shoot! Not until tomorrow, huh? Okay. We'll meet you at police headquarters in the morning at 7:00." After the agent snapped his phone shut, he said, "Mr. Hastings. That was the technician I was telling you about. He can't get here until early tomorrow morning." Sam handed Tom his card. "My number is on the card. Call me if you hear anything."

Tom accepted the card. He stared at it for a few moments as the agents left. After laying it down by the phone, he sat down on the couch worried that the head FBI agent wasn't taking his daughter's kidnapping serious enough.

Klaptin would say something and look off in the distance as if his mind was on something else. Not much I can do about that, Tom thought. I'm sure glad that the other agent, Corey Downer, is along. That one appears to be more interested.

———

KRIS HASTINGS HAD BEEN TAKEN OUT THE BACKDOOR of Terry's at gunpoint. A masked assailant forced her to walk to a van. Her head tilted sharply as the side of her skull hit the van's rear doorframe while being pushed onto the back seat.

Her assailant, who sat down beside her, took off the uncomfortable gag and said roughly, "One yap out of you and you're a dead lady." He tied her hands behind her back and placed a bandana over her eyes.

Kris had been trained in some of the martial arts. She hadn't ever had the occasion to utilize her training. By being patient, she figured, she might get lucky and have an opportunity to escape. For right now, she would go along with their requests, just as long as they didn't touch her body. First, she had to learn the reason why she was being kidnapped.

Kris estimated they were in the car for less than an hour when it came to a stop.

"Come on, lady, you're getting out here," she was told as a set of strong fingers grabbed her arm.

She was led up a sidewalk and through a doorway and pushed onto a bed. She could feel and smell the hemp as it was being used to tie her ankles.

The other voice said, "If you'll behave, nothing will happen. Any attempt to escape will mean sure death. Do you understand?"

Kris heard the door slam—one of them must have left. That's good, she thought—*what should I do if I need to go to the bathroom?*

The room got real quiet, but she could hear the rustle of a newspaper and an occasional clearing of a throat.

————

TOM MIXED A SCOTCH AND WATER and sat on the couch after the FBI agents left. Thus far, my winter vacation has been a disaster, he thought. First, Julie canceled her visit because of a family emergency in Colorado, then the Pamela games and the Guni. The cause of it all is greed...for money. Now Kris is missing.

Guilt feelings overcame him. He should have refused to assist Pamela after arriving at Park Place. Even though helping her at the accident in Tennessee was the proper thing to do, he realized it was because of his dealings with her that Kris was kidnapped. He felt alone and miserable.

The only solace he had came from the FBI Agent Downing. His interest in Kris's disappearance appeared genuine. Tom was glad that Police Chief McSorley was not involved any longer. He didn't like that man.

The phone call came shortly after 10:00 p.m. The man talking sounded like he had crackers in his mouth.

"I have your daughter. If you want to see her again, alive, listen carefully."

"Who is this?" Tom frantically questioned. "Why are you doing this?"

"The Guni—it's the stone for your daughter."

"I don't have the...Guni, or whatever it's called...never did."

"Yeah, tell me another one. Ha, if you don't, then come up with five million—take your choice."

"Someone else has it—not me," Tom pleaded.

"I'm not going to play games. Be home tomorrow at noon and you'll hear from me then."

Tom heard the click on the other end. *Oh, how did I ever get into this mess—my poor Kris?* How could this be happening?

He filled the glass with scotch a second time, knowing that sleep was going to be impossible otherwise. After a failed attempt at sleeping, he got up and slipped out a sheet of computer paper from the printer. He wrote:

Serin stashes the Guni in Pam's bag at the airport.
Serin kills Pam's aunt by mistake, but fails to find the Guni.
Pam hides the Guni in my closet.
Serin shoots the police officer after failing to find the Guni.
Adam Stokes finds the Guni in my closet.
Someone hits Adam over the head and takes the Guni.
Adam Stokes thinks that I have it.
Adam and at least one other person kidnapped Kris.

Tom sipped the scotch and studied his notations. He assumed that Adam Stokes was the kidnapper. The missing piece of the puzzle was—who had the Guni? If he called the FBI right now about the phone call, they were going to be all over this place. There is no way he could come up with five million dollars and he didn't have the

Guni. W*hat to do*? He asked himself while frustrated to the hilt.

I think Kris is safe as long as Stokes thinks I have the gem or can come up with the money. The FBI may not agree with my thinking. I'll probably lay awake all night.

38

SLEEP FOR TOM HASTINGS FINALLY CAME at close to 4:00 a.m. He tossed possibilities from one side of his mind to the other for hours. The sleep was deep when a knock on the door awakened him at close to 9:00 a.m.

Groggily, he put on his robe and made his way to the door.

"Who is it?" he asked.

"It's Haldor, the manager."

Tom opened the door and said, "Come on in, Haldor, you've probably heard what's been going on."

"Man alive, is there anything I can do to help?"

"Yes, there is, Haldor. Have a seat. I'll get dressed. A short time later Haldor led Tom to the condo that Adams Stokes had rented.

"Mr. Stokes is still officially renting it, but it's empty."

"Have you cleaned it yet?"

"No, we haven't. The FBI people have just been here and they took the tape down."

"You asked if you could help. I would like to have a look around," said Tom.

"Sure, go ahead. There's nothing in there. All the Stokes stuff is gone. They even took the phone and answering machine."

Entering, Tom's heart began racing—he was invading the kidnapper's lair. Cautiously moving from room to room, he peered in all the wastebaskets. All were totally empty except the one in the kitchen. It had extra white, tall kitchen plastic bags folded across the bottom and a bit of trash that had spilled over the edge of the original bag.

Looking up, he saw that Haldor was looking out the window. Tom picked up the trash items and began dropping them back in, one at a time. His hope was to find some sort of clue as to where Adam Stokes had gone—that's where Kris would be. There wasn't anything.

"Thanks a lot, Haldor. Sure is cleaned out, isn't it?"

"Yup, sure is."

Tom returned to his condo after thanking Haldor for his concern. He entered his bedroom and noticed the piece of paper on the dresser top. Picking it up, he read the words, *234 Cypress Lane*. Tom remembered Adam Stokes's pocket—it was turned inside out. Could this note have come from there? *Am I tampering with evidence?*

Searching the city of Key Marie on the Internet, he typed in a destination address of 234 Cyprus Lane. The location was about six miles south on Keys Highway.

Tom reached and picked up Agent Klaptin's card—he saw the cell phone number. Common sense told him that he should call the agent. The address on that slip of paper might not mean anything. It could have come from anyone parking in the garage. Agent Klaptin didn't seem too enthused, anyhow. A false lead might make it worse.

Half-an-hour later, Tom turned off Keys Highway and onto Cyprus Lane. The traffic was slow but he had seen it worse. The lane was short, about two blocks long. There was a motel on one side and a line of residences on the other. Driving to the loading zone and pausing, he verified the address, a number over the double door reading 234. Driving on, he parked across the lot so he could face the motel.

The two-level motel had a railed walkway going around the entire perimeter, except for beachside. The other side of the motel was accessed by a short lane, next to the highway. Since he had been watching, only one vehicle had used that route.

Tom drove around to the other side and continued along the entire length of the building. Turning around, he drove back to the Cyprus Lane side, again parking to afford a good view.

Reaching into the back seat he put on a wide brimmed straw hat. After adjusting it, he attached sun shields to his glasses. He guessed it was a long shot that Adam Stokes would eventually emerge. If

Stokes was the kidnapper, he might leave the motel to make the call at noon. Tom reasoned that Adam Stokes *had to go out for something to eat before calling.*

The minutes crawled by and Tom's guilty feeling grew. The agent's card was in his shirt pocket, just in case. The FBI phone technician is coming this morning, he thought. The agents and technician are probably already at my condo.

Another ten minutes went by and Tom was getting drowsy. His chin jolted upward when he saw Adam Stokes emerge on the walkway on the second level. Tom's heart jumped into his throat. His eyes locked on Adam coming down the steps.

His hunch had been right—the paper had come from Adam's pocket. What unit did he come from? He asked himself. Damn, I missed it. Tom did calculate that it was a few doors past the office, toward the highway. He watched as Adam Stokes got into a rusty blue van and drove onto Key Highway, heading south.

Tom's cell phone fell out of his hand while he was attempting to punch in Klaptin's number. A second attempt to reach the agent resulted in total frustration—Tom's phone had malfunctioned.

Throwing the cell phone on the passenger seat, Tom started his car. He moved it into a position where he had a better view of the section of the motel that Adam had emerged from. He waited as his frustration grew. Finally, the blue van returned. Checking his watch, the van had been gone for forty-five minutes. Tom watched as Adam got out and carried two bags up the steps. *Food for my daughter,* he thought. Thanks, sleaze-bag.

Watching—waiting, Tom saw Adam stop, set the bags down and place a key into the door of room number 237.

Fighting for restraint, Tom gripped the steering wheel with his hands and parked his forehead on his knuckles. He wanted to break into that room and take on whoever was there.

Tom thought about finding a phone in the lobby and calling the police. Surely, Kris's kidnappers have guns. I need time to think. Tom drove frantically, needing to get home as soon as possible to call someone...the police...the FBI. His frustration was exaggerated by the slow moving traffic.

––––

ARRIVING BACK AT PARK PLACE, Tom parked and ran up the stairs. He found the manager, Haldor, standing in front of the doorway.

"I had to let them in, Tom. You didn't answer the phone and they were insistent."

Tom hurried into his condo.

"Good morning, Mr. Hastings," said Sam Klaptin. "I want you to meet Perry Smith. He's going to help us with communications. You remember Corey Downer."

Tom nodded and exclaimed, "I found them...Adam Stokes! He's holding my daughter at a motel south of here...Cyprus Gardens it's called."

"How the devil did you figure that out?" asked Sam.

"I found a piece of paper in the garage near Adam's car...before he got taken away by the ambulance...thought nothing of it at first. I saved it and looked at it later. There was this address. I had to check it out."

"Did you see your daughter?"

"No, I didn't, but where else could she be?"

"Mr. Hastings. We don't know for sure that Adam Stokes is the kidnapper."

"Well, why the hell don't we check it out? Let's get going," responded Tom, frustrated.

––––

SAM KLAPTIN DIDN'T FEEL WELL. His pending divorce and the discomfort of being away from his home was weighing on him. Tom's announcement about the paper didn't impress him...it was a fluke, he thought.

"Now, calm down, Mr. Hastings. Let's sit and work this through. I have other information. Adam Stokes's real name is Vince Gulloti. He's spent time in a federal prison, early in the nineties, but is presently supposed to be living in Atlanta, Georgia.

"We suspect he masterminded the Guni heist in New York. It went wrong for him in Indianapolis when one of his henchmen was picked up and the other was forced to place the rock in Pamela Zachary's carry-on bag."

Tom was still deep in thought about his discovery at Cyprus Lane. Was he certain Kris was in room 237? He looked at his watch. It was close to 11:30 a.m. Adam said he would call at noon.

The phone rang. Tom dashed to get it. Perry Smith pressed a button on his equipment and lifted a receiver. He nodded to Tom.

"Hello."

The cracker-crunching sounding voice spoke. "Mr. Hastings, I'll give you until tomorrow to deliver the Guni or come up with the money. You will drive to Sarasota and park in any of the lots that are used for the art fair. Give me your cell phone number and I'll call you there at noon tomorrow. Cell phone number, please."

"It's 218-837-4923. What if the phone doesn't work?" asked Tom frantically.

"Charge it overnight and it will."

Tom heard a click.

Perry Smith pressed another button and said, "Should have the trace in two to three minutes, Sam."

"Mr. Hastings, can I see the slip of paper with the address?"

"Sure," replied Tom and turned it over.

"How long ago was it since you saw Stokes at the motel?"

"Not much more than an hour ago. The darn traffic really held me up and my cell phone wasn't working."

"The vehicle that Stokes was driving—what was it?"

"A partially rusted light blue van."

"Corey, call Tampa and get the swat team down here right away. Where is this place, Hastings?"

"Six miles south on Cyprus Lane, just off Keys Highway. It's a room on the second floor of a motel, number 237, I'm quite sure."

"What's the name of the motel?"

"Ah, don't really know. It's the only motel on Cyprus Lane."

Tom sat down on the couch. Sam came over and sat down beside him.

"We could hit the place with just the three of us. Maybe that would be better. Yet, if something went wrong, it could be fatal for your daughter—we don't want that. My experience tells me we best wait for the swat team," said Sam.

Tom's mouth fell. He got up off the couch. "Wait? Isn't there a faster way? Every minute that my daughter is in that creep's hands is critical."

"I understand your feelings, Hastings, but the swat team is on its way and we'll all be moving over there shortly. It's better to be prepared than going off half-cocked. A short period of time isn't going to make much difference in this case. The kidnappers are still in the negotiating stage."

"How about setting up roadblocks?" asked Tom frantically.

"Well, we don't know for certain that your daughter is at that motel. I'll take your word for it that Adam Stokes is there. Soon as the swat team gets on the island, we'll meet them at the motel."

Klaptin addressed his fellow agent, Corey. "Would you stay in touch with the swat team? I want to time their arrival to our drive to Cyprus Gardens."

Klaptin asked Perry, "Anything on the phone call yet?"

"Yes, just now. The call came from a pay phone at the strip mall not far from the address you gave me—six miles south of here."

Tom sat back down on the couch and put his head between his hands, feeling helpless.

39

KRIS NEEDED A BATHROOM—she waved her rope-bound wrists at her guard.

"What is it, lady?" Emil asked.

"She pointed her chin to the lower part of her body.

"Bathroom. You need the bathroom?"

Kris nodded her head.

"Okay, but don't try anything funny. You could get hurt real bad...like dead."

Emil untied Kris's legs and helped her off the bed. He left the gag in place and guided her to the door. Kris motioned toward her hands.

"Okay, I'll untie them, but I'll be sitting right over there with a gun and I love to use it."

Kris entered the bathroom. After rubbing her wrists and ankles for a few minutes, she did some stretches.

She walked out of the bathroom and stopped, glaring at her captor.

Emil laid the gun on the table, came over to Kris and said, "You lay back down, lady."

Deep resentment and anger infiltrated Kris's mind. She felt her heart rate increase, her stomach knot. A tremendous flow of energy took over her body—karate, right now. Placing both her palms together, she struck Emil on the side of the head, knocking him to the floor. Gasping for air, she pulled the gag away from her face. Before Emil had a chance to get back on his feet, Kris leaped over to the table and grabbed the gun.

She held it in both hands and pointed it at Emil, her hands shaking.

"Its not loaded, lady. Besides you couldn't hit anything, anyhow."

"Oh yeah, just try me you bastard," responded Kris as she steadied the weapon and straightened her elbows, her finger tightening on the trigger.

Emil's forehead became a sea of perspiration beads. Kris took a step away from the door with both arms out front, holding the gun. She didn't notice Vince sneak in behind her. He wrapped both arms around her waist and forced the gun downward. As they continued to struggle, their bodies rotated. Kris's finger pulled the trigger—the ensuing explosion in the room shattered the window. Emil leaped forward and wrestled the gun from her hand.

Vince pushed her onto the bed, "Stay put you broad, unless you really want to get it. Right now!"

They retied her wrists and ankles.

"We better get out of here, Emil. There's glass all over the walkway. A hundred people probably heard the shot. Say, what's the deal, anyhow, you imbecile, how did she ever get the drop on you? Were you asleep? Huh?"

"Oh, never mind. Let's get the hell out of here."

Emil dashed into the bathroom, throwing his stuff into a bag. Vince didn't have anything in the motel. His office was empty and everything retrieved from his rental at Park Place was in the van.

Forming a controlled procession, the two men escorted Kris down the steps and shoved her into the back of the van.

"Aren't you going to check out?" Emil asked.

"Hell no. Are your brains totally missing?"

Vince drove the van out onto Keys Highway and headed for Sarasota. Keeping her cool, Kris worked an earring free and allowed it to drop on the seat next to her. The beginning of a trail, she desperately hoped.

———

TULLY SMITH TOOK THE CALL from the motel manager at Cyprus Gardens, "There's been a gun fired...up there...a broken window. Can you send someone down to check it out? Please hurry."

"I'll send two officers right out," Tully answered.

The motel manager attempted to calm a group of people in the lobby, who had heard the gunshot. One of the women said, "We're not going back to our room until the police arrive. I'm scared!"

Four minutes later a squad car driven by Officer Lam Anderson pulled into Cyprus Lane.

"There's the office over there," said Officer Nate Bloomberg from the passenger seat, pointing.

The squad car pulled into the canopied loading zone and stopped.

"Check it out, Nate. I'll stay here."

Nate Bloomberg opened the door leading to the lobby. The manager left an anxious group of tenants and strode to meet the officer.

"Oh, Jeez, am I ever glad to see you. I'm afraid something has happened up there, real bad. Everybody is scared to death to go anywhere, including me. There's been a shot and at least a broken window."

"Do you know which room number it is?"

"Not for sure, but it's about 235. The broken window should give you a clue. Here, take this key. It'll open any of the rooms up there."

Nate went back outside and waved to Lam, who bumped into a maintenance cart while trotting over. The two officers removed their guns from their holsters and cautiously made their way up the stairway.

Stopping at 237 where there were glass pieces and splinters scattered all over the walkway, Lam said, "This has got to be it."

Lam peered into the room through the broken window. Nate knocked on the door and yelled, "Anyone home?"

Waiting a few moments and after no one answered, he checked the door. It wasn't locked.

Nate and Lam readied their guns. Nate turned the knob and kicked the door open. He ducked while entering the room. Lam was close behind.

"Wow, smell that gun powder," said Nate.

———

AGENT COREY DOWNER HAD CALLED THE KEY MARIE POLICE DEPARTMENT to announce they were going to launch an assault on Room 237 at the motel on Cyprus Lane.

"Ah, sir, I just sent out a couple of officers to that area. Yes, it was Cyprus Gardens on Cyprus Lane."

"You did! For what?"

"The manager called. He reported a gunshot and broken glass."

"Just a second...hold on."

"Sam, we may be too late. There's been a gunshot reported over at Cyprus Lane. A couple of the local police officers have gone there to check it out."

"Here...give me that phone. Get me in touch with the officers right now," Sam told the dispatcher.

"Okay, I'll try." A few seconds later Tully came back on the line. "I can't reach them. They don't answer."

"Now listen and listen carefully—keep trying to reach the officers. If you succeed, tell them to hold. The FBI is on its way to the motel."

Klaptin hung up and exclaimed, "What's the latest on the swat team, Corey?"

"Ah...they just crossed the bridge. They should be on Keys

Highway in a couple of minutes."

"Good. Let's get going. We'll meet them over there."

Corey Downer got behind the wheel and Sam slipped into the passenger seat. Agent Perry and Tom Hastings got in the backseat. They turned onto Beach Street.

Even though they had the siren blasting and the overhead lights flashing, the going was slow. "Gads man, this is going to take forever," said a frustrated Corey as he sneaked through a stoplight intersection.

"Not much you can do about this traffic, Corey. No way we can get around some of it."

Tom squirmed in the back seat for what seemed to him forever. At last he heard Agent Klaptin say, "Okay. Cyprus Lane should be next, Corey."

All eyes in the gray sedan were looking for the camouflage. "Look, Sam. There's the squad car. It's parked in the loading zone."

"Anybody in it?" asked Sam.

"No. It's empty."

"Hey, the swat van just got here," announced Perry from the back seat.

The square cornered vehicle drove into the parking lot and stopped across from the office canopy. Perry exited the back seat, stood and waved at the odd looking vehicle. One of the occupants, dressed in military fatigues, got out and approached the gray sedan.

"Hey, Dave," said Agent Klaptin from behind the rolled down window.

"Good afternoon, sir. What's the deal?"

"We're here to abort a kidnapping, but I've got the gut feeling that the principals are gone. See that police car over there. Our target is in room 237. The officers could already be in there. Get the team out and check out the situation. Don't go in too casual. Be prepared to do battle."

"All right, sir." The leader of the swat team returned to his vehicle. He commanded the remaining occupants out into the parking lot. They were all armed with automatic weapons. Dave ordered two of them to the west-end stairway and two to the east-end stairway. He and the remaining team member went up the steps next to the office.

Corey and Tom had gotten out of the car. They watched as the swat team ignored the broken glass and burst through the door of room 237.

Someone yelled, "FBI. Freeze!"

Nate Bloomberg was on his hands and knees searching under the bed. The other officer was sitting in a chair examining pieces of rope.

"We're police officers!" exclaimed Officer Lam Anderson.

The two swat team members who had entered the room put down their weapons. "Sorry! We're just following orders. We couldn't take any chances. The kidnappers could have been in here as far as we knew."

Agents Sam and Corey entered the room. "What's happened here?" Sam asked Nate.

"Don't know. We just got here. There's been a shot. Doesn't seem to be any blood. There are some loose pieces of rope lying around."

"This room may be involved in a kidnapping...a federal case. I'm Agent Klaptin with the FBI and we're going to take over the room," said Sam.

"No Problem, " said Nate as he dropped the pieces of rope on the bed.

Tom Hastings peeked through the door. His facial expression showed deep fear and anxiety.

"Mr. Hastings, I'm sorry, but your daughter is not here. This unit has been vacated. We are sealing the room and if your daughter was here, we should know shortly. Good news though, there are no signs of blood."

Sam called headquarters in Tampa. He asked his office to notify law enforcement in central Florida to be on the lookout for a slightly rusted blue van, make and model unknown. He used Sarasota as the center of the focus. Rather than a roadblock, he requested that the two bridges connecting the keys to the mainland be placed under surveillance.

———

NO BLOOD—how can I feel good about that? Tom asked himself.

Does that mean there's going to be blood later? I have to keep my act together—falling apart won't solve anything.

40

KRIS'S EARS WERE STILL RINGING. She was lying on the floor of the van and was grossly uncomfortable. Every bump on the road reverberated through her hips and shoulders. Her head began to throb. She could see the backs of the heads of her abductors. When Emil leaned left to glance in the back, she saw his ugly sneering-face. *If only I had pulled the trigger when I had the chance.*

After an agonizing, bumpy hour for Kris, the van came to a stop. Kris felt relief—her mind and body collapsed into a troubled sleep. Emil remained in the van while Vince negotiated with a motel clerk for a room. His fake ID worked and the clerk didn't bother to check the license number of the vehicle.

He got back in the van and drove it around the building to the other side.

"Let's get her in there, Emil. Then I need to park this thing somewhere else. The cops are going to be looking for it."

"Okay, boss. Why don't you open the door and I'll bring her in."

Kris had fallen asleep when the van stopped. She had experienced a bad dream. *Looking for her car in a parking lot, it was nowhere in sight. The parking lot was getting bigger and bigger—huge vines were growing through the cracks in the pavement.* Pain flashed through her body as Emil slid her out of the van—reality returned.

"Look, baby, it'll be a lot easier for you if you cooperate and walk." Grabbing the rope that bound her wrists, he pulled her across the sidewalk and into the room. Kris was quite certain that her life was over, but when she felt the comfort of a mattress, she collapsed into a deep sleep.

———

OFFICER'S NATE BLOOMBERG AND LAM ANDERSON discussed strategy with the FBI agents and Tom Hastings. Sam said, "Until Tom gets another call, finding the van is our priority. We appreciate any help from you guys. We'll take over for now. Just go about your business."

Klaptin ordered Dave, the swat team leader, to call headquarters in Tampa and find a place to stay nearby. "We better get you and Perry back to your condo. There's likely going to be a phone call," he said to Tom.

"Corey, I want you to stay here until the technicians arrive. I'll drive back to Park Place."

Corey watched from the upper level walkway as the FBI's gray sedan turned left onto Keys Highway. Looking out toward the ocean, he noticed a maintenance cart was approaching on the walkway. The middle-aged woman who was pushing it looked determined. She stopped when getting to the first pieces of broken glass.

"You'll have to pass on number 237 for now. When the tape is gone, you can have the room back. Until then, no one is to go into that room, understand?" Corey told the woman.

"I just came over to clean up the glass," the woman answered.

"Oh, okay, just don't go inside."

Corey stooped down, picked up four of the largest pieces and dropped them in her cart. He stood and watched until most of the pieces were recovered. He didn't think the bullet would be on the walkway, but wanted to be sure.

Across the street from Room 237, Corey saw four small bungalow houses that were surrounded by advanced shrubbery. Each had a double driveway leading to a carport. The houses were obviously built by the same contractor. A narrow cracked-up sidewalk ran parallel to the lane.

After checking the dial tone of his cell phone, Corey walked down the steps, across the parking area and across the sidewalk. Looking back at the broken window, he guessed the bullet would have landed somewhere at the base of one of those houses.

Corey noticed a woman in a picture window watching him as he sauntered back and forth on the sidewalk. The woman, whose hands were firmly planted on her wide hips, flipped up her hands and disappeared. Corey noticed a white van turn off Keys Highway and reduce its speed as it approached the four homes. It turned into the driveway of the house where he had seen the woman.

He spotted the large letters on the side of the van, *TV REPAIR*. Anxiously Corey moved toward the satellite dish, strongly suspecting that's what the bullet had struck.

Squatting in front of the dish, he heard someone yell, "What are you doing on my property?" Turning he saw a woman on the front steps of the house.

"Ma'am, your television dish is now evidence in a federal kidnapping case. I'm Agent Downer of the FBI. A bullet coming from over there struck it. " He pointed to the motel. "The bullet is lodged in your dish."

"That's your problem, mister. I want my television fixed, and right now."

"Sorry ma'am, you will have to wait," he said while holding the badge out front for her to see.

41

RICHARD SCHWEITZER WAS LOOKING OUT THE WINDOW of his condo when the gray sedan turned into the parking lot at Park Place. He saw Tom Hastings open a backseat door. Two other men got out—one of them he had seen before. The other man was new, but Richard assumed he was also an agent. The three men disappeared from sight as they headed for the stairway leading to the second floor.

Richard returned to the kitchen where his wife Corrith had set two plates.

"What's the matter, honey? Why so serious?"

"Tom Hastings is back. Something must be going on. I think the FBI agents are here again."

Lucy Barrows and Dale Strong were sitting next to the pool and they observed Tom and the two agents wind their way up the stairs. She looked at Dale and noticed his face pale.

"When will this terrifying business end?" she asked.

"It's all about money," Dale replied.

"Money! What do you mean?" Lucy asked.

Dale turned to look at Lucy. "All wars are fought over money." He got up and headed back to his unit.

Marv and Ann Plum were watching from their window.

"Looks like the FBI is back," said Ann in her high-pitched voice.

"That's all we need around here, more cops," responded Marv, as he gave Ann a slight shove and stomped into the kitchen.

"Hey watch it, you bum. You lay another hand on me and you'll be sorry. I'm glad the cops are around—keeps you in check."

"Ah, shut-up, you bitch."

Bitch, that's what he thinks of me, thought Ann, frustrated. Why that no-good, barrel-chest husband would be nowhere without my dad's money. I've had it with that goon. My problem is lack of money. He's gone through most of it. Her anger increased thinking of the withdrawals her husband had made from their bank account during the past year.

———

TOM FELT DEPRESSED AFTER RETURNING to his condo with the FBI agents. He sat on the couch and watched as Perry worked on the electronics connected to his phone. Even though there wasn't any blood in the motel room, he knew his daughter was in mortal danger. *At least she was alive!*

Sam's phone rang. After listening for a minute, his facial expression changed to a smile. Tom watched anxiously as the agent appeared enlightened and responded, "Uh-huh. Where was that? Yeah...okay...stay on it." Sam hung up the phone.

"Mr. Hastings. Was your daughter wearing earrings when you went shopping on Sunday—the day she was kidnapped?"

"Why...yes...I believe she was. Oh, yeah, they were real big round ones. Why do you ask?"

"An earring was found on the back seat of a van which we picked up in Sarasota."

"What does that mean?"

"That you'll be getting a call real soon. The abductors can't be very far away. I suspect that your daughter is being held within five miles of where the van was found, probably in a motel in Sarasota.

"The Sarasota police and Florida highway patrol are canvassing all the motels. We should find your daughter soon."

42

PAMELA ZACHARY WAS SUFFERING from severe mental turmoil. The hour for her appointment with Bruno was approaching. She had not yet informed Dale that the Guni was taken from her. Would he believe me? She asked herself.

She had called Rhoul earlier in the day and told him about the kidnapping of Tom Hastings' daughter. Rhoul was very interested. Pamela told him that she thought it was because Adam Stokes had determined that Tom possessed the Guni.

"Do you believe that Zachary woman? That Tom Hastings has the Guni?" Rhoul asked sternly.

"No, I do not. He doesn't have it."

"And why is that?"

"Because he would turn it over to the FBI."

"Who do you think has it?"

"Whoever hit Adam Stokes over the head with the tire iron. I don't know who that was."

Pamela heard a gentle tap on her door. "I've got to go. Someone is at the door. I'll call you later, Rhoul."

"Have a good day and *ma'assalama*, Pamela. Good-bye."

Pamela glanced at her watch and headed for the door. It was just after 3:00 p.m. The outside screen door was locked. She opened the inner door. A woman that she had met recently was standing there—Ann Plum, smiling.

"Yes, can I help you?" asked Pamela.

"We need to talk. It's about the gem," said Ann firmly.

"The gem! What's going on?" Pamela unlocked the screen door and re-locked it before guiding Ann to the couch in the living room.

" I'll get right to the point. I have the Guni...oh, it's not on me...it's in a safe place."

Pamela was stunned. "So, it was you. You hit Adam Stokes on the head!"

"Never mind about that. I have a proposition."

Pamela sat on a chair near the couch. She couldn't believe what she was hearing, her knees shaking.

"I know you have a meeting at 5:00 to sell the Guni. I know that Dale Strong set it up with a buyer. I want you to go ahead with the meeting."

Pamela's expression showed doubt and disbelief. She was trying to visualize Ann hitting Adam on the head. While absorbed in thinking about salvaging some type of payoff from the gem, she had given up trying to guess who had it, who took it from Adam Stokes?

"Stay calm, Pamela, and you can still get something out of this. Do you understand?"

"Why, ah, no...well, yes...this is all so shocking."

"Pamela, I have the Guni hidden in a safe place. If anything happens to me, the FBI will be notified immediately and they will take possession. No one will get anything."

Pamela was leaning forward on her chair, not knowing what to do or think.

"I want you to renegotiate the payment...five million dollars...no less. I want three of it. You will get one-and-a-half million. Dale gets a half million. Is that clear?"

"Ann, five million is more than the dealer was willing to pay. What if he turns me down?"

"He won't. How much was he offering?"

"Four."

"Ah, hell, maybe we should go for six. Forget it, five is what we go for."

"How about if I get two?"

"Forget it, Pamela. I'm not budging on anything. Take it or leave it."

Ann got up off the couch and said, "Please do as I tell you and no one will get hurt, including you."

"What about Tom Hastings' daughter? Her life is at risk. She has nothing to do with any of this. Doesn't that bother you any?"

"That's not my problem. I'll call you at ten sharp, tonight. Be home."

"Okay...I'll be there."

———

PAMELA LOCKED THE DOOR WHEN ANN left and returned to the couch. Her mind was saturated with possible decisions. She narrowed it down to four possible options:

Call the FBI.

Call Tom Hastings.

Call Dale.

Call the Saudis.

If she called the FBI, there would be no money for her. If she called Tom Hastings—also no money, but his daughter would be spared. If she called Dale, there would be a million-and-a-half. If she called the Saudis, there would be a quarter-of-a-million.

She picked up the phone and rang a number.

"Hello."

"Dale, this is Pamela. Something has come up."

"What?" Dale questioned with a hint of anger in his voice.

"It's good—I'm going to insist on another million from Bruno. That means an extra hundred thousand for you."

"What if he turns you down?"

"He won't."

"Okay. I'll pick you up at 4:30."

"No, Dale. I'm driving by myself. See you at Jasper's at 5:00."

43

TOM HASTINGS' PHONE RANG at 4:00 on Monday afternoon. The cracker-chewing voice said, "Listen carefully. There's an art fair in downtown Sarasota. Tomorrow at 6:00 p.m. sharp, I want you to be at the pay phones in the west wing of the city library."

"I don't have it...damn-it...I don't." Tom pleaded, but his words didn't get results. The caller hung up.

A minute later, Perry announced, "It came from one of the phones at the library in Sarasota."

Corey Downer had returned from Cyprus Lane. He had information that had established Kris's presence in the room at Cyprus Garden's motel.

Klaptin walked to the sliding door that overlooked the courtyard. "Great! This gives us close to twenty-five hours to find where the kidnappers are holding your daughter, Tom.

"Corey and I will be heading to Sarasota shortly. Perry, I want you to stay by the phone for the rest of the day. If there aren't any calls by, say 9:00, you can head to your room at the motel.

"Tom, I don't think the kidnappers will be calling any more today, but it would be wise if you hung around too, just in case."

"Yes, I certainly will hang around, but I'll need to go out for something to eat later."

"No problem. Well, Corey, let's get going. Call me on the cell, Perry, if anything changes."

"Okay, boss."

Tom walked the agents down to the garage. "Good luck, fellas. I appreciate all that you're doing." He felt the butterflies in his stomach as he observed the gray sedan turn onto Beach Street and head south.

It wasn't that Tom disliked Sam Klaptin—as he did Police Chief McSorley, but he felt something was lacking with the agent's enthusiasm. Everyone is human, Tom thought. Klaptin is not the man for this job. How can I as a private citizen remove him and put Corey in charge? There's no way. I'll need to take a more aggressive role if Kris's life is to be saved...heaven help us all.

———

JASPER'S BAR & GRILL WAS QUIET ON MONDAY AFTERNOON. Other than the bartender, there were only two patrons present. They were sitting at a table in a far corner.

At three minutes to 5:00, Dale Strong entered. He looked around and took a table near the opposite wall, a secure distance from the other patrons. Minutes later, Pamela Zachary arrived. She spotted Dale and sat on the chair next to him.

"Pamela, I don't think Bruno is going to go for the extra million. You've already made an agreement. In fact, he might get rather obnoxious...mean as hell."

"There isn't much choice on my part, Dale. I don't have the gem anymore."

"You what! You don't have it? If not, who the crap does? Is that why the extra million?"

"You're catching on, Dale."

"Who has it?"

"I can't tell you right now. Later, you'll find out who has it, if Bruno agrees to the new deal."

———

THE CLOCK ON THE WALL AT JASPER'S BAR & GRILL showed 5:00. The door opened and two men entered. One of them was Bruno. He headed for their table. The other remained standing by the door. He was carrying a briefcase.

"Okay, let's have it," Bruno announced as he sat down.

"I have some questions," Pamela announced.

"What questions? We made a deal."

"There's been a change. The price has gone up a million."

"Woman, we made a deal. Don't you dare try and play games with me." Bruno retorted sharply, his large round face reddening.

"I don't have any choice—there's a new player."

"A new player—now what the hell does that mean?"

"It means more money. Do you want the Guni or do I go elsewhere?"

Bruno angrily said, "Okay! I'll think about it. Here, write down your phone number." He pushed a napkin across the table.

Pamela wrote down her number and pushed the napkin back.

"I'll call you back and let you know," said Bruno angrily as he got up, wheeled and stormed out the door.

"Whew," responded Dale as he wiped his forehead. "I've got to hand it to ya', Pamela, you've got guts."

44

TOM HAD MIXED FEELINGS after Agents Klaptin and Downer left. Thus far, they had failed to recover his kidnapped daughter. They seemed to be one step behind the local police. He dreaded the thought of what may have happened if the swat team got to the motel while his daughter was still in there. Likely there would have been a shoot-out. Kris may have been killed. Tom had lost confidence in Klaptin's approach to the kidnapping.

Feeling the need to get out of the condo, he decided to walk the beach and have a drink at Overly's. "Perry, I'm going out for awhile—Overly's Bar & Grill, actually. I'll probably be gone for a couple of hours."

"Okay, Tom. Hey, let's look up the phone number for that place in case I need to reach you."

The surf looked angry that evening. Large breakers rolled onto ancient wooden works that protruded through the sand in front of Overly's. Tom paused and watched for a few minutes before entering.

"A scotch and water, please," Tom anxiously told the woman bartender after he took a position on a barstool.

The first drink went down rather fast. "Sure, I'll have another one," Tom said when the bartender turned his way. "Would you get me an order of nachos, too?"

Tom spent the next hour rolling his drink around in his hand and thinking. His mind was floating from the effects of the scotch. He had nibbled through about half the nachos when a piece of paper was laid on the counter next to his glass. Turning, he saw a cocktail waitress.

She said, "A man over by the door asked me to give you this."

Tom glanced toward the door where several people were milling about. There was no sign of anyone that was acknowledging sending over the slip of paper.

Unfolding the paper, it read, *Bring Guni or money to Key Marie wharf at noon tomorrow. You walk up the middle of the pier. No cops or your daughter dies.*

Tom leaped off his stool and ran to the door. Seeing no one in the entryway, he dashed out into the parking lot—no one. Whoever gave the waitress the note had gone. But wait—he considered the possibility that whoever sent him the note was still in the restaurant. Tom returned and walked up and down the aisles in the dining room, looking for a suspicious glance. He saw none and returned to his barstool.

Tom lifted the half-full glass of scotch and brought it to his lips. He put it back down on the counter.

He looked at his watch. It was 9:00. "My bill, please."

———

TOM'S FEAR TURNED INTO ANGER—the kidnappers were playing games. He hated them. The pay phone instruction at the library near the art fair was a decoy. The FBI people were wasting their time over in Sarasota. Kicking the sand with his foot on the way back, his irritations grew—*something positive better happen and soon.*

Tom knew that Adams Stokes and his followers would not hesitate to kill to gain possession of the gem. He strongly feared that the FBI, using the swat team, could result in Kris's death, especially with inept leadership.

Agent Perry was dozing on the couch when Tom returned. Hearing the door open, he sat up.

"Anything happening?" asked Tom.

"No, not a darn thing. Ah, heck, I might as well go to my room. It's only about a twenty minute drive from here."

Tom decided not to pass on the new information he had received at Overly's. He needed some time to think. After Perry left, Tom called Richard Schweitzer.

"Richard, you must know all about the kidnapping."

"Yes, I do. Corrith and I are just sick about it."

"Thanks for your concern, would you mind doing me a favor?"

"Sure, what is it?"

"Do you know anyone who has a gun?"

"Sure do. I have one."

"You're kidding. Where? Here?"

"Yeah, I keep it in a nightstand drawer in the bedroom. One never knows."

"The favor, Richard. Can I borrow it? Better yet...buy it, if that's a problem."

There was a pause at the other end. "Okay, Tom. Do you want to pick it up now? What the samhill do you need a gun for, anyhow?"

"I'll be right over."

A minute later, Tom knocked on the door of Unit 280.

"Come on in, Tom," Corrith said after opening the door. "Have a seat right over there."

Richard came in from the bedroom. The gun was a .32- automatic, neatly tucked in a holster. Tom was pleased because it was similar to the gun that was lying on his bedroom closet shelf back in Minneapolis.

"I hate to ask you for more, but do you have any shells?"

"The clip is full. Need any more?"

"I don't know, Richard, but it wouldn't hurt to have extras."

Corrith's facial expression changed to one of grave concern. She asked, "What in heavens sake is going on, Tom?"

———

TOM TUCKED THE GUN into his glove compartment and drove down Beach Street just after midnight. He turned onto Keys Highway and headed for the wharf. Light rain began splashing on the windshield. The rhythmic swoosh-swoosh sound of the wipers calmed his mind during the drive. Tom pulled into the parking lot that was used for both the pier and Jasper's.

Tom had found Adams Stokes before He was confident that he could find him again. If he did, he knew that his daughter would be near. After parking, he got out of the car and looked around.

There were only half-a-dozen vehicles in the parking lot, one of which was a light gray van. Drawn to it, Tom saw rust patches around the fenders as he got close. Grabbing a rear door handle, he pulled and it opened, splashing light on the seat. He froze—an earring was lying there. Kris had left a trail.

Returning to his car, he retrieved the gun from the glove compartment. Looking toward the pier, he noticed a building. It bordered the planking near the parking lot. Jasper's Bar & Grill was the name on the blue-yellow neon sign fronting the building. There were bluish lights showing through small side windows.

Tom walked onto the pier and paused at a bench that was abutted against the outside wall of Jasper's. Kris is near here, he reasoned. Could she be in a boat? Sitting down, he observed a long row of boats that spanned about half the length of the pier. They were parked in slips dimly lit by pole lamps.

Many of the boats were cabin cruisers. One of them could be where Kris was being held. The kidnappers would try to avoid roadblocks by using a boat, thought Tom. It made sense to him.

Quietly, he walked up the slip's side of the pier. Stopping and looking back toward Jasper's, he was about halfway up the line of vessels. Passing a large sail boat, he stopped—the large cruiser beyond the next slip had a light showing through a window in the middle level. The upper and lower sections were dark.

Getting close to the boat without risking exposure, he stared at the lighted window. He could see someone sitting and smoking a cigarette. The face looked familiar—Was it Adam Stokes? Tom's eyesight wasn't sharp enough to be positive at first.

Remaining dead still, he strained his eyes to be sure. There wasn't a sound except for the vessels bobbing and rubbing against the slip bumpers. *It was Adam Stokes!* Tom was tempted to shoot the man through the window. If he missed or it wasn't Adam Stokes, the result could be tragic. Besides, if it was Stokes, there was likely at least one other kidnapper in the boat.

Turning around, Tom rapidly walked back to his car. After putting the gun away, he started the engine and headed back toward Park Place. His mind was totally absorbed in thinking about Kris and Adam Stokes.

A direct attack by him on the kidnappers could be a sure way of getting his daughter killed. Calling the FBI, led by the swat team with inadequate leadership, could have the same result. He needed to be sure Kris was in the boat. The lower cabin was the most likely place where she would be held. He remembered noticing a small window.

Arriving at his condo, Tom redressed, pulling on a pair of swim trunks, a warm-up suit and a T-shirt. Before leaving his condo, he searched the drawers in the kitchen closet. His face lit up when seeing a jack knife.

Thoughts of cold water didn't dampen his spirit as he returned to the pier parking lot. The jack knife lay on the seat next to him. Stepping out, he took the warm-ups off. Standing by the car, he surveyed the line of boats that bobbed unceasingly. About half of them were sailboats. The boat that he was looking for was a large cabin cruiser next to the vacant slip.

After taking his watch off, he noticed it was just before 2:00 a.m. Tossing the watch onto the passenger seat, he reached in and picked up the jack knife. Opening his trunk, he lifted out a belt life preserver and strapped it around his waist. He chuckled nervously when thinking how long he possessed this life preserver. His two children weren't even teenagers then.

Richard's gun was lying on the passenger seat. He looked at it and considered taking it along. It would get wet and be useless, he concluded. Leaving the gun in the car, he headed for the pier. The drizzle had intensified, reducing the density of light that was radiating from the poles.

He shivered when sitting on the pier and dipping his feet in the water. His thoughts of the gross discomfort that he was about to experience were lost in a surge of anger. Tom thought about Kris and the pain she was going through. Slipping into the water to his waist, he held onto the edge of the pier and gradually adjusted to the cold.

Making sure the jack knife blade was closed, he securely clenched it in his left hand. Letting go of the pier, he dropped into the water, exposing only his head, neck and the top of his shoulders. By paddling with his hands, he began moving and came along side the first boat. Tom pushed off and moved on to the next. Pausing occasionally, he listened and rested. It took close to an hour to get down the line of boats and approach the one where he had seen Adam Stokes through the window earlier.

The next craft that his fingers touched was his target, the boat that he suspected held his daughter. Working his way around the other side, he saw a small hexagonal window about three feet above the water level.

Tom quietly drifted toward the window, using his fingers as a guide. Carefully, and without putting much pressure on the surface, he elevated his body and peeked through. Even with the dim light, he could see someone lying on a bunk. After allowing enough time for his eyes to adjust to the darkness, he saw a rope tied around a pair of ankles. Suddenly, he felt intense tension inside his stomach. The person lying there had to be Kris. Not trusting his eyesight, he attempted a second look—there was no doubt. He had found his daughter.

Keeping his body against the boat, he put his nose up against a plastic screen that covered the window. The spirits were with him that cold drizzly evening. The round glass window was open.

Allowing some time to pass and emotions to drain, he whispered,

"Kris."

She didn't move.

"Kris," he whispered a little louder.

She stirred.

Again, he whispered, "Kris."

Her eyes opened.

"Shh, it's your dad. Nod if you hear me."

Kris nodded.

"Listen carefully. I'm going to cut out the meshwork in the window. It's going to take a while."

She nodded again.

Moving the knife from left hand to right, he pulled out the small blade and carefully thrust it through the meshwork. Slowly and meticulously, he began cutting through the plastic screen. The portal window was about twelve inches in diameter. It took close to half-an-hour to cut through enough mesh to allow bending it away from the frame.

"Kris, nod if you hear me?" Tom whispered loudly.

Kris nodded.

"I'm going to toss this jack knife onto the bed. At close to noon tomorrow, prepare to do battle. Do you understand?"

Kris nodded.

Tom carefully tossed the knife and it landed next to her stomach. He anxiously watched her fingers grasp the handle.

"Keep the knife hidden until then. Use it to free yourself and use it as a weapon when you need to. Do you understand?"

Kris nodded.

Tom felt a lump growing in his throat. Thinking how this mission was critical for his daughter's survival, he regained composure and pushed the mesh back close to its original position. He raised the fingers of his right hand over the opening and waved. Feelings of deep sorrow almost overcame him—Realizing that this could be the last time he would ever see his daughter alive. Tom was certain that if he barged into the boat right now, both he and his daughter would be killed.

Slipping away from the window, he quietly moved away from the cruiser. Pausing at the sixth craft, he looked back and felt deep remorse by leaving his daughter in the hands of scoundrel criminals. Tom had always prided himself in the fact he didn't usually overreact—kept his cool.

He continued paddling until a secure distance from the cruiser. Pulling his cold, wet body onto a dock, he hastily walked the pier back to the parking lot. Grabbing a towel from the back seat of his car, he dried himself and pulled on the warm-ups.

Tom showered and was in bed by 4:00 a.m. Before going to sleep, he thought of calling Klaptin first thing in the morning. He visualized the swat team people running up the pier toward the cabin cruiser, guns blazing. Tomorrow morning...he would deal with it. Exhaustion brought on a deep sleep.

45

BRUNO GAZED AT THE PHONE NUMBER on a small piece of paper. One of his contacts had informed him the previous night that the local wharf was going to be the site of a kidnapping payoff. He got upset when the contact told him the payoff was going to be made with the Guni. "What are these guys pulling on me?" he whispered.

Perhaps Zachary could be trying to pull a fast one, he thought. I may be dealing with the wrong people. He looked at his watch. It was close to 9:00 a.m.

Ringing Pamela's number, he had told her that the meeting needs to take place today at Jasper's, at 11:00 a.m. "Are you sure you have the Guni?"

"Yes. If you've got the money, I'll have it there."

After Bruno hung up he still had doubts. She seems too sure of herself. If the meeting fails again, he was counting on a secondary option. According to his well-paid informant, there was an outside chance that Hastings had the Guni and he'll be one doing the kidnapping payoff on the pier at noon.

———

PAMELA SMILED AFTER ENDING THE PHONE CONVERSATION. This is easier than I thought. That Ann is a real pro. *"I'll have it there,"* I told that brute-of-a Bruno.

She tossed away feelings of sympathy for Tom Hastings and his daughter. They have to fare for themselves. I have a life ahead of me. First, I need to take care of Pamela. She called Dale.

"Dale, it's on for 11:00 this morning at Jasper's."

"Great, you still want to go it alone?"

"I'm going to have Ann with me. Just the two of us."

"Ann! She's got the Guni?" Dale asked excitingly.

"Yup."

"How in the heavens did...she clobbered Stokes? Naw...."

"You better believe it. Are you coming or not?"

"Okay, I'll see you at Jasper's at eleven...unbelievable."

———

MARV PLUM KNEW SOMETHING WAS UP. His wife had that excited look in her eyes, and it wasn't about him.

She was in the bedroom and he entered. "You're as nervous as a cat. What's going on?" Marv asked.

"Nothing that concerns you, you big lug."

"Now baby, let's not be that way."

"Ah, as usual, you wouldn't be interested. I'm going shopping with Pamela Zachary in a little bit."

"What, Pamela Zachary? Now what the hell is going on between you two? You know that she's in a lot of hot water of some kind...shopping, my butt!"

"Never mind, you big dope. It's none of your business."

"Ah, the hell with you guys, I'm going out for a drink."

"Go ahead, and if you don't come back, that would be just fine."

Marv slammed the door, took a few steps and tiptoed back to the front door. He stood by the edge of the screen door and put his ear next to the screen. He saw Ann come out of the bedroom and pick up the phone.

Marv looked up at the sky. He stared at the large white billowing cloud that hung over the complex. Something big is up—a lot of money perhaps. I'll talk to Richard, he thought. He may know what's going on.

––––

ANN PUNCHED THE PHONE SEVEN TIMES. "Pam, the big dope is gone. What happened over at Jasper's?"

Pamela laughed hysterically. "You were right. Bruno is going for the five million—it's a deal. I can't believe it. I love you."

"I told you so. When do we meet?"

"11:00 this morning. Come on over about 10:30. We'll take my car."

"Okay, see you then."

––––

RHOUL MASSIF AND BERN TALLIN were parked across the street from the main structure of Park Place. They were slumped down in the front seat.

"There she goes," said Bern.

Rhoul turned his head and lifted slightly. He could see a blue Honda backing out of a parking space.

"There's someone with her—a woman, " Bern added.

When the Honda was about a block away, Rhoul sat up and turned the ignition key. He U-turned on Beach Street and slammed down the accelerator.

––––

TOM ENTERED AN OFFICE SUPPLY STORE when it opened the next morning. Even though he hadn't slept much, he felt sharp. After purchasing a satchel, he made sure there was room for his right hand when the strap was buckled loosely.

"Anything else, sir?" the clerk asked.

"No, that's all."

Walking up the steps of the condo, he refused to think about the potential danger that existed for him if he went through with what he had planned—his priority was Kris.

His hope was that there weren't more than two kidnappers. One of them was Adam Stokes, Tom was certain. The .32-automatic would take care of Stokes. Tom assumed the other kidnapper was the man he saw with Stokes at the Beach Café. Kris had the knife. Tom felt confident his daughter was capable of holding up her end. He remembered as a father he had scoffed at the idea of her taking a course in martial arts. Parents aren't always right, he thought and smiled.

Agent Perry was due back at Park Place about 9:00. The agent's phone number was on his card, lying right by the phone. Tom took a deep breath. Should he call the agent and tell him about the note. If he did, the agent would call Klaptin and the swat team would hit the pier. Tom visualized the cabin cruiser speeding away from a spray of bullets. The FBI could call the coast guard, but it would be too late— Kris would be dead.

Quickly, Tom made last minute arrangements. The gun was in his car. He had stuffed the satchel with newspapers, leaving a little room at the top for the gun. That was also in the car. Only one obligation left—he needed to open the door for Agent Perry.

The agent knocked on Tom's door at 9:05, right on schedule. "There's coffee in the pot. Help yourself," said Tom.

At 10:15, Tom got up off the couch. "Perry, I've got some errands to run. Could you hold the fort down?"

"Sure. I expect to hear from Klaptin sometime this morning. Hopefully, they will have rescued your daughter by then. You should be here when he calls."

Tom nodded and walked out the door.

———

SAM KLAPTIN HAD CALLED IN THE SWAT TEAM a second time since he was sent to Park Place. His search of the Sarasota downtown area yielded a positive result about mid-morning on Tuesday. Two men and a woman with something covering her face were seen entering a room at Midtown Motel three blocks away from where the blue van was found.

The camouflaged van pulled into the parking lot next to the gray sedan. Sam Klaptin and Corey Downer emerged from the sedan and entered the door leading to the lobby. They came out minutes later and walked down the sidewalk, glancing at the unit number.

They stopped—Sam turned and waved. Moments later, six swat team members trotted single file to take up positions along the vehicles parked in front. Two of them joined Sam and Corey. Upon signal, they burst through the door with their weapons, ready to fire.

"Nobody here," said one of the team members when he reappeared in the doorway.

Sam and Corey entered the room. The bed had not been slept in but there was evidence that someone had laid there recently. There were two cigarette butts in the ashtray.

"They were here," said Corey.

Sam looked at his watch. It was slightly after 11:00 a.m.

"Let's get back to Park Place. Perry should be there by now. Tom wasn't supposed to do the delivery until 6:00 p.m. We should have plenty of time."

Sam realized that he had been foiled a second time. He was distraught. Besides failing to capture the kidnappers and save Hastings' daughter, his stomach was acting up bad. He wondered if he wasn't getting an ulcer.

He was just one frustrating hop behind the kidnappers, but right now a dead end. Either his men get lucky or they had to return back to Park Place and wait for the next phone call. The local police had beaten him to the first hideout, then the kidnappers must have seen them coming in the second situation.

Sam had a horrible thought. *What if this site is a decoy?*

———

MARV PLUM WAS DRIVING and Richard was in the passenger seat. They were headed for Jasper's. Marv flicked on the wipers to clear off the mist that was spreading over the windshield.

"What do you think is going on at Jasper's?" asked Richard.

"My wife and perhaps more. Ann's up to something. Like hell she's going shopping with Pamela Zachary," answered Marv. "She's up to more than something...perhaps she's coming into some money. It's only a hunch, but she had that look."

Richard glanced at this watch. It was 10:50 a.m. He had reluctantly agreed to go along with Marv. The gun that he had loaned to Tom Hastings might be at the pier. If so, there would be other guns. He wanted to ask Marv to turn around, but somehow couldn't. He didn't tell his wife where they were going, but the look in her eyes—she knew something big was up. She'll really be worried. "God," he heard her whisper. "I hope this is over soon."

———

CORRITH SCHWEITZER WAS IN THE PARKING LOT with Lucy Barrows when the FBI vehicles arrived back to Park Place.

"Well, look who's here," said a smirking Lucy Barrows. "The army."

"Holy buckets, Lucy, that's not the army. It's the FBI."

Corey Downer was driving the gray sedan when it pulled into the parking lot at Park Place.

"Sam, remember that woman? That's Corrith Schweitzer and she looks scared."

Sam Klaptin got out of the car just as the camouflaged van pulled into the adjoining parking space.

"What's the problem, ma'am? You look worried."

"My husband, Richard...Richard Schweitzer and Marv Plum went somewhere about an hour ago. They should have been back by now. I think Marv had a gun."

"Corey, would you dash up to Unit 230 and check on Hastings?"

"Hastings isn't there. I saw him leave a while ago, also," responded Corrith.

"Not here!" The agent looked at Corey and added, "Let's go up and check it out with Perry. Something is going on—I feel it in my stomach."

They dashed up the stairs. "Hastings never came back. He went out to run some errands," Perry had said sleepily.

Sam read the concern in Perry's face.

"Corey, would you check with Chief McSorley. Maybe he's got some news. Meanwhile, Perry, call Dave and have the swats stand by right here."

46

TOM FELT GUILTY SMUDGING THE TRUTH WITH PERRY. The agent didn't catch on that Tom had no intention of returning. Tom's plan on how to rescue his daughter had to be his number one priority. How would he ever forgive himself if his plan backfired and Kris were killed? If I can draw Adam out of the boat, Kris will take care of the other guy, he thought confidently. "She's gotta'," he whispered out loud.

The slow traffic didn't bother Tom. He had plenty of time—about an hour. He looked at his wristwatch. It showed almost 11:00. Passing by the street that led to the pier, Tom pulled into the parking lot of the church that he and Kris attended on Sunday. He spent the next half-hour meditating and reflecting on family life in the past. Life was wonderful until the plane crash.

Becky looked so beautiful when he dropped her off at the airport. "I'll see you in a few days," she had said. "We'll get dressed up and go out for dinner." That was the last time he saw his wife alive. The plane crashed and killed everyone aboard, including his sweet Becky.

The anger and disgust that he felt about the hijackers was transferred to the kidnappers. Kris is not going to die. *I must succeed.*

Again, Tom checked his watch. It was time. He got back in the car and headed for the pier. Tom took a deep breath after his car came to a stop in the parking lot. It was now or never, he thought as he pushed open the car door.

He took the .32-automatic from its holster. Pulling back on the mechanism, he let go and it snapped forward. A live bullet slipped into the barrel. He laid the gun down on top of the newspapers in the satchel. Carefully, he pulled on the strap, making sure his right hand fit through the opening near the top.

Grabbing the satchel, he stepped out and stood by the car. Rethinking his strategy, he removed the gun from the satchel and placed it into his hind pocket. If someone asks me to drop the satchel, he thought. Richard's gun will go with it.

Looking down at his shoes, he reached down and tightened the Velcro straps on both of his tennis shoes. He felt a bit whacko while thinking about a big league baseball player—this certain infielder for the Minnesota Twins who was a fanatic with the Velcro straps on his batting gloves, tightening them many times over—eventually the player was traded to the Yankees.

After tightening the strap on the satchel, he picked it up with his left hand and slowly walked onto the pier, staying close to the right-side railing. Stopping and glancing back toward the parking lot, he noticed two large men get out of a car. Geez, it's the two Saudis. What the devil are they doing here? Tom asked himself. I don't need complications.

———

THE WHARF IN KEY MARIE consisted of a pier at least four football fields long, extending eastward into a large shallow bay. The mainland to the east was easily visible on a clear day. Heavy-duty planks, about twenty feet long, were laid down perpendicularly for the entire length.

Visitors to the pier shared a large asphalt parking lot with patrons of Jasper's Bar & Grill The building that housed Jasper's was old with aging olive green vertical wood panels. It was supported by pilings and jutted out partially over the water.

The trim around the small windows had patchy gray spots where the paint had peeled away. A large antiquated front door was held in place with rusty, large strap-hinges. Tom could see that the bench hunkered under a small, fogged-up front window was empty.

Beyond Jasper's were a series of slips occupied by sailboats, cabin cruisers, and other forms of watercraft. A wooden railing that was built for safety purposes lined most of the pier. On the south edge, across from Jasper's and beyond, a series of benches were conveniently located for people fishing and sightseeing. The bench on the terminal end of the pier extended the full width of the planking.

The swampy area between Jasper's and the parking lot was overrun with shrubs and plants camouflaging the water underneath. On a rise of land in the swamp, next to the pier, stood a small wooden shack. The rear door of Jasper's opened onto a narrow wooden walkway that continued around the parking lot side and connected to the pier.

Tom took a few more steps until he was abreast of Jasper's. He stopped and again looked back at the parking lot. The Saudis had moved closer to the pier.

Screeching gulls were swooping close to his satchel as if expecting a handout. They settled down on the pier in ever-changing clusters, staying close to the damp footprints that Tom left behind with each step. Except for some people he saw occupying the bench at the far end, the pier beyond him appeared unoccupied.

Again, Tom stopped and anxiously turned to look toward the parking lot. The two Saudis were standing next to the bench that was hunkered next to Jasper's, not far from the front door.

Two other men walked onto the pier, also coming from the direction of the parking lot. Tom recognized Marv Plum, but *who's the other guy?* Then he realized it was Richard Schweitzer. *What the heck are they doing here?* It was too late to worry about their motivations. He turned away and continued to walk.

The boats parked in the slips along the other side of the pier looked different during the daylight hours. Tom was glad that he had counted the number of slips when he left Kris the previous night. He was certain the cabin cruiser was next to the empty slip that he could see in the distance.

He felt the dampness of the mist on his hands and wondered if some of it was cold sweat. Reaching upward with his right hand, he felt his nose. Geez, it's cold. He stopped and flexed his right fingers a few times. Reaching back into his hind pocket, he felt the even colder metal of the gun.

Tom was about half the distance between Jasper's and the empty slip when a person stepped onto the pier. He had come from the dock section next to the empty slip. Tom stopped and watched as the person walked across the pier to the railing. The man turned and began walking toward him. Tom put the fingers of his right hand around the gun handle, his forefinger gently touching the trigger.

Half the man's face was covered with white whiskers, which tapered into a narrow beard. The stride of the man's walk was steady with his long empty hands swinging freely. A maroon beret covered the top of his head. Was it Adam Stokes wearing a disguise? Tom asked himself anxiously. Pulling the gun out of his hind pocket, Tom concealed it behind the satchel. After advancing two steps, Tom stopped. He could feel his heart racing as the white-whiskered man got closer and closer.

The man slowed considerably before coming abreast. Tom was watching his hands. The man stopped and his husky voice uttered, "Set the satchel down and walk back to your car. Your daughter will come to you...there."

——

KRIS WAS EXTRA ALERT. She felt the time was drawing near. Her growling stomach said it was close to the noon hour. She could hear the muted sounds of her abductor's voices from up above.

Footsteps on the floor above resounded through the lower cabin. Someone was coming down the steps. Narrowing her eyes to slits, she saw the door partially open. A man's head peaked in. Without saying a word, he closed the door and went back up the steps.

Kris was waiting for the right moment. When she felt the boat move slightly, she surmised that one of her abductors had left the boat. Working herself into a sitting position, she grabbed the jackknife with her right hand. Leaning forward as much as possible, she extracted a blade. Carefully Kris cut the ropes that bound her ankles.

Swinging both legs to the left and allowing her shoes to touch the floor, she secured the jackknife between her knees. By moving her arms forward and back, the blade began cutting into the rope. At last the final threads of the first strand of rope split apart. Setting the knife down on the bed, she worked her wrists free.

Being very careful not to make any sound, she wiggled the gag with her hands until it fell to her shoulders. Grabbing the material in her left hand, she cut through it with the blade. Standing up, she became dizzy. Feelings of vertigo forced her back onto the bed. The loud squeak from the mattress sent her heart racing. She was relieved when her feelings of vertigo had dissipated.

Kris held her breath for a few moments, hoping not to hear anyone descending the steps. The pulsation in her neck declined as her lungs filled with oxygen. After taking a series of deep breaths, she took a step. The plastic mesh that her dad had pushed back into place during his dramatic visit had slipped inward. Fortunately for her, the most recent visitor had not noticed.

Kris heard a door open up above. She held her breath again, attempting to listen. She heard it slam shut and felt the boat move slightly. Next, she heard the sound of feet moving—one of her abductors must have gone up to the operator's station. The boat jerked slightly when the engine started, generating cramps in Kris's stomach. Quickly, she moved to the door, ready to strike with the knife if anyone entered.

47

JASPER'S COCKTAIL WAITRESSES WORE SHORT BLACK SKIRTS. They matched their fake leather eye patches that were held in place by a dark string. Red bandanas were tied around their necks and covered part of their white blouses, which ended just short of the waist to reveal the navel.

Even though most of the tables were occupied, the conversations were subdued—occasionally spiked with loud laughter. Heavy plumes of smoke gathered above some of the tables and eventually rolled against the metallic squares in the ceiling. Two men and two women were sitting at a far corner table. There was a briefcase on the edge of the table in front of one of the men.

The two bartenders working that Tuesday were busy filling mugs with beer from spigots and mixing bar drinks. The taller of the two, Clifford, saw two men leaning against the wall by the door. He had seen them before—bad things happened when they had last visited. When time would allow, he anxiously glanced at the door. Two other people, both men, had just entered. Clifford's motion froze when he saw one of the men by the door place a hand in his jacket pocket.

"Gus, don't look now, but we could be in for some trouble," Clifford told his partner.

Gus looked up and saw the two latest arrivals take a table next to the far wall. "Is it those two, that just came in?" he asked.

"No, the other two guys standing by the door. I think they're with that bald guy—the one at the table with the briefcase setting on top.

Gus stood on his tiptoes to get a look at the table in the far corner. He saw a bald man, sitting down with a hand over the top of the briefcase. The big mouth in the middle of his round head was saying something to a woman with long dark hair. A cocktail waitress interrupted Gus. He moved over to the server's station to take her order.

———

NEITHER PAMELA NOR ANN HAD SEEN Marv Plum and Richard Schweitzer enter. Marv led the way to a table near the opposite wall. He raised his chin and stretched his neck, looking for his wife.

"She's at that table, Marv—in the far corner. That looks like Dale Strong there, too," said Richard.

"Oh yeah, I see 'um....What the...what the devil is Dale doing there? Uh-oh...Pamela Zachary, too. Something big is going on."

Richard added, "That bald guy seems to be doing most of the

talking."

"Oh yeah, can you see what's going on?" asked Marv.

"Not totally, but wait...now your wife and the guy with the large bald head are having a few words."

Marv kept watching the corner. When a cocktail waitress arrived, he said, "Scotch on the rocks."

"Ah, nothing for me, thanks," Richard added.

———

ANN DEMANDED, "I want to see the money!"

"Only after I see the Guni," the bald man said firmly while pressing down on the briefcase.

"Okay," she said and reached down into her pocket. She brought out the large green glittering gem, but drew it back when Bruno reached.

"Not so fast...the money. I need to see the money."

Pamela and Dale saw Bruno make a nodding gesture toward the door. Dale's forehead began to perspire.

Ann stood up and said, "Well, let's have it, Bruno, or we're leaving."

She didn't hear the man come up behind her. He put his hand over her mouth and drew her head back. As her arms extended, Bruno jumped up and grabbed her wrist. He wrenched the Guni from her clenched fingers. The man behind displayed a knife in his other fist to discourage any interference by people at the nearby tables.

Gus, the bartender, hastily punched the phone three times.

Bruno was standing. He looked at Pamela. "There's money in that briefcase. It's not the full amount. You know the reason why. You dishonored our original deal. Now it's going to cost you."

Ann attempted to break free of the henchman's grasp. In doing so, her neck came into contact with the knife. Dale Strong and Pamela Zachary remained in their chairs and watched with shocking fear as Ann dropped to the floor, blood oozing from her neck. The chair she had been sitting on tipped over.

Bruno left the briefcase on the table and said to his henchman,

"Come on, let's get otta' here."

———

PAMELA STOOD AND LOOKED DOWN AT THE FLOOR where Ann was tangled in the legs of the fallen chair. *Not the full amount*—what is that supposed to mean? She thought. Is there still four million? She reached across to grab the briefcase, but Dale had taken it off the table and set it down on a chair.

His fingers were fiddling with the latch, trying to get it open. Pamela dashed around to the other side of the table. "That's not yours, Dale. It belongs to me and Ann."

"I want my share, four hundred thousand," Dale said firmly. "I'm getting it right now. Nothing you can do right now will stop me."

"Oh no you don't. You get ten percent, no more," responded Pamela angrily.

———

RICHARD HAD GOTTEN OFF HIS CHAIR. He stood and couldn't believe that Ann's husband, Marv, was smiling.

"Hey, Marv, don't you want to help your wife?" he asked.

"She got herself into this. Let's see if she can fight her way out."

"My God, Marv," snorted Richard in disgust.

———

BRUNO AND HIS HENCHMEN DASHED THROUGH THE DOOR and onto the pier. They stopped abruptly when two large dark-skinned men emerged onto the planks from behind the small building.

"Come on, boys, take care of them," shouted Bruno.

His henchmen pulled out pistols. Rhoul Massif and Bern Tallin ducked back behind the small building. The stillness of that early afternoon in March was interrupted by a gunshot. Bruno was the first to fire his gun. He directed the shot toward the small building and retreated back to Jasper's, hiding behind the corner of the building. One of his henchmen found refuge behind the bench next to Jasper's. The other ran across the pier and crouched behind a bench there.

"Pete," Bruno said firmly. "We've got to make a run for it. Those two big lugs could be bluffing. The Saudis aren't allowed to carry weapons."

"Hey, Steve; let's go! Back to the car," Bruno shouted across the pier.

The three men began running toward the parking lot. A second shot rang out—Bruno was hit. The Guni spurted from his hand and clunked down on a plank, bouncing three or four times and rolling before coming to a stop in a crevice between two planks. Bruno's henchmen fired a couple of shots at the small building before dashing back to their original positions. Bruno had fallen.

48

TOM HAD SET THE SATCHEL DOWN on the planked surface, concealing the gun behind his back. The white-bearded man continued walking toward the beginning of the pier, his pace increasing to a trot. Tom's attention was drawn to the sound of a gunshot coming from the direction of Jasper's. Well beyond the bearded man, he saw the two Saudis duck behind a small building, more shots followed. Three men began advancing from Jasper's toward the parking lot. They all had guns. Tom saw the man in the middle fall down.

He returned his focus to the slips, nothing was happening. Tom heard another volley of gunshots coming from the Jasper's area. Looking again, he saw two of the men retreating and dropping down behind benches. The white-bearded man who Tom had met earlier had stopped and lay down on the planks.

Turning sharply, Tom caught a glimpse of movement on the dock between the empty slip and the large white cabin cruiser. There was a man standing on the dock—it was Adam Stokes and he was holding a gun.

Tom stopped breathing. He felt dizzy. "Get away from that briefcase," Tom heard him yell.

Still holding the gun behind his back, Tom forced his legs to move and began backing away. When he got close to a bench, he quickly ducked behind. He heard the bark of a gunshot and saw a splinter of wood fly over the backrest. Pointing the .32-automatic in Adam's direction, Tom pulled the trigger. Adam dropped to one knee and fired again—the bullet whistled just over Tom's head.

———

NATE BLOOMBERG WAS PATROLLING on Keys Highway when receiving the call from Barb.

"Nate, Jasper's Bar & Grill called. They need help and fast."

"Ah, heck—that place always needs help."

"Nate, this sounds serious."

"Well, okay, I'll give it a look."

Minutes later, Nate pulled into the parking lot shared by the pier and Jasper's. Casually, he opened the car door.

"Holy Jesus, those are shots!" he exclaimed loudly.

Staying low, he reached into the car and brought out the mike.

"Car one, car one—from car three. Are you there, Chief?"

"Nate, what's the hell's goin' on?"

"I'm over by the wharf, next to Jasper's. Someone's having a shoot-out. I need backup and quick."

"Stay put, Nate, I'll be there in five."

Police Chief McSorley flicked the switches that activated the siren and the lights. He pulled onto Keys Highway and headed for the wharf. He was a couple of miles away when his phone rang.

"Chief McSorley, this is Sam Klaptin of the FBI. We just got back to Park Place from Sarasota, following up on a lead regarding the Hastings kidnapping case. Tom Hastings is gone and I suspect he's making a delivery to the kidnappers. Do you have any information about any violent activity going on at Key Marie at this time?"

"Yeah, there's a disturbance in progress at the wharf, a place called Jasper's. According to my man, Nate, there've been some shots."

"Gunshots! McSorley, thanks...hold the fort down...we're on our way."

"Great! We appreciate any help that we can get. Nate's down there alone right now."

———

"COME ON, COREY, LET'S HEAD OVER TO THE WHARF. Someone's fired a gun over there." Sam hastened over to the swat van, poked his head in the window, and trotted back to the sedan and got in.

Corey flicked on the siren switch and planted the flashing red light on the roof of the sedan. He drove onto Beach Street and in minutes became totally frustrated because the traffic was heavy and many of the vehicles were not responding.

"Damn-it, those people can't hear or see!" exclaimed Klaptin.

———

KRIS HAD HEARD GUNSHOTS AND OPENED THE CABIN DOOR. She was extremely relieved that there was no one in the middle cabin. Creeping up the next set of steps, she saw a man standing next to the captain's chair, peering through the windshield. The gunshots that I had heard earlier were distant, she thought. The shot that I heard right now came from the dock next to the boat. She saw the man duck and the windshield shatter—that shot came from the pier, Kris realized. Another bullet whistled overhead. The person on the dock had fired again.

Taking advantage of the action outside and the noise of the engine, Kris stole up behind the man and with both hands on the handle plunged the knife blade into left side of his back, just under the rib cage. The man yelped and turned, grimacing in pain—Kris gave a vicious Karate chop to the side of his neck. Before he had a chance to recover, she struck him again, this time to the other side of the neck—another...another and another. The man dropped the gun and fell to the floor, unconscious.

Kris turned the boat engine key off and pulled it out of the ignition. She picked up the fallen gun. Though she had never operated a pistol before, she placed it in her right fist and put her finger around the trigger. More shots were being exchanged between whoever was on the dock and someone on the pier. Stepping onto the support base of the captain's chair, she cautiously peeked through the broken windshield.

It's my dad! She saw him lying down behind the bench—peering from underneath. She could see a puff of white smoke and heard another bullet scream by the boat. My dad's got a gun! He's shooting! Someone is shooting at him! I've got to do something. The person on the dock fired again. This time the bullet ripped into the wood of the bench, sending splinters flying.

THE NEXT BULLET FIRED BY KRIS'S ABDUCTOR hit a metal brace, sending it careening close to Tom's baseball cap. The man fired again and Tom felt a stinging burn in his right arm. Watching from underneath the bench, he could see Adam Stokes advancing, gun in hand.

Tom's right forefinger was on the trigger, but it was paralyzed because of the wound in his arm. Attempting to switch the gun to his left hand, it dropped to the plank. Tom lay helpless behind the bench. Adam picked up the satchel and walked over to where Tom was lying. He pointed the gun at Tom's head.

Tom closed his eyes and put his head down and began mumbling, *"Our Father...."* He heard a shot...another one...and another one. Tom opened his eyes in time to see blood spurt across several planks, creating a long, narrow, dark-red pyramid. Adam Stokes had whirled and reeled, attempting to keep his balance. As he fell more shots followed him down. He dropped into a heap and the gun clattered as it landed on the planks.

KRIS, CROUCHING A FEW YARDS AWAY, was still holding Emil's gun in both hands, smoke emitting from the barrel. One of Adam Stokes's feet kicked, as he lay, pushing against the satchel and sending it over the edge, into the water. Kris kept her gun pointed at Adam Stokes's body even as it convulsed only a few feet from her father.

"Dad! Dad, are you okay?"

Tom sat up, holding his shoulder. "I've been hit in the shoulder, but it doesn't feel too bad. Better check out Stokes. Get his gun."

———

TWO FRUSTRATED AGENTS FINALLY TURNED OFF KEYS HIGHWAY and onto Wharf Street. When they arrived at the parking lot, two police cars were blocking the entrance to the pier. Officers were crouched behind the cars.

Corey stopped the gray sedan near the officers. Sam got out and held his hand up, signaling the swat van to stop and hold. He and Corey approached the officers.

Sam asked, "What's going on here? Is it what I think it might be?"

Chief McSorley spoke. "Well, I'm not sure, but there're two wars going on—one of them right over there. Two men behind that small building, the Saudis, I think. They've been exchanging gunfire with two people—one person by Jasper's and the other behind that bench on the pier. About halfway up the pier there were more shots. At least two persons are down. One that you can see over there and another farther up, on the pier. The shooting has stopped for the moment."

"Is there any sign of Hastings?" asked Corey.

"No. We haven't seen him or his daughter. I don't know where they're at."

Sam looked back at the van. He was on the verge of launching an attack when his stomach erupted in pain. He doubled over and retched.

"Are you okay?" the chief asked.

"Yeah, I'm fine. Just a little upset stomach."

Sam had a decision to make. From what he had observed there were two hostile persons on the pier, well in range. Further out, he could see a man lying on the planks next to a bench. Beyond him were more people. Someone was lying on the planks and two persons were behind a bench—gunfire had ceased in that area. Looking back at the van, the swat team members were out of the vehicle and appeared ready.

———

MOST OF THE PEOPLE REMAINING AT JASPER'S were down on the floor as a result of a bartender yelling for everyone to get down when the shooting had started. The windows inside the Bar & Grill were located such that no one could see the pier out front, or the parking lot.

During a pause in the shooting, Pamela Zachary crawled over to Ann. The knife wound in Ann's neck appeared superficial and the bleeding had stopped. Pamela rose to her feet and helped Ann get up. "Let's see how much money is in the briefcase," she said.

Dale was still on the floor on the other side of the table. He had gotten the briefcase open. "There's not much in here, just one bundle, probably not more than a hundred thousand," he said.

"Why that dirty, cheating bastard," said Ann angrily, her shrill voice carrying across the room.

"Dale, you stay right here with that briefcase or we'll kill you. Come on, Ann, let's see what's going on out there."

While the two women headed for the back door, they didn't notice that Dale was down under the table and transferring bills from deeper down in the satchel to his jacket pocket. The two women went out the back door and crept alongside the parking lot side of the building. They were hidden from the pier and the small building by a cluster of tall weeds and bushes.

———

MARV STOOD UP AND SAID, "Come on, Richard, the girls went out the back door. Let's see what's going on."

"I don't think so, Marv. You go ahead. I'm staying right here until this madness is over with."

"Okay, you do what you want, but I'm going out there," said Marv.

He went out through the back door and over to the walkway that Pamela and Ann had taken. Peeking around the corner, he saw the two women. Pamela was crouching next to the pier and Ann was back a couple of steps leaning against the outside wall of Jasper's.

Two shots rang out. They both ducked.

"I don't like this, Pam—not worth getting killed over," said Ann.

A couple of minutes went by without any more gunfire. Pamela stood up, took another step—then she saw it. The Guni was lying in a crack between two planks, only inches away from the edge, but a few steps away from where she stood. Instinctively, she stepped onto the pier and ran toward the gem. As she stooped down to pick it up, two shots rang out—she fell.

Serves you right you idiot, Ann thought.

Marv came up behind Ann and they watched in horror while a bloody froth spread and covered Pamela's lips.

Marv grabbed his wife's arm and pulled her back. "Get back, go inside. I'll take over here."

He had a gun in his hand and advanced to the edge of the pier. He fired a shot in the direction of the bench across from Jaspers. After firing another at the small building, he dashed over to Pamela and grabbed the Guni from her clenched fingers.

One of the Saudis emerged from behind the small building and yelled, "Stop! Bring it here, or I'll shoot."

A shot rang out from the bench across from Jasper's and the Saudi fell. The second Saudi fired and hit Marv, who dropped to one knee before falling to the planks with a thud. The next few moments were deadly quiet.

A loud penetrating voice broke the stillness. Corey, using a loudspeaker, boomed, "Put your guns down and come out with your hands up!"

Nothing happened. "Dave, go take out those two on the pier," ordered Klaptin.

The swat team raced around the police cars and converged onto the pier. The man behind the bench, next to the railing, tossed his gun onto a plank in front of him. He stood and put his hands on his head. Moments later the man behind the bench in front of Jasper's also tossed his gun out and surrendered.

The Saudi still standing laid his gun on a plank and put his hands up as the swat team ran by. Nate and McSorley, along with the two FBI agents, advanced toward the fallen bodies. Agent Corey stooped and picked up the Saudi's gun from the planks. Rhoul was attending to his fallen comrade, Bern.

"How is he?" Corey asked anxiously. "The ambulance should be here any second."

Rhoul had ripped open his fallen comrade's shirt. He placed the palm of his hand on Bern's forehead. "Allah is on our side, Bern. Your wound doesn't look serious." Rhoul took a deep breath and looked up at the sky.

As Corey knelt down to help, the sound of a siren penetrated the air.

———

MARV PLUM WAS GROANING AND LYING ON HIS STOMACH. He began crawling toward the Guni, which had fallen from his hand. It lay on a plank a few feet from his clawing fingers. Next to him lay the still body of Bruno. Pamela Zachary was lying on her stomach, her lips bathing in a pool of blood, one leg dangling over the edge of the pier planking.

The chief knelt down by Pamela and lifted her hand. "This woman is dead," he said.

Sam walked over to Marv Plum, whose hand was inches away from the Guni. Sam leaned over and picked it up. "Remain still, please. Help is coming." He held the gem against the sky. "This isn't worth dying for, Plum."

The ambulance had arrived and was waved onto the pier.

Bern Tallin had gotten to his feet. Assisted by Rhoul Massif, they moved away from the small building and strolled over to where the three bodies lay.

"My man is going to be okay," Rhoul told Sam.

"Rhoul, is this the Guni?" He held it up for Rhoul to see.

"It appears to be...it is," said Rhoul after taking a closer look.

"I'm going to have to hold onto it for the time being. If everything is in order, it will be returned to the Prince."

"Thank you, my friend."

———

TOM HAD GOTTEN UP AND WAS SITTING ON THE BENCH. He had nestled his wounded right arm against his stomach, supporting it with his left hand.

Kris stood after examining her father's shoulder. "The shooting has stopped over there. It looks like the army has taken over. I better check on the guy inside the boat."

"That's Klaptin and his swat squad," Tom responded. "They look beautiful. Let them take care of the guy inside, Kris."

"Can you walk?" asked Kris.

"Yeah, I think so."

Kris laid the gun down on the bench.

Tom stood up. He looked down at the body of Vince Gulloti and didn't feel any remorse. That man had caused him and his daughter a ton of grief and deserved what he got—it was all about greed.

The Florida sun had broken through the clouds. Tom looked around and listened to the sound of gulls. He and Kris began walking toward the cluster of people milling next to Jasper's.

Tom watched the swat squad team break away from the others and run towards them. "Look, Kris, what a beautiful sight," he said while looking out over the bay.

EPILOGUE

Pamela Zachary died from the wound that she had gotten during the exchange of gunfire between the Saudis and Bruno's henchmen. Her greedy attempt to retrieve the Guni succeeded, but only for a few moments.

Omar Vallif, the Arabian prince, finally got back his birthday present, the famous Guni. Rhoul Massif and Bern Tallin delivered it in person and were honored by the prince's father.

Vince Gulloti, also known as Adam Stokes, died from the bullets fired by Kris during the gunfight on the pier. Emil, Vince's henchman, was taken to the hospital in serious condition, suffering from a knife wound and beating at the hands of Kris Hastings. He recovered, was tried and sentenced to twenty years in prison.

Bruno, the gem dealer, died on the pier from a bullet fired by one of the Saudis. His two henchmen were not shot during the gun battle, but both are currently serving ten-year prison terms.

Ann Plum had fallen and broken her ankle after her husband Marv pushed her away from the pier. The day after the shoot-out, she held a stack of bills in her fist as she watched Dale walk across Beach Street with his share, only five thousand dollars. She wondered why Dale wasn't upset. Ann had forty-five thousand in her stack. That's all that was in the briefcase—fifty grand. She had counted it herself.

Dale didn't need to hang around Lucy Barrows any longer. He didn't need her money. He smiled whenever he thought about either Ann or Bruno—and the briefcase—the mostly empty briefcase—

Dale reached around and padded his wallet, which was slightly protruding from his back pocket.

Marv Plum spent a month in the hospital recovering from the gunshot wound that he had received while attempting to pry the Guni from Pamela's fingers. On the day he was released, a deputy sheriff served him with divorce papers.

The swat team, Corey Downer and Sam Klaptin returned to Tampa Bay—none of them were injured. Agent Klaptin was hospitalized for a bleeding ulcer. Later, he and his wife reconciled and he resigned from the FBI.

The local Lion's Club of Key Marie honored Chief McSorley with a plaque at a luncheon in his honor. He was credited with solving the kidnapping.

Patrolman Nate Bloomberg was promoted to Sargent for the part he played in the kidnapping and gunfight.

Richard Schweitzer ran onto the pier after the swat team had run by. He assisted Kris in helping her dad to the bench next to Jasper's while awaiting a second ambulance. His wife, Corrith, was greatly relieved when he returned to Park Place unharmed.

Tom Hastings spent three days in the hospital recovering from his arm wound. By the following Saturday afternoon, he was sitting in the stands with his daughter, Kris, and friend Julie, watching a spring training baseball game between the Pirates and the Yankees.

Tom was munching from a bag of popcorn and told them about exercising his re-purchase option on his former property in central Minnesota. He had decided to move back.

Kris Hastings continues to work for the airline. A year after the kidnapping, she was assigned a security guard position for international flights.

NEW RELEASES

As It Happened
Over 40 photos and several chapters containing Allen Saunders' early years, tales of riding the rails, his Navy career, marriage, Army instruction, flying over "The Hump", and his return back to North Dakota. Written by Allen E. Saunders. (74 pgs) $12.95 each in a 6x9" paperback.

Great Stories of the Great Plains - *Tales of the Dakotas - Vol. 1*
The radio show "Great Stories of the Great Plains" is heard on great radio stations all across both Dakotas. Norman has taken some of the stories from broadcasts, added some details, and even added some complete new tales to bring together this book of North and South Dakota history. Written by Keith Norman. (134 pgs.) $14.95 each in a 6x9" paperback.

Early History of Sargent County - *Volume 1*
Over seventy photos and thirty-five chapters containing the early history of Sargent County, North Dakota: Glacial Movement in Sargent County, Early History of Sargent County, Native Americans in Sargent County, Nicollett and Fremont, The Quartzite Border, Acquiring Land in North Dakota / Sargent County, Weather, Ransom City and Memories of the Summer of 1883, Fight for the County Seat, The Little Old Sod Shanty on the Claim, Prayer Rock, Townships and Surveyed Maps from 1882. Written by Susan M. Kudelka. (270 pgs.) $16.95 each in a 6x9" paperback.

Beyond the Heart & Mind
Inspirational Poetry by Terry D. Entzminger
Beyond the Heart & Mind is the first in a series of inspirational poetry collections of Entzminger. Read and cherish over 100 original poems and true-to-the-heart verses printed in full color in the following sections: Words of Encouragement, On the Wings of Prayer, God Made You Very Special, Feelings From Within, The True Meaning of Love, and Daily Joys. (120 pgs.) $12.95 each in a 6x9" paperback.

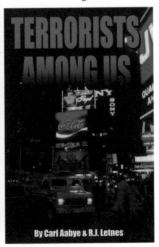

Terrorists Among Us
This piece of fiction was written to "expose a weakness" in present policies and conflicts in the masses of rules which seem to put emphasis on business, money, and power interests at the expense of the people's security, safety and happiness. Shouldn't we and our leaders strive for some security for our people? Written by Carl Aabye & R.J. Letnes. (178 pgs.) $15.95 each in a 6x9" paperback.

THE HASTINGS SERIES

Blue Darkness *(First in a Series of Hastings Books)*
This tale of warm relationships and chilling murders takes place in the lake country of central Minnesota. Normal activities in the small town of New Dresen are disrupted when local resident, ex-CIA agent Maynard Cushing, is murdered. His killer, Robert Ranforth also an ex-CIA agent, had been living anonymously in the community for several years. to the anonymous ex-agent. Stalked and attached at his country home, he employs tools and people to mount a defense and help solve crimes. Written by Ernest Francis Schanilec (author of <u>The Towers</u>). (276 pgs.)
$16.95 each in a 6x9" paperback.

The Towers *(Second in a Series of Hastings Books)*
Tom Hastings has moved from the lake country of central Minnesota to Minneapolis. His move was precipitated by the trauma associated with the murder of one of his neighbors. After renting an apartment on the 20th floor of a high-rise apartment building known as The Towers, he's met new friends and retained his relationship with a close friend, Julie, from St. Paul. Hastings is a resident of the high-rise for less than a year when a young lady is found murdered next to a railroad track, a couple of blocks from The Towers. The murderer shares the same elevators, lower-level garage and other areas in the high-rise as does Hastings. The building manager and other residents, along with Hastings are caught up in dramatic events that build to a crisis while the local police are baffled. Who is the killer? Written by Ernest Francis Schanilec. (268 pgs.) $16.95 each in a 6x9" paperback.

Danger In The Keys *(Third in a Series of Hastings Books)*
Tom Hastings is looking forward to a month's vacation in Florida. While driving through Tennessee, he witnesses an automobile leaving the road and plunging down a steep slope. He stops and assists another man in finding the car. The driver, a young woman, survives the accident. Tom is totally unaware that the young woman was being chased because she had chanced coming into possession of a valuable gem, which had been heisted from a Saudi Arabian prince in a New York hotel room. After arriving in Key Marie Island in Florida, Tom checks in and begins enjoying the surf and the beach. He meets many interesting people, however, some of them are on the island because of the Guni gem, and they will stop at nothing in order to gain possession. Desperate people and their greedy ambitions interrupt Tom's goal of a peaceful vacation. Written by Ernest Francis Schanilec (210 pgs.)
$16.95 each in a 6x9" paperback.

Purgatory Curve *(Fourth in a Series of Hastings Books)*
A loud horn penetrated the silence on a September morning in New Dresden, Minnesota. Tom Hastings stepped onto Main Street sidewalk after emerging from the corner Hardware Store. He heard a freight train coming and watched in horror as it crushed a pickup truck that was stalled on the railroad tracks. Moments before the crash, he saw someone jump from the cab. An elderly farmer's body was later recovered from the mangled vehicle. Tom was interviewed by the sheriff the next day and was upset that his story about what he saw wasn't believed. The tragic death of the farmer was surrounded with controversy and mysterious people, including a nephew who taunted Tom after the accident. Or, was it an accident?   Written by Ernest Francis Schanilec (210 pgs.) $16.95 each in a 6x9" paperback.

March on the Dakota's - *The Sibley Expedition of 1863*
Following the military action of 1862, the U. S. government began collecting an army at various posts and temporary stockades of the state, in preparation for a move northwestward to the Dakota Territories in the early summer of 1863. The campaign was organized by General John Pope, with the intent to subdue the Sioux. Two expeditions were planned, one under General H. H. Sibley, organized in Minnesota, and the other under the Command of General Alfred Sully. Interesting facts, actual accounts taken from soldiers' journals, campsite listings, casualties and record of troops also included. Written by Susan Mary Kudelka. (134pgs.) $14.95 each in a 6x9" paperback.

War Child - *Growing Up in Adolf Hitler's Germany*
Annelee Woodstrom was 20 years old when she immigrated to America in 1947. These kind people in America wanted to hear about Adolf Hitler. During her adolescence, constant propaganda and strictly enforced censorship influenced her thinking. As a young adult, the bombings and all the consequential suffering caused by World War II affected Annelee deeply. How could Annelee tell them that as a child, during 1935, she wanted nothing more than to be a member of Adolf Hitler's Jung Maidens' organization? Written by Annelee Woodstrom (252 pgs.) $16.95 each in a 6x9" paperback.

The SOE on Enemy Soil - *Churchill's Elite Force*
British Prime Minister Winston Churchill's plan for liberating Europe from the Nazis during the darkest days of the Second World War was ambitious: provide a few men and women, most of them barely out of their teens, with training in subversion and hand-to-hand combat, load them down with the latest in sophisticated explosives, drop them by parachute into the occupied countries, then sit back and wait for them to "Set Europe Ablaze." No story has been told with more honesty and humor than Sergeant Fallick tells his tale of service. The training, the fear, the tragic failures, the clandestine romances, and the soldiers' high jinks are all here, warmly told from the point of view of "one bloke" who experienced it all and lived to tell about it. Written by R.A. Fallick. (282 pgs.) $16.95 each in a 6x9" paperback.

Grandmother Alice
Memoirs from the Home Front Before Civil War into 1930's
Alice Crain Hawkins could be called the 'Grandma Moses of Literature'. Her stories, published for the first time, were written while an invalid during the last years of her life. These journal entries from the late 1920's and early 30's gives us a fresh, novel and unique understanding of the lives of those who lived in the upper part of South Carolina during the state's growing years. Alice and her ancestors experiences are filled with understanding - they are provacative and profound. Written by Reese Hawkins (178 pgs.) $16.95 each in a 6x9" paperback.

Tales & Memories of Western North Dakota *Prairie Tales & True Stories of 20th Century Rural Life*
This manuscript has been inspired with Steve's antidotes, bits of wisdom and jokes (sometimes ethnic, to reflect the melting pot that was and is North Dakota; and from most unknown sources). A story about how to live life with humor, courage and grace along with personal hardships, tragedies and triumphs. Written by Steve Taylor. (174 pgs.) $14.95 each in a 6x9" paperback.

Phil Lempert's HEALTHY, WEALTHY, & WISE
The Shoppers Guide for Today's Supermarket
This is the must-have tool for getting the most for your money in every aisle. With this valuable advice you will never see (or shop) the supermarket the same way again. You will learn how to: save at least $1,000 a year on your groceries, guarantee satisfaction on every shopping trip, get the most out of coupons or rebates, avoid marketing gimmicks, create the ultimate shopping list, read and understand the new food labels, choose the best supermarkets for you and your family. Written by Phil Lempert. (198 pgs.)
$9.95 each in a 6x9" paperback.

Miracles of COURAGE
The Larry W. Marsh Story
This story is for anyone looking for simple formulas for overcoming insurmountable obstacles. At age 18, Larry lost both legs in a traffic accident and learned to walk again on untested prosthesis. No obstacle was too big for him - putting himself through college - to teaching a group of children that frustrated the whole educational system - to developing a nationally recognized educational program to help these children succeed. Written by Linda Marsh. (134 pgs.)
$12.95 each in a 6x9" paperback.

The Garlic Cure
Learn about natural breakthroughs to outwit: Allergies, Arthritis, Cancer, Candida Albicans, Colds, Flu and Sore Throat, Environmental and Body Toxins, Fatigue, High Cholesterol, High Blood Pressure and Homocysteine and Sinus Headaches. The most comprehensive, factual and brightly written health book on garlic of all times. INCLUDES: 139 GOURMET GARLIC RECIPES! Written by James F. Scheer, Lynn Allison and Charlie Fox. (240 pgs.)
$14.95 each in a 6x9" paperback.

I Took The Easy Way Out
Life Lessons on Hidden Handicaps
Twenty-five years ago, Tom Day was managing a growing business - holding his own on the golf course and tennis court. He was living in the fast lane. For the past 25 years, Tom has spent his days in a wheelchair with a spinal cord injury. Attendants serve his every need. What happened to Tom? We get an honest account of the choices Tom made in his life. It's a courageous story of reckoning, redemption and peace. Written by Thomas J. Day. (200 pgs.)
$19.95 each in a 6x9" paperback.

9/11 and Meditation - *America's Handbook*
All Americans have been deeply affected by the terrorist events of and following 9-11-01 in our country. David Thorson submits that meditation is a potentially powerful intervention to ameliorate the frightening effects of such divisive and devastating acts of terror. This book features a lifetime of harrowing life events amidst intense pychological and social polarization, calamity and chaos; overcome in part by practicing the age-old art of meditation. Written by David Thorson. (110 pgs.)
$9.95 each in a 4-1/8 x 7-1/4" paperback.

From Graystone to Tombstone
Memories of My Father Engolf Snortland 1908-1976
This haunting memoir will keep you riveted with true accounts of a brutal penitentiary to a manhunt in the unlikely little town of Tolna, North Dakota. At the same time the reader will emerge from the book with a towering respect for the author, a man who endured pain, grief and needless guilt -- but who learned the art of forgiving and writes in the spirit of hope. Written by Roger Snortland. (178 pgs.)
$16.95 each in a 6x9" paperback.

Blessed Are The Peacemakers *Civil War in the Ozarks*
A rousing tale that traces the heroic Rit Gatlin from his enlistment in the Confederate Army in Little Rock to his tragic loss of a leg in a Kentucky battle, to his return in the Ozarks. He becomes engaged in guerilla warfare with raiders who follow no flag but their own. Rit finds himself involved with a Cherokee warrior, slaves and romance in a land ravaged by war. Written by Joe W. Smith (444 pgs.)
$19.95 each in a 6 x 9 paperback

Pycnogenol®
Pycnogenol® for Superior Health presents exciting new evidence about nature's most powerful antioxidant. Pycnogenol® improves your total health, reduces risk of many diseases, safeguards your arteries, veins and entire circulation system. It protects your skin - giving it a healthier, smoother younger glow. Pycnogenol® also boosts your immune system. Read about it's many other beneficial effects. Written by Richard A. Passwater, Ph.D. (122 pgs.)
$5.95 each in a 4-1/8 x 6-7/8" paperback.

Remembering Louis L'Amour
Reese Hawkins was a close friend of Louis L'Amour, one of the fastest selling writers of all time. Now Hawkins shares this friendship with L'Amour's legion of fans. Sit with Reese in L'Amour's study where characters were born and stories came to life. Travel with Louis and Reese in the 16 photo pages in this memoir. Learn about L'Amour's lifelong quest for knowledge and his philosophy of life. Written by Reese Hawkins and his daughter Meredith Hawkins Wallin. (178 pgs.)
$16.95 each in a 5-1/2x8" paperback.

Outward Anxiety - Inner Calm
Steve Crociata is known to many as the Optician to the Stars. He was diagnosed with a baffling form of cancer. The author has processed experiences in ways which uniquely benefit today's readers. We learn valuable lessons on how to cope with distress, how to marvel at God, and how to win at the game of life. Written by Steve Crociata (334 pgs.)
$19.95 each in a 6 x 9 paperback

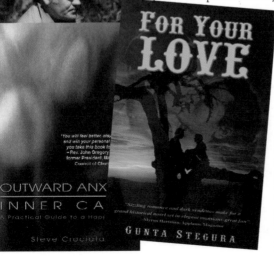

For Your Love
Janelle, a spoiled socialite, has beauty and breeding to attract any mate she desires. She falls for Jared, an accomplished man who has had many lovers, but no real love. Their hesitant romance follows Jared and Janelle across the ocean to exciting and wild locations. Join in a romance and adventure set in the mid-1800's in America's grand and proud Southland.
Written by Gunta Stegura. (358 pgs.)
$16.95 each in a 6x9" paperback.

Bonanza Belle

In 1908, Carrie Amundson left her home to become employed on a bonanza farm. Carrie married and moved to town. One tragedy after the other befell her and altered her life considerably and she found herself back on the farm where her family lived the toiled during the Great Depression. Carrie was witness to many life-changing events happenings. She changed from a carefree girl to a woman of great depth and stamina.
Written by Elaine Ulness Swenson. (344 pgs.)
$15.95 each in a 6x8-1/4" paperback.

Home Front

Read the continuing story of Carrie Amundson, whose life in North Dakota began in *Bonanza Belle*. This is the story of her family, faced with the challenges, sacrifices and hardships of World War II. Everything changed after the Pearl Harbor attack, and ordinary folk all across America, on the home front, pitched in to help in the war effort. Even years after the war's end, the effects of it are still evident in many of the men and women who were called to serve their country.
Written by Elaine Ulness Swenson. (304 pgs.)
$15.95 each in a 6x8-1/4" paperback.

First The Dream

This story spans ninety years of Anna's life - from Norway to America - to finding love and losing love. She and her family experience two world wars, flu epidemics, the Great Depression, droughts and other quirks of Mother Nature and the Vietnam War. A secret that Anna has kept is fully revealed at the end of her life. Written by Elaine Ulness Swenson. (326 pgs.)
$15.95 each in a 6x8-1/4" paperback

Pay Dirt

An absorbing story reveals how a man with the courage to follow his dream found both gold and unexpected adventure and adversity in Interior Alaska, while learning that human nature can be the most unpredictable of all.
Written by Otis Hahn & Alice Vollmar. (168 pgs.)
$15.95 each in a 6x9" paperback.

Spirits of Canyon Creek *Sequel to "Pay Dirt"*

Hahn has a rich stash of true stories about his gold mining experiences. This is a continued successful collaboration of battles on floodwaters, facing bears and the discovery of gold in the Yukon. Written by Otis Hahn & Alice Vollmar. (138 pgs.)
$15.95 each in a 6x9" paperback.

Seasons With Our Lord

Original seasonal and special event poems written from the heart. Feel the mood with the tranquil color photos facing each poem. A great coffee table book or gift idea. Written by Cheryl Lebahn Hegvik. (68 pgs.)
$24.95 each in a 11x8-1/2 paperback.

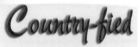

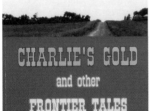

Damsel in a Dress

Escape into a world of reflection and after thought with this second printing of Larson's first poetry book. It is her intention to connect people with feelings and touch the souls of people who have experienced similiar times. Lynne emphasizes the belief that everything happens for a reason. After all, with every event in life come lessons...we grow from hardships. It gives us character and it made her who she is. Written by Lynne D. Richard Larson (author of Eat, Drink & Remarry) (86 pgs.) $12.95 each in a 5x8" paperback.

Eat, Drink & Remarry

The poetry in this book is taken from different experiences in Lynne's life and from different geographical and different emotional places. Every poem is an inspiration from someone or a direct event from their life...or from hers. Every victory and every mistake - young or old. They slowly shape and mold you into the unique person you are. Celebrate them as rough times that you were strong enough to endure. Written by Lynne D. Richard Larson (86 pgs.) $12.95 each in a 5x8" paperback.

Country-fied

Stories with a sense of humor and love for country and small town people who, like the author, grew up country-fied . . . Country-fied people grow up with a unique awareness of their dependence on the land. They live their lives with dignity, hard work, determination and the ability to laugh at themselves. Written by Elaine Babcock. (184 pgs.) $14.95 each in a 6x9" paperback.

Charlie's Gold and Other Frontier Tales

Kamron's first collection of short stories gives you adventure tales about men and women of the west, made up of cowboys, Indians, and settlers. Written by Kent Kamron. (174 pgs.) $15.95 each in a 6x9" paperback.

A Time For Justice

This second collection of Kamron's short stories takes off where the first volume left off, satisfying the reader's hunger for more tales of the wide prairie. Written by Kent Kamron. (182 pgs.) $16.95 each in a 6x9" paperback.

It Really Happened Here!

Relive the days of farm-to-farm salesmen and hucksters, of ghost ships and locust plagues when you read Ethelyn Pearson's collection of strange but true tales. It captures the spirit of our ancestors in short, easy to read, colorful accounts that will have you yearning for more. Written by Ethelyn Pearson. (168 pgs.) $24.95 each in an 8-1/2x11" paperback.

The Silk Robe - Dedicated to Shari Lynn Hunt, a wonderful woman who passed away from cancer. Mom lived her life with unfailing faith, an open loving heart and a giving spirit. She is remembered for her compassion and gentle strength. Written by Shaunna Privratsky. $6.95 each in a 4-1/4x5-1/2" booklet. *Complimentary notecard and envelope included.*

(Add $3.95 shipping & handling for first book, add $2.00 for each additional book ordered.)